To Beryl!

Hope you find it amusing

[signature]

DEDICATION

I wish to dedicate this book to my wife, Mary, whose tireless work as my secretary and editor has made my dreams possible

BONNYWEATHER

TERENCE J O'BRIEN

authorHOUSE®

AuthorHouse™
1663 Liberty Drive
Bloomington, IN 47403
www.authorhouse.com
Phone: 1-800-839-8640

Published by AuthorHouse   06/11/2012

ISBN: 978-1-4678-8350-4 (sc)
ISBN: 978-1-4678-8351-1 (hc)
ISBN: 978-1-4678-8352-8 (e)

CONTENTS

CHAPTER 1

Ambrose Bonnyweather was a man whose life had used up fifty summers—half a century of being out and about on planet Earth. *Amazing, really,* he thought. For half a century he had been gathering experience to make him the man he was today, and that made him smile (perhaps a little smugly). He left the smile on his face to show people that he had something to smile about.

Ambrose Bonnyweather was not a big man physically. He was well built and burly, not fat. His burliness was accentuated by the old-fashioned, blue chalk stripe suit he was wearing. His homburg hat sat sternly like a helmet, and the thick, ebony stick with which he struck the pavement made him look like Mussolini carrying a large plastic bag by its neck. He looked conspicuous. And he knew he did. The half-smile playing at the corners of his mouth made his face look benign to the multitude of fellow humans accompanying him at half past nine that morning on Oxford Street. And he could tell people viewed him as something of an enigma. He strode, another thing few people did. He strode manfully and purposefully down the pavement. His brisk striding was a sort of personal demonstration against what he thought was missing from modern society. And what was missing, he was quite categorical about: briskness, a sense of purpose, and a conviction that it was how you looked and acted that mattered. Oh yes, he was an enigma all right; it would take a good man to guess what he did for a living. The unfortunates around him devoted their lives to career structures and uniformity, which was certainly not for him. He thanked God he was a thinker, and that was what he was doing now. It was his work that he was thinking about.

When he saw the red setter, the corners of his mouth lost half their smile and his face hardened. His eyes assayed the dog as they would a nugget, and his first attempts at affectionate noises to attract the animal made three or four people turn to him quickly—but their reflexes belied the looks they gave him. The dog didn't even turn its head. He called, "Here, here, then," and pushed his way through the passers-by. "Here boy. Here, then, boy" were variations he used as he marched purposefully after the setter. The dog disappeared from his view momentarily, and he lurched forward quickly (his stick smartly rapping the leg of a large, grey-suited, briefcase-carrying man who didn't like it).

"Hey, now. Just steady on," the man said in a sort of pained snarl, and Ambrose Bonnyweather gave him a sharp glance without decreasing the speed of his movements. He said, "Sorry" as his shoulder pushed into a woman, making her take two or three paces more quickly, involuntarily. He muttered, "Sorry" again when he saw the look on her face as he left her behind.

The man said, "God, some people really are uncouth," and the woman said, "Right in the back. I could have had a kidney complaint." But they were soon swallowed and carried on with the ebb and flow of the people. Bonnyweather went on through the people because he knew from experience that a dog would be even more perverse if he broke into a trot. His prey turned to give him a cursory look, and there was a head held high with haughtiness in the way it pitter-pattered while accelerating. He increased his pace, and his voice hardened noticeably as he commanded the dog to come to him.

"Here, here, boy. Come here, boy," he said sharply. And he said, "Sorry" and "Excuse me, please" testily to the people who impeded him. And so the chase went bumpily on, up to the corner of Adam and Eve Court where there was a fruit barrow. Quickly, almost as if that was what the dog had been planning, it put its paws on the barrow, grabbed an apple, and cantered up Adam and Eve Court, easily avoiding the stallholder, who was upset.

"Bloody mongrel. Thieving bloody hound," the man shouted as he rushed round his barrow and collided with the hurrying Bonnyweather. Bonnyweather had been turning the corner and putting even more imperious urgency into his command: "Come here, come here, boy."

"Hey 'ere, is that your dog then?"

Bonnyweather flicked a mere glance at him before he was stopped in his tracks, his arm held in a vice-like grip.

"I said is that yours, guv. That bleeding dog?"

"Here! Come here, boy!" Bonnyweather shouted loudly after the setter, but he knew that he'd lost.

"That's the third bleeding day running it's nicked a Granny Smith, that'll be 90p."

"What?"

"90p. Three bloody-good Granny Smiths.

He realised that the man thought it was his dog and said, "It's not my dog."

"Come on, squire. There's no need for all that, is there?"

"How do you mean? It's not my dog." And as an afterthought, he questioned with indignation, "90p for three apples?"

"Aw come on, jock, get your hand down. I mean its black and white, innit?"

Ambrose Bonnyweather disliked intensely the term *jock* because, in London, he knew it was an insult. Here, jocks were Harry Lauders with their cider bottles and the assumption that King's Cross was the only part of London you knew.

Anyway, he didn't even talk like one now. He gave the man a withering look, but the man was not to be withered.

"Do I have to get a copper then?" he asked amazed, "Just for 90-bleeding-p?"

Bonnyweather took the man's hands off his arm, wishing that he'd gone to karate classes during the winter, and he took a pound from his pocket.

"Here," he said with disdain, "But I would like you to know that it was not my dog."

"You're a great jock," the man said as he went back to the other side of his barrow. "You shouldn't have taught it to eat bleeding apples, should you have then?"

He dismissed Bonnyweather by returning to his business saying, "Yes, laidy, what about it—can I tempt you?"

They both knew that the incident was closed.

It was no use following the dog now—it could be anywhere. But red setters weren't cheap, they were always worth a bit of effort. *Fuck it,* he thought, and he was immediately horrified that he could lose control so easily and allow his background to burp back at him in such a common way.

Ambrose Bonnyweather's background was important to him, important in the sense that it was his secret. He had come a long way, and it was a source of extreme annoyance to him that working class people seemed to assume so readily that he was one of them. Even worse, by the use of the soubriquet *jock,* they quite deliberately inferred that he was some way down even the working class pecking order. It wasn't just a question of racialism; it was a question of pride.

For fifty years, he had been a Scotsman. A Lowland Scotsman, it's true. But when he moved south to London, he had been surprised and dismayed by what seemed to be the role his fellow expatriates played in the metropolis. It had been almost a year before he met a fellow Scot who wasn't drunk. Then he had met the pleasant man at the job centre whose obvious status and comforting Doric had made him feel that his accent was less of a handicap than he had thought. Nevertheless, like an actor from Sunderland hoping for a part in a Noël Coward play, he had tried hard to learn to pronounce his words in a way that those who say they adore regional accents pronounced their words. The last couple of years of thinking and pausing before he uttered anything had given him an accent which, other than the occasional lapse when irritated or relaxed, could have been from anywhere, he believed. Specifically, any part of the English-speaking world where they had learned to think and pause before they spoke. He pulled himself together and told himself that he would be a fool to let either the dog or the trader colour his day. After all, he was his own master, and that was more than a lot of people could say. He shrugged the incident from his thinking and resumed his enjoyment of the noise and bustle of a great city going about its business.

But it was symbolic, the business about the dog, absolutely symbolic. It was the sort of thing that had happened too many times of late. Things were becoming a little too capital intensive, and there seemed to be no luck. During the last few months there had been a marked lack of excitement in his work, and in fact, he had been about to define for himself what he meant by *excitement* when the red setter had come into view. It was luck that brought excitement. *Luck,* he thought, *was a vital factor in any cash flow situation,* and that, simply, was what was missing. He turned into Tottenham Court Road, already clearly divided by the morning sunlight. His side was the dark side, and somehow, it made him more appear more suitable: hatted, sticked, and tight suited in the shade. He strode along Tottenham Court Road, looking enigmatically in front of him. He noted with quick glances that people were trying not to notice him. He finally stopped in front of the glass-doored entrance to the Bloomsbury art gallery, property of Marylebone Council. He shaded his eyes to peer beyond the glass and was apparently satisfied. As he closed the door after himself, his face was hidden by a notice that said "Open Daily, 10 a.m. to 5 p.m. (except Sunday), Admission Free."

His office, the web from which his operations extended, was in the Bloomsbury art gallery, and today—although he didn't know it—was going to be the start of a full and eventful week.

If Ambrose Bonnyweather enjoyed the feeling that he was an enigma, it was because he felt that Beatrice Thompson probably thought he was. And although he was not a naturally demonstrative man, he did have some concern about what she thought of him. Beatrice Thompson was not herself an enigma. At least it was not a word that would have entered her thinking. She counted change into her purse outside the newsagent's shop and wished he would buy all the newspapers on some sort of account, to be repaid; it was more, well normal, to have accounts for newspapers and things. Beatrice Thompson was from a background of account holders, accounts at reasonable places of course, such as Harrods and Fortnum's. Buying things with cash puts you on a different level. Having to wait for change, checking that it was right, and that sort of thing made it a different matter altogether. Although really, she always did enjoy the way the young man in the newsagent's shop looked at her . . . and the way he called her "my darling" with such coarse affection. Jolly cheeky, but awfully nice hair. She clasped the papers to her after she'd hitched the large shoulder bag more securely onto her shoulder and marched off down Tottenham Court Road.

Beatrice Thompson had a willowy figure—*rangy,* someone once had called her—and still thirty-one, she was a taut-skinned girl of whom Ponds and Elizabeth Arden would have been proud. The weathering and muscle-knotted healthiness of a country girl had, as yet, only given her crinkles round the eyes from keen-eyed observing in the sunlit, fresh air and a hairstyle designed for a riding hat. From her appearance and dress, she would have been thought "country" if she lived in a provincial town. In London, she was more of a Sloane Ranger without a 4x4. Clothes from Harrods (worn like the Queen at Sandringham) made Beatrice Thompson look like the wife of an army man, but she wasn't.

She was the daughter of an army man, a colonel. She was single and unattached, and she had been bored at home in Gloucestershire. Now she was—as she called herself—a working girl. A working girl who thought her job was quite fun at times, but she wished her employer, Ambrose Bonnyweather, would open some accounts at places and allow her to tell people that she worked for him.

She rather worshipped him, in a way, because he was so unlike all the other men she knew. She rather enjoyed the mystery and the way everything was so incredibly different in her job (as compared to the sorts of tasks performed by the one or two people she knew who had decided to get a job in town). In many ways, it was jolly lucky that she'd found the job with Bonnyweather. She was finding out what it was really like to be a woman who was especially needed, and she would never have had the opportunity of meeting a man like him anywhere else. So strong, so literary, so articulate—and yet Scottish. And totally unused to the sort of life she'd known. He was very impressive considering what he'd had to overcome.

Her thinking was interrupted by the smiling face of a man in Bonnyweather's age group. His smile was broad as he paused and waited until she reached him.

"Hello, Miss Thompson. There is a beautiful morning."

She had no idea who he was. The man smoothed the moustache closely wrapped around his still smiling mouth.

"Hello," she said and paused, quite unsure.

"You think I am in good disguise?" he asked, then he threw his head back and roared with laughter. She looked at him with a perfunctory smile. He stopped laughing suddenly, looked each way before leaning toward her, and spoke in a low voice, "Ruskin's Bird Seed, Ruskin's Bird Seed, Miss Thompson," he said and laughed again, willing her to join him.

"Oh," she said as it dawned on her, "Mr Napiorkowski from Aquarius."

Of course, he'd grown a moustache.

"You like? I am smart?" he asked her.

"Oh yes, jolly smart. Yes, lovely."

He leaned toward her again. His breakfast sausage had marked its territory well, and she closed her eyes like horsewomen when horses break wind.

"*Solidarosh,*" he said. Then with his face quite serious, "*Solidarosh,* we must be proud like you English, eh?"

"Oh," she said again, then, "Well I really must, you know." She backed away and smiled.

"I will today see you, maybe, eh?" he said and waved as if she was on a train. "*Solidarosh,*" he called quite loudly, and she unwittingly raised her voice as she backed along the pavement.

"Yes, yes of course." Then very loudly, because she thought it was Polish for goodbye, she said, "*Solidarosh.*"

Two postmen who were passing interrupted their deep conversation to stare at her until she saw them and lost her smile quite quickly and deliberately. *Still,* she thought, *that is really why I came to London. It's different than Gloucestershire.* She wondered if Ambrose would make one of his rare visits to her place tonight—she loved the fact that anything she cooked was always new to him. Even things her mummy always made (which weren't terribly extraordinary)—food she'd always eaten. He, on the other hand, never told her what sorts of things he'd had in his Scottish home. And his sexual foibles fascinated her: so quietly intense, so much more mysterious and poetic than the "shall we get 'em off then, old girl?" chaps she met at parties and hunt balls.

Her situation made her feel that, somehow, she was serving him. She was lucky to have him as her mentor, and she loved to hear him asking for things. But Jenkins, *God,* he was different—incredibly different. He was just an old goat, and God knows why he couldn't find the sort of woman he was used to. But Ambrose was the sort of person she could like because he was so incredibly new to her—and that's what was on her mind as she approached Bloomsbury art gallery.

Clutching her newspapers more tightly to her bosom, she cautiously climbed the two steps to the glass and gunmetal doors. At the doors, she peered in. If that awful man was there, she would go away, ring Ambrose, and tell him to keep that man away from her or fight him or something. She might even tell Ambrose that she wouldn't come in at all—it wasn't terribly pleasant having to deal with a person like Jenkins. She could see no sign of life through the doors, however, so she went in quickly.

The foyer of the art gallery (the *fwayer,* Mr Jenkins called it) was not large. It contained the glass entry and exit door, a wall covered with notices and posters advertising events and exhibitions at other galleries, and a couple of statues. They were modern, symbolic statues, and they stood near a chair and a table, half covered with postcards. This was the head caretaker's table. There were two exits from the foyer into the interior: one straight into "Modern Works & Exhibitions," and one with a sign that led upstairs to "Post-Renaissance." It was not large as foyers go, but it was the hub—in fact, the operational headquarters—of the head caretaker, and he often referred to it as his office. Roy Jenkins was the head caretaker, but he had no subordinates other than the three cleaning ladies who came in each morning between 7:30 and 9:00. On his table were two signs, both neat and not too obtrusive. And both were neatly (if not quite evenly) printed in Letraset. One said simply: "Postcards 80p each," and the other said, "Please ring for attention," but it gave no indication what one had to ring.

Mr Jenkins reluctantly respected Mr Bonnyweather and worshipped Miss Thompson His worship of Beatrice was activated by a lust that was both sexual and snobbish.

Beatrice was relieved to find the foyer empty and went over to the table to see if today was the day for the mysterious monthly letter—the brown, cheap envelope addressed in illegible scrawl, which was the only correspondence that ever arrived for her employer. There was no letter to be seen. She stiffened, head still. In the distance was the sound of whistling, someone whistling the first two lines of "I Could Have Danced All Night," apparently under the impression that those two lines were in fact the whole tune. The whistling was subdued; it was as if the whistler had more blow than whistle or was perhaps preoccupied. A moment was enough for Beatrice to recognise not only the tune but the whistler. She clutched her newspapers even more tightly and went quickly into "Modern Works & Exhibitions." The whistling ceased. After a few quickening footsteps, Mr Jenkins appeared from "Post-Renaissance." "Miss Thompson? Miss Thompson, is that you?"

He looked down through the other doorway and raised his voice: "Miss Thompson? Beatrice?"

He followed her.

She pulled the office door shut smartly behind her, and there was a frantic air about the way she clutched the newspapers and the key ring. The weight of her shoulder bag added to the sense of frantic scrambling as she clawed her fingers at the lock to be sure that she was safe. She was. The door was locked and she breathed a sigh of relief, hurried to a small table, and dumped the papers and jumbo-sized bag.

"Miss Beatrice, can I have a word?"

Jenkins was on the other side of the door, and she turned to look at it.

"Beatrice, it won't take a minute."

He sounded more persistent than usual, and she walked slowly back toward the door. Her gaited mirrored that of someone going toward a dangerous animal that is caged behind a barrier, but nevertheless worrying. She stopped a couple of paces from the door and said as peremptorily as she could, "Will you go away?"

"What?" he asked.

She took a pace nearer and raised her voice, putting some of her station into her voice: "Go away. Stop harassing me."

There was a pause. She stared coldly at the door, and on the other side, Jenkins looked at it wistfully, desperate for a ploy.

"I've got feelings haven't I?"

She looked at the door as if she knew exactly what his feelings were, but she didn't answer.

"Can I see you at dinnertime?"

"Oh do stop being so difficult, Mr Jenkins," she replied, but there was just the tiniest hint of feminine tolerance in the way she said it.

"Let me in, Beatrice. He's no right to change these locks—I have to answer for this property."

My *God!* The man was exasperating. She turned her back to the stupid man and saw Bonnyweather at the other end of the room. He was hanging small items of clothing on a clothes horse.

"Have you been there all the time?"

"What?" Jenkins asked.

"Go away," she shouted, and as she walked back to her table, she demanded assistance.

"Tell him to go away. He's a menace, an absolute menace!" and she added with venom the only suitable words she could think of: "He's disturbed."

Jenkins voice sounded plaintively distant.

"Dinnertime, eh, Beatrice?"

Beatrice shouted at the door, "I am not having lunch today." It was as if she wanted the whole world to know. And she hoped Bonnyweather would respond to her call.

"Well? Say something to the idiot."

He had gone back to the washbasin and was hidden from view by a large rack filled with dusty, brown, paper-wrapped parcels; old picture frames; and numerous dirty busts. He was wringing out a pair of socks.

"Poor sod," he said, "He worships you, that's all."

Jenkins, thinking she was softening, said gently to the door, "What?"

Bonnyweather put his head round the rack and raised his voice.

"It's all right, Bernard. I'll see to it."

"Oh," Jenkins was surprised and a little taken aback, "Righto, Mr Bonnyweather. I didn't know you were in."

"Righto then, Bernard," Bonnyweather shouted at the socks he had wrung out. There was a pause and Beatrice sat at her table. She was grateful for Bonnyweather's aid, but she was still a little irritated that he hadn't made his presence known a little sooner.

"Good morning," Jenkins said, still at the door. Beatrice and her employer exchanged glances.

"Morning, Bernard. Thank you," Bonnyweather said before lowering his voice for her, "You can let the heat out of your legs now."

She wasn't too sure what that remark meant, but she was glad he had interfered and put a stop to that stupid man.

"He's a menace, an absolute menace."

Bonnyweather seemed unable to find anything important in the subject. His theory was that there were people and people in the world, and Jenkins was so obviously one of the others. He hung the last of his washing on the clothes horse.

"He's harmless. Thinks highly of you—that's all."

She wished he wouldn't keep excusing the man, particularly when he seemed to suggest that a sort of drooling sexuality was excusable—especially because Ambrose seemed to be above such motives. She wished Ambrose would bother her like Jenkins did.

She couldn't help voicing her irritation: "Why can't you use the launderette like anyone else?"

He rinsed out the washbasin and dried his hands in silence, making it obvious that he was not going to answer her question.

She went to the window and opened the top six inches. She looked out for a pause at the little bit of Percy Mews that was visible. It was so barren, never anything living to see. There were just walls, a low roof, the parapet behind and below which there might have been a yard or a garden, and some ten feet of roadway. Percy Mews turned sharply away from the window view. There was the sky, of course, rising from a ground of castellated chimneys, and a flat roof with a curious wire netting railing round it. She couldn't understand why he stood gazing at this view so often, but to show that she was irritated, she now stood, looked out for a long pause, and answered his silence with her own before going back to her table.

Bonnyweather's office was long and narrow and had been designed as some sort of storeroom or maybe a workshop. By the door, which allowed people into or out of the office, there was a large multi-curved Edwardian hat cum umbrella stand. The view from there started with a desk and a large and very old-fashioned armchair that was adjacent to the front of the desk.

A piece of well-used carpet covered the floor from the desk to a solid-looking table at the edge of the carpet. If the carpet represented the playing area, then Beatrice's small but solid table at the edge of the carpet represented all too clearly the junior player. Beyond the carpet, the room carried on for a third of its length, had shelving down one wall, a door into another room, and the previously mentioned rack. And, of course, the room contained the washbasin from which, during any silence, could be heard the subdued but insistent screeching of a steady trickle of water. Above Bonnyweather's desk was a large poster or print of the head on view of a goldfish looking lugubriously contemplative. And on the wall near Beatrice's desk was a poster of a girl kneeling. It hung flush from the ceiling, the juncture of wall and ceiling beheading the girl or giving the impression that her face would be found gracing the skirting board of the room above. Poster aficionados would possibly recognise the body of a nude Jane Fonda, but no reason was ever offered as to why Bonnyweather disapproved of her face. One could guess that it may have had something to do with Vietnam. Beatrice used to be terribly embarrassed about the poster, but now—having gotten to know her employer better—she realised that it was his way of showing profound respect for and fascination with the female form. As he once said, "Priapism is nature's solipsistic tribute to its own beautiful creation, the breasts." She was still a little embarrassed (but incredibly impressed) when she discovered what he meant. So she had become used to the poster. It was an art object, and bringing it to his attention could create rather heady moments in him, which she liked.

"Been out?" he asked as he came to the desk, "Or are you late?"

"No," she said and rummaged in her copious bag, "There was a phone call yesterday afternoon." She gave him a glower and said, "When you said you had to be back by four o'clock." But there was no response or explanation as usual. She found what she was seeking in the bag, a packet of birdseed.

"Borzoi seems an awfully nice man. He was very keen," she said and put the bag down on the floor. "He had a dreadful sense of loss. Apparently it was all his own fault."

"Borzoi?" he asked as he watched her take the birdseed to the other room, "I would have thought they'd have been hard to lose." "He says he'll pay cash and a good bonus if we can deliver in a week."

She raised her voice as she left the office, "I arranged to see him in Aquarius, hence the birdseed."

He leaned back in his chair, locked his hands behind his head, and contemplated the headless nymph.

"Soon be summer," he said, "Open windows." He spoke to the poster as if encouraging it quietly. If she heard his response she ignored it.

"He was terribly interesting. He was at the same school as my brother. I met his aunt in Provence a couple of years ago."

She came back into the office and said, "She was with that awful James woman—writes novels or something—maybe she's on the stage." She closed the door to the other room behind her and went to her table. The newspapers had to be gone through.

"He did ask if you would be interested in doing a small investigation on his typist, but I told him you never touched humans," she quipped, opening one of the papers, "Apparently he thinks she might be less uppity if he can get something on her."

"Such as?" Ambrose asked the poster.

She was searching through classified adverts and replied, "Well he's tried following her, but she uses buses, which terrify him. He never knows about fares and where to get off and things. He's terribly keen about it all, though. He thinks he's seen her picture in *Forum*. Anyway, I told him we were sorry, and the Borzoi's name is Tsarevitch."

Bonnyweather took his hands from behind his head.

"My god he's one of your lot all right. Tsarevitch? You know you could change that birdseed for cat food if you talked nicely to Mrs Napiorkowski."

"*Ska.*"

"What?"

"Napiorkow*ska*. She's a female."

He sat up straight.

"I know she's a bloody female—my God I know that! I'm not one of your wet guards officer telly producer twits."

She looked up from the paper, taken aback by the heat of his response. She was always surprised at the sort of things he could get upset about.

"I was raised on porridge in a good, honest, working-class environment where pocket money had to be earned. I know what a woman is."

He opened a drawer and busily searched through it. She lowered the paper and looked at him with a sort of maternal serenity. Then she smiled a gentle, understanding smile. He didn't look up. Instead, he took a file from a drawer and looked at the papers in it.

"Are you sulking?" she asked with a twinkle in her voice. He closed the file as if satisfied and drummed with his fingers as if in deep cogitation. He then stood, clasped his hands behind his back, and purposefully but slowly walked to the window.

"Would you listen to a carpenter?" he asked, looking out.

"What?"

"What notice would you take of a carpenter? A carpenter in his twenties? Eh?"

She didn't answer because she couldn't think of an answer. She assumed he was going to be brutally clever again. She watched him, watched his back, and she waited for the fingers of his hands to move and seek new positions.

"These days, it wouldn't really matter what he was. I mean, if he was on television and things, they wouldn't necessarily say he was a carpenter, would they?"

There was a pause: he was looking out and she was looking at him looking out.

"No, he'd never get the opportunity now. Not if he was religious," Bonnyweather said. And he added as an afterthought, "And a Jew."

She couldn't get the drift, but she was aware that he might just be playing with her.

"They're called Orthodox, aren't they? Religious Jews," she added as a sort of explanation. After gazing at his unresponsive back for a pause, she said, "Are you out of sorts or something?"

"Don't be childish, Bridget."

The smile left her face.

"Will you stop calling me Bridget?" she sounded grim.

"Any messages?"

"A red setter and a budgie," she snapped, looking at the newspaper again.

"How old?"

"How old? Which?"

"The setter."

"Three."

"Odd. That's odd."

He still made no move to turn away from the window, and she told herself that she was too preoccupied to look at him.

"Must have had a good reason. They're usually quite settled at that age."

She turned the page of the paper and folded it back before she deigned to reply, "Oh." He still didn't turn. He had heard the rustle of the paper and knew that she wasn't looking at him. "And its name was?" "Still is. Kev," she replied, and against her judgement looked up as he turned.

"Kev? Unusual. Probably a malapropism." He gave her a quick, brief smile as he went back to his desk, "Now that is a really unusual name for a red setter. This could be an unusual case."

He stood thoughtfully tapping his desk and said, "Dodgy, though—can be vicious buggers, red setters," and as an afterthought noted, "and they eat bloody expensive apples."

She looked at him. She was puzzled by his last remark but aware that he rarely, as he remarked, said things that did not have a meaning. She couldn't see the relevance of apples, and she knew hundreds of people—some, anyway—who had setters and never described them as vicious. The apple reference mystified her. But she knew him well enough not to volunteer for a discussion she was going to lose.

She took the parcel from her bag and stood up to unwrap it. It was a top hat, a top hat for use in horse riding. Beatrice looked at the hat in her hands with a mixture of pride and anxiety.

"It's a bit posh, isn't it?"

He didn't answer. There didn't seem to be an answer. She took the hat with her to the washbasin.

"I hate these, really, but Tweaker was quite insistent. She thinks side-saddle is terribly in. Anyway, it could give me a hundred points if Poppy's judging."

"You're not doing that horse thing again, are you?"

He did his interpretation of an upper class horse rider's accent, "And where are we *orf* to this time? Are we chasin' at the white city?"

She tried the hat on and rather liked what she saw in the mirror. And she didn't reply until she saw herself from various angles and finally took it off.

"Don't be infantile," she said with disdain as she went back to the table. But she couldn't help it, she had to confide: "I'm terribly excited. Paddy's let me have 'The Boy.'" She resumed her seat and pulled a carrier bag out from under the table before saying, "It's a hoot, really. Tweaker is quite put out."

He watched her take a pair of riding boots from the carrier

"But does 'The Boy' want you?"

There was a smile on his face; he enjoyed being flippant.

But Beatrice hadn't been trained to recognise flippancy, there was no such thing in her background.

"Oh don't be so brittle! You know jolly well if it wasn't for my venting I'd be absolutely supine with boredom."

She lowered her voice to make her confidence more impressive: "Mark had him for nearly a year, you know. It's a terrific feather in his cap."

"Had who?"

"'The Boy,' of course." He could be exasperating.

"Oh," Bonnyweather said as he thought about which direction to go. He then said, "Decadence, that's all it is. Decadence. Parasites on honest, working-class society."

"Oh balls."

"How long are you having off?" he questioned. The conversation was ceasing to amuse him.

"Only Friday. It's dressage on Friday," she said with a hand down one of her boots, turning it admiringly, "Gosh, these have come up well haven't they?"

She put the boots on the table and folded the newspaper neatly before looking at him.

"Have you had coffee?"

"No, haven't had time," he said and nodded in the direction of the washbasin, "That tap's gone again."

She went over to the washbasin and tightened the tap. That was usually all that was needed, but this time the water still ran, albeit a little slower. She took two mugs from the shelf and asked, "Have you arranged to see Errol Billington yet?"

"Isn't he the bloke in *The Guardian*?"

Sometimes his sense of fun irritated her, like it did now as she went to the door.

"I just hope that Jenkins fool isn't there. If he is, I'm coming straight back—you can make it."

He smiled amiably, "Don't be so silly, Bridget. He only worships your body—it's quite natural."

She stopped and gave him a very cross look and was determined to be determined.

"You are not going to provoke me," she said and carried on toward the door. "At least he can remember my name," she noted. But thinking about Jenkins made her pause again, her determination melting into anxiety, "But if he's there, I'm coming back."

"Nonsense," Bonnyweather said before spoiling his reassurance by saying, "He worships you, that's all."

"Well he can jolly well stop worshipping me. I'm just not having it."

The telephone on the desk rang. They both looked at it, and as he did every now and then to confirm his position, he stood up. No point in having a dog and barking yourself.

She marched to the desk with a glare and pushed the two mugs at him, which he involuntarily took. She picked up the phone saying, "Perry Ironside Agency, Beatrice Thompson speaking," and she watched him walk to the window as she listened.

"Oh yes, of course. Just hold the line a moment," she said, and he watched the phone being placed tightly to her breast. "It's him: Errol Billington."

He turned quickly back to the window, "Good, I thought that would be his next move."

"He wants to see you."

"I wonder . . ." he mumbled and unconsciously moved back a pace from the window, "Yes, arrange to have him met. Get him up here."

She looked at him for a moment, standing there holding the mugs before saying, "Hello, Mr Billington? Mr Bonnyweather may be interested. When can you be seen?"

Ambrose spoke in a low voice toward the window, "Next hour. After that it could be too late."

Beatrice merely flicked her eyes at him as she spoke into the phone, "What about now? Good, splendid. Do you know the Bloomsbury art gallery?" She listened for a pause then spoke as if she was concerned about what had been said, "Of course, yes. Well just opposite is a pet food shop. What? Aquarius . . . No, opposite the gallery. Right, it's now after 10. Go to Aquarius. Be there at 11:05." She seemed irritated, "Yes, of course. Inside buy a pound of Ruskin's birdseed, and I will identify myself. Oh and no talking, Mr Billington—Mr Bonnyweather doesn't like that." She replaced the receiver and looked at him.

"He sounds quite young. It's a pity he didn't say much about himself in his letter, his education sounds a little doubtful."

He came back to the desk slowly, smiling. "You mean he didn't know which end of a horse you go venting with?"

"You know jolly well I didn't mean that. All I meant was, you couldn't tell which school he'd been to."

He put the mugs on the desk, put his hands on her shoulders, and said gently, "You asked for birdseed again."

She looked up into his face. That slightly bewildering feeling swept over her as usual: the touch of his hands, the nearness of him—it was all a sort of awesome thrill.

Her voice softened, "I can change it when I meet him."

He turned away from her, his face filled with thought and focused on his desk. She watched him, warm with a strange emotion. Her face was filled with a smile that was seraphic. He looked up at the goldfish, and his voice was dreamy, poetically dreamy: "You know, there is a simple profundity in the very least of God's creatures."

"Do you . . . do you want something?" she asked, with hope in her query. They gazed at each other, and she took a pace to the desk, drawn to the offer of his eyes. Then the telephone rang.

"Oh bother," she said as uncertainty left her.

"Perry Ironside Agency. Beatrice Thompson speaking," she said and smiled at him as she listened to the phone.

"Who?" Oh hello, Nicky. How are you?" She looked guiltily at Bonnyweather and laughed. For some reason he felt hurt.

"Oh, God, no. I left him at Ferny's when we went off to Ronnie Scott's. Did you? What a hoot . . . Three of you? Oh you really are an old goat, Nicky."

Bonnyweather was taking a dislike to Nicky.

"Of course," she said rather proudly, "I've got 'The Boy.'"

Then turning her back to Ambrose she said with exaggerated nonchalance: "Oh you know, Daddy had them to dinner a couple of times, and they like the house . . ."

He winced like he always did when she said "hice" or "abite." He said out loud, plaintively, "Oh, God, not another highborn pillock."

She turned to glance at him, gave him a quick smile, and said, "Good Lord, really?"

That was it; she was in conversation. *They should have taken the bloody thing off its cradle,* he thought as he looked at her standing there. For a second he was almost fired again by the way she gave him a brief smile as she listened and absentmindedly smoothed her breast.

But it was no good: his need had fled.

"Of course, of course we will . . ."

"Fuck it," he mumbled. Now she was arranging something— something with someone else. And he didn't notice his expletive.

"Look, our Mr . . . our best man will be along within half an hour. Are you still in Jermyn Street?"

He gave her his attention and stopped thinking about himself.

"I know, I know. I think it's terribly sad."

He stood up and proclaimed, "So am I. If it's a job, it's going to cost him a lot of pocket money." He then went to the window and looked out without joy.

"Okay, okay."

He winced again at the way she made it sound like *eeeokay.* Why these toffee-nosed twits should rewrite the bloody language . . .

"Yes, of course. In a flash . . . Oh how sweet. Bye, byeee." She put the phone down and smiled at him.

"That was Nicky Fairburn-Twigg. You know, Celia's brother? He really is a hoot," she said and went to her table.

"Fairburn-Twigg?" he asked as if he had never heard of anything so outlandish, "Fairburn-Twigg? Where do they get these bloody names?"

She paused for a moment, looking at him.

"From their parents, of course, you oaf. He's lost a horse—rather valuable, too."

"*Lorst* a horse?" He liked to irritate her. "In *Jermyn* Street?"

She decided to ignore his childishness. It had been unfortunate that the phone had rung.

"No, silly, from their place in Burford."

She fluffed her hair with her fingers, as if it might have been rumpled during the warmth of their moment. "I said you'd go round and chat and things."

Bonnyweather stood up, seemed to change his mind about saying something, and walked to the hatstand, looking as if he'd made up his mind.

"Did you tell him it would be expensive?"

She took her boots off the table and put them neatly together on the floor, "My dear, the horse is more important than money. I'd hate to be the idiot who's made off with it."

That settled it. That was all he wanted to hear. At least there would be a twenty-quid consultation fee and expenses for the next month's cash flow—even if he never went near Burford, wherever that was.

"Right," he said briskly, donning his homburg and patting it into place.

"32A. He has a flat above the doctor. Oh dear, I have forgotten his name. He was the one who took the thingy off Fiona."

He took his stick from the stand and gave her his William Powell look.

"You realise that I'm only doing this for money?"

"Of course," Beatrice replied. She had never heard of William Powell.

"Good."

"I say," she tittered, "I think you'd better do some locking up."

He'd put his stick down to button up his trousers, slightly embarrassed as always when such things were mentioned. Their eyes met as he picked up his stick again, and there was something rather disconcerting about the serious, glazed smile and the slow way her eyes moved up from his flies.

"Right, schlom," he said and went out, closing the door.

Her smile was an unconscious outward sign of the comfortable, happy feeling she had in her head. It was so marvellous to be needed, to feel that you could make someone happy. She sighed happily. She remembered something she had read in *Cosmopolitan* last year about an explosion of heat and satisfaction and excitement that surged from her abdomen up, filling the body like a volcano of erupting fulfilment. That wasn't exactly how she felt, but perhaps she had all that to come? She took her coat from the stand and hoped that someday—no, some night—Ambrose would really make their marvellous intimacy last longer. She would even get black sheets and that sort of thing if he wanted them. He did remind her so much of that chap, Mellors—sort of surly, but terribly satisfying and useful.

Although, really, unless it changed before the end, she maintained tremendous sympathies for Lady Chatterley's husband. Sophie had given her the book last Christmas, and although it was hard going in parts, she was more than halfway through it. She used to read quite a lot of it each week, but she was rather a slow reader, and anyway, she didn't have such a lot of time now that she was working. She opened the door, her pleasure seeping away into irritable anxiety—something that always happened when she had to get out of the gallery. Beatrice peered out and listened, and then she went out, leaving the door not quite closed in her haste.

CHAPTER 2

He heard her go, heard her expensive and useful court shoes go tip-tapping down the corridor from "Modern Works & Exhibitions" into the foyer. Then the silence. She'd gone out, and he'd missed her.

"A customer already Jenkins?" Mr Pugh asked and smiled because he wanted to look pleasant. He felt pleasant.

"That's what I like to see: queuing at the door, waiting for us to open, eh?"

"No, sir, I think it was a cleaner."

"A cleaner? At this time?"

"Probably in the washroom, sir," he replied, and he curled up his mouth to make it look like a smile, "Getting herself done up—you know—ready to go."

"But somebody just came in."

"No, out, sir. She went out."

Pugh looked at Jenkins for a moment and realised that the man's idiot grin could mean he was trying to cover something up.

"She?" He questioned, unsure how Pugh could be sure which sex it had been.

"Cleaner. Cleaner, sir," Pugh remarked, and he added in explanation, "They're women."

Pugh was of two minds: get to the bottom of all this nonsense about cleaners in the building at ten o'clock in the morning, or be magnanimous as someone in his position probably should be with subordinates.

Jenkins went to the window and said, "Probably in the staff room. Been getting ready to go. Making up and that sort of thing."

Pugh realised he'd got a bird: one of the cleaners obviously stayed on after time for a bit of that there. He supposed it was a legitimate perk, but he'd have to watch the situation. He smiled knowingly at Jenkins—not too man to mannish, but well, tolerantly.

"In the staff room, eh?"

Jenkins looked at his smile and said, "Yes."

Then another thing occurred to Mr Pugh: though he was the assistant director of galleries and had been for three weeks now, he was still unsure of the geography of the galleries under his aegis. He couldn't remember a washroom at the Bloomsbury—there wasn't the staff to warrant one.

"Do you mean the loo?"

Jenkins was peering out of the window with some intensity. He'd spotted Beatrice taking her lovely body up toward Goodge Street.

"At the end of the exhibition room, sir."

"Oh," Mr Pugh replied and went to join him at the window, "I didn't know we had one here." He looked out into Tottenham Court Road and asked, "A sort of staffroom is it?"

Beatrice disappeared from view, and Jenkins reluctantly turned his attention to the assistant director at his elbow.

"There is only one, sir," and he added, "For both sexes."

"Oh." Again, Pugh had a wave of doubt as to what they were talking about.

"Does it have cooking facilities—kettle, you know?"

Jenkins looked at him. He'd obviously missed something when he'd looked at Beatrice.

"Yes, there is a kettle, sir. Would you like some tea?"

"Yes," Pugh replied. He had watched Jenkins's mouth curl up again at the ends, "No. I mean, no, not really. Haven't time." He remembered quickly the advice given by his uncle who'd been responsible for people for years that officers should always be charming and slightly vague because it makes their men regard them with affection. So he smiled as happily as he could and said, "Jolly good. Nice of you to offer," in a way he thought an officer should. He lowered his voice confidentially, "I wouldn't make it too obvious, though—they're supposed to be out of the building by nine."

Jenkins looked puzzled, "Who?"

Pugh winked with difficulty. It was years since he'd winked.

"Attractive cleaning ladies who have to make themselves up in the staffroom, eh?"

"Oh." It was Jenkins's turn to wonder what they were talking about, "Oh yes, sir."

Barrymore Pugh had been senior resource officer of museums and galleries in Croydon until three weeks ago—up to getting his current job as assistant director of galleries. And he realised that now he was a top management man—a principal officer, no less—perhaps he shouldn't get too involved with staff like he used to.

"There seems to be a dearth of space—storage space—in the borough," Pugh said and folded his arms, wanting Jenkins to know that he was sharing his thoughts with him, "Any spare rooms here?"

"No." He'd said it too quickly so added, "I mean there's the staffroom downstairs, sir."

Barrymore Pugh thought that Jenkins had a fixation with washrooms and staffrooms.

"Staffroom?"

"Well," he began. He hoped to God this new ad wasn't going to make a habit of all this visiting. Mr Honeywell had only been three times in two years. "There's really only a tap and cold water, but we call it the washroom. Would you like to see it, sir?"

"Well yes, but not now."

Staffroom, loos, washrooms. Couldn't he think of anything else?

"What about storerooms?"

"I said there's a washroom or staffroom if you like. The cellar."

"Oh, oh right." He moved to go and then said, "Well I'll have to have a good gander round in a couple of weeks' time. There seems to be quite a bottleneck occurring at central. I think we'll have to shift some of it here."

"Three-dimensional or two-, sir?" This was going to be a right cock-up if it was three dimensional. He'd have to use Ambrose's office, and Ambrose wouldn't like that.

"Eh?"

"Sculpture or paintings?"

"Oh, you know: I suppose there's some of each."

"Well we could probably accommodate some modern pieces, sir, but wall space for canvasses is just about complete. What sort of work is it, sir?"

"Oh, well," he started as he threw his head from side to side to indicate the vastness of the possibilities, "could be anything. I'm not quite sure what they have down there to be honest, but it's a bottleneck."

It dawned on Jenkins that this man was not the sort who would get a job with the arts council.

"I wouldn't worry, sir. I'm sure there's lots of storage facilities at the other, larger galleries."

They were moving to the foyer.

"Well," Pugh began. He had the impression that Jenkins was trying to push his luck. "We'll have to see," the superintendent said, "Bloomsbury's had a bit of space."

"Oh did he?" The superintendent was Jenkins's superior, Mr Murphy, an Irish berk in Jenkins's opinion. The superintendent, for his part, wasn't too happy about Jenkins. In increasing efficiency and cutting back on services, the council had of course halved the expenditure of the recreation and culture department immediately. And the department had been rationalised. No curators were to be appointed to minor galleries until the economic situation improved. Plus caretakers were given a supplementary allowance for the extra responsibility of completing weekly statistics on attendances and compiling each cleaner's timesheet. Mr Murphy felt that the extra responsibility given to Mr Jenkins had gone to his head.

"I think Mr Murphy is probably confusing us with somewhere else," he said, putting his grin on again.

"It does happen sometimes, you know, sir. He's a little isolated, being confined to an office as he is."

He could be right. Barrymore Pugh hadn't been too sure of Mr Murphy either.

"Well," he said, "we'll have to bear everything in mind, but see what you can manage. Let me know what facilities there are."

"Let you know direct, sir? Or tell Mr Phillips?"

Mr Phillips was senior resources officer of galleries, and Barrymore Pugh didn't like the look of him either. His secretary, Miss Trimble, seemed rather apprehensive of Phillips as well. Perhaps he'd been trying something on with her? He supposed it would be more correct for Jenkins to deal with Phillips. "Yes, of course, but let me have a memo. I want to keep in the picture."

That sounded fairly impressive he thought, how principal officers should talk. He couldn't think of anything else to ask, so he looked at Jenkins kindly.

"Watch the cleaner business. We don't want Mr Murphy getting anxious, do we?"

He personally couldn't give fourpence about Mr Murphy, but it was the sort of thing Jenkins would like to hear him say he supposed. Jenkins didn't know what he was talking about.

"Cleaners, sir?" He didn't like the way Mr Murphy's name kept coming into the conversation.

Mr Pugh tapped the side of his nose, "Nuff said, eh?" And he smiled as he went to the foyer.

"Where do you keep your bits and pieces then? Have you an office?"

"No, sir," and he made it sound sad, "No, I have the *fwayer*." He switched his quick smile on again. "That's the hub of my little empire, sir."

"Oh." Pugh wasn't really interested, but he forced himself to be chatty, "Do you jot down the attendance figures and things?" Jenkins gave him a swift look. He'd been late these last two weeks with his weekly statistics, had Murphy been shopping him?

"Oh yes, sir. It's just difficult sometimes to get them down to the office in time," and he added maliciously, "Mr Murphy locks his door at dinnertimes, and he knows I have the same hour."

"Does he?" He made it sound as if Jenkins had quickened his interest, "Does he eat in the canteen?"

"I don't know," Jenkins sounded hurt at this irrelevancy, "but if the door's locked, I can't . . ."

"Yes, yes, of course. I should have a word with him."

"I will, I will, sir."

"Good, well." They were in the foyer and Pugh was moving his briefcase from one hand to the other, "Don't forget to jot something down now and then, and I'd like a situational report—you know, on the storage possibilities. As soon as you can." He went to the doors and added, "I'm not too happy at the extent of the centralisation in this borough."

"Right, sir," Jenkins replied and wondered how these people got their jobs. "Oh, sir, will you be coming again?"

Pugh had the door handle in his hand.

"What?" *Good Lord!* He'd made a hit with this one all right. "I'll try. I'll try and come again quite soon," he chuckled to show his mateyness, "Priorities. I only have so much time, you know."

He turned in the open doorway, smiled reassuringly, and said, "But I'll try. I'll try to get down in a couple of weeks or so. Bye, Mr . . . Bye."

"Bye, sir." Jenkins watched the door swing shut after him and thought again about the unfairness of job selection—not that he'd want to compete in the same field as that stupid clown.

"My God, he probably thought that French impressionists were continental Mike Yarwoods, and he permitted himself a smile for thinking of such an intellectual joke. People underestimated him, thought he was just a thick manual worker, didn't know the books he had been through. He must try and remember that joke to tell Beatrice, that might show her what sort of mind he had.

He continued thinking as he went through Modern Works & Exhibitions, aiming for the toilet at the end but unable to pass the corridor roped off and signposted: "private staff only." That corridor led to the door of Bonnyweather's office, two storerooms rented to Bonnyweather by Roy Jenkins as a private enterprise arrangement. The corridor also led to a small cellar with a tap—the washroom, as already mentioned—and being L-shaped, no doors were visible to casual onlookers. One had to move down and turn along another leg to reach the doors. Jenkins looked at the rope and sign and realised that he was going to have to do something. It was too tempting for the Mr Barrymore Pughs of this world. But of course—and he smiled modestly to himself at the ingenuity of his thinking—he could put a hessian fold-stand in front of it. A painting on each side and a couple of modern pieces at its feet, and no one would think there was an opening behind.

Maybe he could use two fold-stands—make an entrance like a men's urinal he'd once seen at a race meeting.

He replaced the rope barrier and mused down the short corridor, immediately noticing that Bonnyweather's door was ajar and that, new lock or no new lock, he could actually get in. He hurried to the door and opened it cautiously. The room was empty, but he called out (not too loudly) just to be sure, "Anybody in?" There was Beatrice's table, so obviously hers: he could see the riding boots and smell her perfume—it hung about the table and excited him. He picked up her box of tissues. Again, her scent. He pulled out two tissues, tearing one in his haste to have something of hers—her smell, something she touched. He put the tissues in his pocket and reminded himself that, more importantly, the open door gave him an opportunity not to be missed.

He hurried back to the foyer for his equipment and decided that the camera would be enough. It wasn't an expensive camera, but it was small. You had to slide one half into the other to operate the shutter. Ideal for surreptitious photography. He'd bought it some weeks ago, but he had not had the opportunity to use it yet. Back in the office he went to Bonnyweather's desk and carefully opened drawers. He was surprised at the number of candles—different colours, different shapes in each drawer. He found what he was seeking: a drawer filled with papers in brown manilla folders. Gingerly lifting out a number of folders, he leafed through them and saw that the name and address of the client in each case was inside the folder. He knew this was his chance.

He tried to focus the camera on the folder, but it was too close. The name and address wouldn't fit into the eyepiece; he needed to be higher, further away from the subject. Standing on Ambrose's chair seemed to give him range, and if he bent down a little it didn't seem too far away. After all, he could get prints enlarged. He took three snaps of the first folder just to be sure—sure he'd moved the shutter without moving the camera—and then he felt rather than knew that someone was watching him.

Errol Billington was standing in the doorway. They had never met before, but Jenkins was the more interested, more observant. Errol was about seventeen, of average height and fairly slim. His punk hairstyle was growing out—and with it the henna dye. He wore a short-sleeved shirt open at the neck and partly hidden by a sleeveless pullover. His trousers were narrow and grey. Surprisingly, his trousers had a smart crease. He carried what appeared to be an old mackintosh.

"Excuse me," he said.

Jenkins observation had been completed in a split second, and his reflexes lowered the camera quickly and made him bend to the desk to stop falling.

"I couldn't find anybody," Errol said, as if in explanation.

"Oh," was all Jenkins could muster. He leaned awkwardly down on the desk, his feet still in the chair.

"I couldn't find the bell. It said ring, but I couldn't find a bell."

"It's in the *fwayer.*" And because the young man seemed not to understand, he added, "The entrance. In the entrance, the *fwayer.*"

"Well I couldn't see it."

They looked at each other for a pause, Jenkins totally unsure and Errol wondering why he was standing on a chair leaning at the desk.

"You doing some exercises?"

"No."

"Oh."

Jenkins didn't want to stand up straight because he didn't want to explain the camera.

"I'll go back and look."

"It's on the desk. Quite obvious. There's a sign."

"I saw the sign. Couldn't see the bell though."

"Well it's there."

"Shall I go back and ring it?"

Jenkins decided that he'd lost the chance for any more photography, so he climbed down from the chair.

"No," he said, "No, there's no need to if I'm here."

He put the folders carefully back in the drawer and was reassured by the uninterested look on Errol's face.

"Right. Let's go to my office then."

He went out, and Errol stood respectfully as Jenkins pulled the door to and indicated that he wished Errol to follow him.

"You haven't closed the door."

"I know," Jenkins said and offered no explanation. Errol followed him to the foyer. Jenkins went round behind his table and gave the young man a critical look before picking up a bell from the floor under the table and plonking it down triumphantly near the notice saying "Please ring."

The young man met his look for a pause.

"Well I wouldn't have thought of looking on the floor for a bell."

Jenkins sat in his chair, took off his peaked cap, and placed it carefully so as not to disturb the postcards on the table. Then he said, "Well can I help you?"

"Is this your office? I thought it was a foyer."

"The *fwayer* is my office. What can I do for you?"

Errol looked round the foyer before he said anything, then he smiled in a sort of pityingly sympathetic way—as he would to a man who thought a foyer was an office.

"Can you tell me where Aquarius is?"

"Eh? I mean, pardon?"

"I'm looking for Aquarius."

Jenkins was puzzled. The young man did not look to be the sort who frequented art galleries—never mind coming in to view a specific work—but he learned that many arty people affected the dress and mannerisms of the proletariat, so he was cautious.

"Is it a sculptural work or two-dimensional?"

He placed his fingers together, prepared to be an expert.

"It's a shop," he said, and added (because of the look on the caretaker's face), "For pets."

"Oh, oh! *That* Aquarius." A bloody shop; he might have guessed. "Just out of here on the left, first turning left. Windmill Street," and he added, "sir" because you never knew.

Errol said, "Right, thanks," before he walked to the exit, pulled the door to its widest point, and went out. He was thinking the door would swing back into place after him, but it didn't—he'd opened it too wide.

"What about the door then?" Jenkins called, irritation in his voice. He put his cap on before standing because the open door, the cool wind, all parts of the outside world made him feel exposed, on view. He knew he should be seen properly dressed.

He wondered why on Earth anybody should come into a gallery to find the whereabouts of a pet shop as he closed the door. He stood looking out through the glass for a pause before he pulled his thinking together. He decided to carry on taking advantage of his opportunity. He quickly went back to Bonnyweather's office with his camera.

He climbed onto the chair twice (and down again to open a folder, photograph the client's name and address, and open another). He had hoped to get as many addresses as he could in what he knew could only be a short time. He was standing on the chair focussing on the third address when he became aware of someone in the doorway. When Errol said "Excuse me," his reflexes again bent him to lean on the desk, his feet in the chair, not comfortable or dignified.

"What sort of shoes have you got on?" Jenkins asked rudely.

"Eh?" Errol looked down at his desert boots, "Why?"

"Because I can't ever hear you. Why don't you ring?"

"Well I knew where you'd be, didn't I?"

With a stranger thinking that he spent his time in Ambrose's office doing this sort of covert business—leaving aside that, as head caretaker, he was perfectly entitled to enter anywhere in the gallery (and it wasn't in their agreement to put new locks on doors)—Errol's presence made him feel guilty. Only through Ambrose's perversity had he had to resort to this sort of thing, but he felt guilty and irritated by this youth who couldn't ring bells.

"I forgot the name of the street. What was it?"

Jenkins stood upright in the chair and proclaimed, "Windmill. Windmill Street."

Although Errol did not seem interested in the reply, he was looking at the modern, three-dimensional work by the hatstand near the door.

"What's that?"

Jenkins followed his gaze. "A statue. A work of modern art." He couldn't hold on to his rancour when he was asked to be an expert.

"Yes, I know that. But what is it? What's it supposed to be?"

"What's it supposed to be?" Jenkins echoed him scornfully, "You don't say 'what it's supposed to be' about works of modern art. You say, 'tell me about it.'"

Errol gave him a look but didn't say, "Tell me about it"; instead he said, "Is it a dog?"

"A dog?" The amazement showed in his voice, "A dog?" That anyone could think that a symbolic, three-dimensional abstract creation was in any way representational seemed philistine. "Like a dog?" he said again and looked at the work, trying to view it through the young man's eyes.

"It doesn't look anything like a dog."

"Well I think so," Errol said adamantly.

"If it represents anything, it represents the convolutions of man's longings, his repression, his . . ." And his eyes caught sight of Beatrice, who was standing behind Errol.

"Oh good morning, Beatrice. This young man thought," and he smirked in a superior way before adding, "that was a dog."

Errol turned to Beatrice, not wholly interested but aware that the caretaker was impressed by her presence.

"I only asked if it was meant to be a dog," he said as he turned back to Jenkins, standing in the chair like an umpire or a conductor, "I didn't think it *was* a dog."

"You said, you said, 'Is it a dog?'" Jenkins voice was dogged.

"I didn't."

"What are you doing in here?" All her distaste at seeing that man in her space, her private quarters, brought detestation into her voice in the way only an upper class accent succeeds in doing: icy, superior, authoritative, contemptuous. Jenkins was uncomfortable. He felt suddenly vulnerable standing on Ambrose's chair.

"I was just passing, and the door was open, and this young man was seeking my assistance . . ."

"You know that you're not supposed to be in here," she cut him off like a headmistress.

This was too much even for Jenkins. Love may be one thing, but being bollocked in front of a stranger for being in a room he was paid to be responsible for? "Not supposed to be in here?" His pride was like a sharp pain. "I'm supposed to be able to go anywhere in this gallery, it's my responsibility. It is quite indiscriminate of Ambrose to change this lock. He had no right to—it was no part of our agreement."

Beatrice and Errol looked at him in silence—she felt curiously safe behind Errol, and he was merely interested (as always) in watching someone lose an argument.

"I have every right to be . . ."

"Get down from that chair at once."

Beatrice was surprised by her courage. She was very angry, her voice authoritative and terse. He climbed down, vulnerability in his every move.

Errol said, "He was taking pictures," and that was too much for Jenkins. He may not be able to rail at his loved one, but he knew where he was with this yobbo.

"All right, all right. That'll be enough of that. He wanted Aquarius, Beatrice, and I thought he meant . . ."

"Aquarius?" Beatrice was surprised.

"This young man was enquiring for the whereabouts of it," he said, feeling just a little bit easier. Maybe her surprise had weakened her position.

"Can I have a word with you, Beatrice?"

He looked at Errol as he would an interloper, "Well, I've told you where it is. Off you go, lad."

"Aquarius?" Beatrice asked Errol this time.

"He says it's in Windmill Street, on the left as you go out," he said as if she'd asked.

"Oh have you bought Ruskin's bird Seed?"

"No, not yet. I'm going over there now."

"I wonder, Miss Beatrice," Jenkins began, not liking the way his adversaries were chatting as if he weren't there, "would you be kind enough to . . ."

"Errol Billington?"

"Yeah," he said surprised, "Yeah, that's me."

"Okay," Beatrice said as she looked at her watch, "10:57." Both Errol and Jenkins felt that the time was significant. She took hold of Errol's arm and her voice had a sort of urgency: "Would you like to stay here with me?"

"Eh?" His surprise was heightened by the grip on his arm. Beatrice was brisk and uncaringly cold to Jenkins.

"I will look after Mr Billington, Mr Jenkins. And I suggest that you don't tamper with things that are outside of your understanding."

"Outside my understanding?" *My God!* Even the one you love can be impertinent! "I can assure you, Miss Beatrice, all this is entirely within my understanding . . ."

"He means empirical," Errol said to Beatrice, and she moved him a pace away from the doorway.

"Come along, Mr Billington. Until you have the birdseed, we have not officially met. And I advise you, Mr Jenkins, to return to your post and leave well alone."

Jenkins was hurt but willing to obey her. He went to the door and mumbled, "You really can't order me about. I mean, I have an important role in this gallery . . ."

"You're the caretaker," she said simply.

"Precisely," he remarked as if she'd at last seen his point, "Oh Beatrice, why do we always squabble? Can't I buy you a sandwich?"

He was close to her, and it was awful, but she held her ground as he moved past her into the corridor.

"No, you certainly cannot."

"But my feelings. I can't hide them, Beatrice." There was a desperation in his voice and he didn't care about Errol's presence—it was so rare to have her face to face.

"Can't you see that together . . . ?"

"I am sorry, Mr Billington. This must be so embarrassing for you."

"Never mind him . . ."

"Shall I go to Aquarius?" Errol asked, unembarrassed.

"Yes, I think that's a good idea."

Jenkins and Beatrice watched Errol go to the turn of the corridor and pause.

"Shall I pretend not to look? You know, as if I know when I get the birdseed?"

Beatrice smiled at a worthy pupil before replying, "That will be splendid."

Now at last, just the two of them. Jenkins was a goer; he didn't give in until he was told to.

"Let me buy you a sandwich this dinnertime," he pleaded.

"Oh you really are ridiculous," she said and shooed him from the doorway, "Do try to be sensible."

He backed away a couple of paces as a reaction, and the telephone rang in the office.

"Just one minute," Jenkins pleaded as Beatrice went into the room, "Just a minute, Beatrice . . ." But she had shut the door, telephones being more important than caretakers. On her way to the desk, there was a knocking at the door and a muffled and plaintive, "Beatrice."

"Perry Ironside Agency, Beatrice Thompson speaking. Can I help you?" Then her voice became more matter of fact, "Oh it's you. Oh you really are 32A. Oh all right, all right. But he'll be cross." She turned her back to the desk, her left arm supporting her bosom and her telephone arm, "Yes, I'm going over to meet him now," and she turned again, ready to put the instrument down. "Well don't be too late," she said almost sharply, "Bye, byeee."

She had been apprehensive—terribly apprehensive—when she'd seen Jenkins in the office, but then it had been so easy. He was just a little man trying to be pleasant in his own very peculiar way. But underneath, he surely realised he was baying at the moon? It was complimentary, she supposed, being worshipped, having someone who was so eager. And perhaps, if he hadn't such a sort of cringing aggression, his worshipping could be interesting. But he really was ridiculous. Why couldn't Ambrose bother her? And what an awfully common boy Errol was. But his use of the word empiric impressed her, as well as the strange air of self-confidence he seemed to have—far too confident for someone from a state school. Perhaps he could be interesting. She dismissed such thoughts as pointless as she put her coat on, prepared to go to Mrs Napiorkowska's Aquarius. She looked forward (as she always did) to the clandestine routine they had for meeting clients.

Mrs Napiorkowska came out from the back of the shop. There was no bell, but she always knew when someone was in. With all the suspicious patience of her Polish background, she stood behind Errol, watching him because she knew what skinheads could get up to. Errol wandered round, gazing (he hoped) interestedly at tins of cat food. He fingered one or two decorative dog collars and read the instruction on a packet of worming powder until he spotted the gerbils. He watched them with all the fascination humans have for caged animals as they worked the treadmill, trod on each other, and buried into hay as if they wanted to do something in private.

"Can I be helping you?" Mrs Napiorkowska asked.

"Eh?" Errol tore his eyes from the gerbils, "Errr, I'm just looking"

"Well this is not a library, you know. This is a shop. Have you animals?"

At that moment Beatrice came in, her coat collar was turned up and she was wearing sunglasses. She went to Errol.

"Good morning, Miss Thompson," Mrs Napiorkowska said, and as always, Beatrice was surprised.

She whispered to Errol, "Go to the counter. I'll join you there."

Mrs Napiorkowska said as she approached, "Ruskin's?"

He turned for assurance to Beatrice, who nodded. He put the packet of flea eradicator back on the shelf.

"Yes, please."

"A pound?"

"Errr, yes," he said and watched her take a packet from the stacked display on the counter.

"45p please."

It hadn't occurred to him that he would have to pay. He searched his pockets—he had 30p.

"Can I have half a pound?"

Mrs Napiorkowska put the packet back with a sigh, glancing at Beatrice who quickly turned to the gerbils. "28p" she said, handing another packet to Errol.

He paid her and turned to Beatrice who indicated the door with a jerk of her head. He took her signal, went to the door, and headed out. She watched the gerbils for a few moments as if compelled to, and then she went quickly to the door.

"Goodbye, Miss Thompson," Mrs Napiorkowska called.

Beatrice didn't answer. She didn't want her to be sure who she was. She went out and saw Errol clutching the birdseed, looking in a shop window.

They didn't speak for a pause after she'd joined him, not until she saw what the shop sold. It only had one small window and called itself a sex emporium. She took his arm, looked at her watch, and said, "It's 11:10. He may not be there, so we'll walk down Oxford Street for fifteen minutes."

And they did.

CHAPTER 3

Jenkins paused and stood in the doorway. He'd followed Bonnyweather to the office and looked in, unsure whether to enter.

"Pressures, pressures, Bernard," Bonnyweather was saying as he hung up his hat and slid his stick into the umbrella receptacle, "I've just been out. Got as far as Devonshire Street and just stopped."

He went to his desk and remarked, "Couldn't remember where I was going. All I knew was that it was about a horse."

"A house?" Jenkins asked, coming forward a couple of paces.

"Horse," he said and sat on the desk. He had to move the phone to get his behind further on. "Equine, you know. Clip, clop, clop. Anyway, pressures. Shut the door, Bernard, security's vital," he said, pausing briefly to watch Jenkins move back to the door. "Pressure. That's the curse of civilisation: stress."

Jenkins closed the door and felt more confident as he uttered, "Exactly, exactly." He came further into the room, headed in the direction of the armchair, and said, "Too many ruts. Life shouldn't be lived in ruts . . ."

"In what?"

"Ruts." He didn't like sitting in the chair, not yet anyway. He added, "We should aim to better ourselves—and be allowed to."

He manoeuvred himself into a position near the chair arm and said, "That's what an education system is supposed to mean." He couldn't help looking toward her table, "Are those Beatrice's boots?"

"Yes," Bonnyweather replied, leaning back on his hands and looking absently at the poster. Jenkins pushed the boots from his vision and looked at Bonnyweather gazing at the poster.

"Education shouldn't be a stereotyped preparation for puerile examinations. A man should be rounded, not blinkered," he said, not realising that he'd sat on the arm of the chair.

"But forgetting Bernard, just like that—it only used to happen to old people in the old days." He walked to the window to gaze out, ruminating on his forgetfulness.

Jenkins watched him; he was enjoying this tête-à-tête. He didn't want to spoil anything, so he waited a pause before he spoke.

"Memory, like a woman, is usually unfaithful."

Bonnyweather turned to look at him.

"That's a Spanish proverb," Jenkins explained.

"Is it?" Bonnyweather went back to sit on the desk and Jenkins wondered whether he'd said the wrong thing. He added, "Women and elephants never forget."

"Who said that?" Jenkins knew he had heard it before somewhere.

Bonnyweather sat on the desk looking at the poster as he always did when women came into the conversation. He look as if he were deep in thought.

"No, you're right, Ambrose," Jenkins said as he slid down into the armchair, "And I don't care who hears me say so: education has no right to demand qualifications when it's the only one that can give them. I mean it's introversion gone mad, isn't it?"

Bonnyweather said absently to the poster, "I think it was Dorothy Parker." But Jenkins was sitting comfortably, his thought processes flowing.

"Victimisation. That's what it is—no more, no less." He paused as he thought about what he'd said, and Ambrose was lost in Jane. Each thinking behind his unseeing look.

"Did you know that 200,000 years ago there was only one female person who had mitochondrial DNA? Just the one woman of the 2,000 on the planet." He looked at Jenkins puzzled face, "Amazing when you think of that, isn't it?"

"Well yes," Jenkins replied, unsure what his companion's gist was. "What happened to her, then?"

"Who?"

"This woman with DNA."

"Mitochondrial DNA, Bernard," he wagged his finger reproachfully; "All Homo sapiens have that now. She was first," he looked sternly at the caretaker for a pause. "Eve: first woman. Although I prefer to think of her as Sophia."

"You mean," Jenkins paused, unsure, "she was Jewish?"

"Bernard, please," Bonnyweather again seemed reproachful, "Sophia is Greek. It means wisdom. The first woman, the mother of God, some people believe."

"Oh." Jenkins was impressed, he hadn't expected to be privy to a conversation of this depth, "But I thought she was called Mary."

"God, Bernard, *God*," he said and wagged a finger again, "She was the wisdom, God was the power," he finished and slid down from the desk.

"How do you know there was only one woman?"

"Palaeobiology. It's all there in the genes, you know. We're living in a mind-boggling time, Bernard. That's what intelligence is for: keeping abreast."

He wandered round the desk to sit in his chair.

"Yes, got as far as that association of youth clubs place and just couldn't remember."

"I know, I know just what you mean," Jenkins replied. He felt he was on more familiar ground. "And that's another thing: there's no youth clubs for people our age, are there? No, everything's for kids. It's a kid's world today."

"Have you stopped smoking, Bernard?"

"Well more or less."

"I thought you had." Bonnyweather moved the phone back to the edge of the desk.

Jenkins refused to be sidetracked: "Oh yes, it's a kid's world, all right—that's why a lot of them stay kids all their lives." He laid back and crossed his legs, thoroughly enjoying a philosophical conversation.

"We're building here in Britain—I can't speak for anywhere else, but I wouldn't mind betting—what we're building here is a juvenile society."

"I think America started it."

"Well it didn't take us long to get the bloody hang of it." There was an explosive bitterness in his voice.

"The class structure didn't help, did it? Too many levels. You don't mind me sitting down?" Jenkins wanted proof that he was being accepted as an equal in this discussion, but he didn't wait for an answer. "Too many levels. What's the value of A-levels if you want to get on and do something in this world?"

Bonnyweather looked thoughtful, "Or venting."

"They're poleaxing the nation's intelligence." It occurred to him that Ambrose had said something so he queried, "What?"

Bonnyweather looked at him for a moment, then he decided there were things to be done. This wouldn't get the baby a new dress, so he opened and shut the drawers of the desk as if busy searching for something important.

"Well Bernard, you're quite right. It's all this unsavoury rushing about for money that's at the root of it all," and he paused. His thoughts—as always when he mentioned money (his mind's code word for status)—moved to Beatrice. He walked to her table and said, "I bet she looks bloody marvellous on a horse," picking up her riding boots.

"Who? Beatrice?"

Jenkins was puzzled by Ambrose breaking off from things like that, and for a moment he thought he was talking about the girl in the poster. He was turning the boots, letting the light show the grain in the leather, examining them with affection on his face. And when he spoke, his voice was soft and caring

"I bet we all would if we'd been mounted as a child."

He put the boots down and looked smilingly at Jenkins. "Ah yes, *ceteris paribus,* Bernard. *Ceteris paribus* and we'd be a happy breed."

"Oh," Jenkins replied. He didn't know any Latin. "About this lock business, Ambrose. I'll have to explain to the assistant director, you know."

Bonnyweather was breezy going to his desk, "Well I don't want to be inhospitable, Bernard, but there's things to be done."

Jenkins stood up, as usual unsure about where he stood.

"Why do you keep calling me Bernard?"

Bonnyweather was busy with a drawer, searching at his desk, and Jenkins knew the discussion was over. Ambrose seemed to have the knack for cutting things off just when they were in full bloom. He looked up and smiled. "Remember, Bernard, 'To make light of philosophy is to be a true philosopher.' Pascal said that," he remarked, and after smiling at the uncertain smile on the caretaker's face, he went to the door and opened it.

Jenkins had never heard of Pascal. Well he'd heard of the sweet firm, but it couldn't be them. Anyway, he felt he ought to pursue this Bernard business.

"My name isn't Bernard," he said as he went to the door that was being held open for him.

"Pop in again sometime. It's always useful to talk things over."

"My name's Roy, not Bernard. Roy Jenkins."

Ambrose looked at him benignly, "It's the attitude that counts. The attitude—not where you get to."

Jenkins turned at the door for a last look at Beatrice's table. "She's beautiful, isn't she?" He looked at her employer with a mixture of wistfulness and envy. "She'd respect a vet, wouldn't she? Does she love you?"

Ambrose looked seriously back at the serious face. "I think so," he said. They paused, both considering what had been said, then Jenkins jammed his cap on and went into the corridor with more spirit.

"My God, if I could only get to college—I'd move into a different class, all right."

Bonnyweather was sympathetic: "We all would, Bernard. We all would," he said as he closed the door.

He was sorry for Jenkins, like he was for anybody who was dissatisfied, anyone who wanted to improve his lot and join the more fortunate but lacked the imagination to change himself.

People like Jenkins wanted to be among the fortunate and still be themselves. They didn't realise that it was the sort of person they were that was keeping them where they were. They didn't realise that you have to change your whole persona if you're going to cross the barrier. It was like a disease, this qualification business. Exams and bits of paper—they don't make you into an enigma, a personality that intrigues the fortunate into accepting you.

Poor sod, hoping, lusting after someone he hadn't a cat in hell's chance of getting. He wondered why he was so needled about education. No, he was born with an inferiority complex. He smiled at the thought of what Jenkins would do if Beatrice decided she liked being worshipped. No, she was too far up the tree for the likes of caretakers. She wouldn't know what to do with one. You have to have class or some sort of eccentricity to make it with upper crust females. You have to be an enigma or keep showing them that you're ten times more intelligent than they are—they respect that. And if they respect you, they'll lead you to the bedroom sooner or later. He himself was taking his time, deliberately building it up just to see what the score was. He wasn't desperate; he hadn't had too much luck in the past with eager females.

He watched a man putting a ladder up in Percy Mews, and he thought, *Yes, there's a man who is quite content to live at his own level, just be happy making money out of people who thought they were more fortunate because they didn't have to hump ladders about for a living.* No, it was no use striving to be something you weren't.

He gazed out of the window at the man with the ladder for a pause before he remembered and sprung his mind into action. She'd be back with this Billington soon, so he'd better make a bit of a show, put another tie on. Ties, Ambrose thought—and in fact, often said—were the way a man could change his appearance without having to buy another suit. A selection of ties can be a selection of changes. He took a tie from the bottom drawer of the desk. He took off the one he was wearing and put it on the armchair before going to the mirror over the washbasin and grimacing at the screech of water squirting from the leaky tap. Yes, he'd impress Billington.

He had knotted the tie and looked closely at the mirror until it was misted by his breath. There was a knock at the door, a special knock: three separate taps spaced out then tree rapid taps then three more spaced out. In Morse code this meant "OSO." He called to the mirror, "*Entre.*"

Beatrice opened the door partly and looked in.

"Can I disturb you, Mr Bonnyweather?"

"Eh?" He cursed himself for being caught out yet again making a stupid response. She took a pace in, holding the door and impeding anyone who may have been behind her.

"Have you time to see Mr Billington?"

He realised she was making it seem that he might be too busy if he wanted to be.

"Oh, oh yes. I'll see him now, Miss Trotter," he said and turned back to the mirror to check his tie and face in the clearing mist.

"Thompson," she said curtly and opened the door wider, "Do come in Mr Billington. Mr Bonnyweather will not be a moment—he just has to collect his wits."

She pointed to the armchair, "Do sit down." Errol went nervously to it.

Errol Billington had always considered himself to be different than
his school friends—and certainly different than those who had become
his closest friends. And the difference had come home to him when
none of them had sought or taken the jobs they had said they were
going to when they were talking among themselves. None of them had
become mercenaries, joined the SAS, gone to work in a fairground
collecting fares on a waltzer, or gone to make a fortune as a pimp.
They'd gone into shops and offices, and one was a gas fitter. But he
hadn't given in. The old feller might be doing his nut, but he wasn't
going to be pushed into a dead-end ordinariness. Mind you, the old
feller's job was interesting, but that needed A-levels and all that. Errol
wanted to get work, be independent, and do a job that used the sorts
of talents he had. This interview with Ambrose Bonnyweather was the
furthest he'd been down the avenue of his ambitions, and he didn't
want to cock it up.

"Have you come far?" Beatrice asked as she closed the door,
talking as if it were the first moment of meeting, as if they hadn't been
promenading up Oxford Street for the last twenty minutes or so. "No,
not really," Errol said, watching her go to her table.

She had been impressed with his strong silences whilst they'd
been walking—and surprised by some of the things he did say. She
was pleasantly surprised—in fact, considering his background—by the
little gentlemanly touches: holding her arm to cross the street, moving
to the outside of the pavement, and exuding self-confidence. But now,
coming in to meet Ambrose, he was nervous and not really at ease. And
she felt protective.

"It's a super day isn't it?" she said and glared at Bonnyweather, still
preening himself, "Rather reminiscent of the Adriatic, isn't it? I love
the Adriatic. There's always more one wants to look at when there's
sun, don't you think?"

She sat at her table and gave him a dazzling smile.

"Well Mr Billings, eh?" Bonnyweather called out to the mirror and
she thought, *Oh God, he's not in that mood, is he?*

Errol had to twist round in his chair to see where the voice was
coming from and said, "Billington."

Bonnyweather was beaming at him as he came from the
washbasin.

"*Chantay monsewer,*" he said, and because Errol just looked at him, he added, "Speak French?"

"No," he replied and pointed down to the washbasin, "You've left the tap on."

Bonnyweather clasped his hands behind his back and stood looking down on Errol. He saw the tie on the armchair, draped over each arm and under Errol. He pulled it with a suddenness that made the young man think he was about to be attacked. He flinched and rocked from side to side as the tie was pulled from under his behind, and then he watched Bonnyweather with wide eyes as he cracked the tie a couple of times like a whip before rolling it round his hand.

"Well, Ambrose Bonnyweather—that's me. And you are Errol Billington, is that right, Miss Trotter?" he asked as he went to the desk.

Beatrice was jolted from her thinking and wondering why Ambrose was being so silly. She thought, *Maybe he's ill at ease? Men are funny.*

"Thompson," she said, like a habit.

"I am an agent, an enquiry agent. You could almost say," he began before pausing, bending over, and approaching the desk to say, "a special agent."

Errol nodded as if he understood.

"Ties, Mr Billington. Ties are important in my game," he said, and Errol wondered why. "What does your father do?"

"Eh?" The question was unexpected, "Oh he wears one."

"Job," he said testily, "Father's job."

"He's a probation officer," he said, and because it seemed he was expected to say more, he went on, "That's why I'm interested in crime, you know, as a career."

"Aha," Bonnyweather said, as if what Errol had said had summed things up, "That could be useful. Make a note of that Miss Thompson."

"Thank you," Beatrice's voiced with irony, but she didn't write anything. She was too interested in watching and listening.

"I'd like to become an investigator." Errol had spoken because they were both looking at him. "Well really, it's either that or something like a drama critic."

"What is?"

"I like finding out things, writing about things."

Bonnyweather felt that he was allowing this young man to control the interview, so he asked if he had left school.

"Tech," Errol said with the pride of someone who had come from further education, "I've done a business studies course at tech—well part of one." And again he felt he was expected to go on, "I was there for eight months. I thought it might be useful."

Bonnyweather neither knew nor cared what a business studies course might be, the young man didn't have to impress him with that sort of garbage. He was above all the artificialities of institutional attainment—"a man's a man"—that was his maxim, and it was up to every man to show he was a bloody man and not hide in the herd. And if there was any impressing to be done, it was the weakest to the wall.

"Well lad, well," he said and leaned on the desk, trying not to look at Beatrice, "Enquiry agents—specialists, that's the word: specialists—" he paused for effect, "Espionage, currencies, immigration, drugs, murder. We're specialists."

He looked hard at Errol who felt a response was needed.

"I know," he said

"I'm a specialist, Mr Thompson . . ."

"Billington," Beatrice corrected mechanically.

"I specialise in pets."

Errol was surprised. "Pets?"

"Just think," and he gave him a second or two, "just think, lad: you've made your pile, got all the furniture you need—big house, cars, cottage in Wales, caravan in the Lake District, kids into good jobs—just you and the wife. Just think."

He looked very serious, and Errol tried to think of just himself and a wife before he went on, "Just think: you're the wife," and Errol wasn't sure for a moment, "Everything's there: mod cons, fridges—those sort of things—maybe even an oh pay. But what is the most valuable thing you can own, eh?"

Errol thought, then he said, "A complete Sony Music Master with tape deck, CD player, and radio."

Bonnyweather just looked at him.

"Quad then—not stereo."

He was severe, but he told himself that the youth was only a boy. "Pets, Mr Billings, pets. Something to lavish care on, something worth paying good money to find if it were lost—that's what middle-aged wives of successful men value: they value pets. And I specialise in helping them."

He sat back in his chair, satisfied that his logic was irrefutable and dazzling in its originality.

"Oh," Errol said.

Perhaps the lad was lost in admiration?

"Right. What do you want to see me about?"

"Do you tail them? You know, work out their movements?"

Errol was having a little difficulty associating private eyes with animals, but he wanted to look keen. After all, private investigators are private investigators—there must be exciting times, car chases, grateful clients . . . the sort of thing Rockford, Cannon, and Columbo did in a day's work.

Beatrice felt a need to be helpful and smiled at Errol. "Mr Bonnyweather traces lost and stolen animals for their anxious owners," she explained.

Errol looked at her, not showing any gratitude for her help before turning back to Bonnyweather. It wasn't easy to face him because the armchair was at an angle that made seeing anyone at the desk or by the window a very uncomfortable ordeal.

"I was looking for a job," he said, "a vacancy."

"A job?" Bonnyweather was taken aback, "You mean paid?"

"Well yes," Errol said and added, "You know, wages."

Both Bonnyweather and Beatrice were looking at Errol, and he couldn't think what else to say. The careers officer had told him to always ask about pay and conditions because that would show he was making a serious application. He said, "My dad said anything over fifty pounds to start with."

After a pause, Bonnyweather spoke slowly, carefully: "I think, Mr Billington, that there is little point in prolonging this conversation. Fifty pounds. A complete beginner? No, Mr Billings, I think we're wasting each other's time."

Errol looked at him and understood what he'd said, but he had been led to believe that you didn't get an interview if nobody was needed. He stood up disappointed. Then he remembered the scheme he'd been told about, "Mr Green said I could ask if you wanted a training scheme."

"A what?"

"I don't know much about it, really. I've got this leaflet."

He searched the pockets of the old mac he carried, watched like an actor by the other two.

"Mr Green says I can get paid for a year by MS or something. Sort of government."

Beatrice felt sorry for him and didn't know why. He finally found the leaflet and straightened it out a little before giving it to Bonnyweather.

"I can get thirty-five pounds per week, and the employer doesn't have to pay anything."

Bonnyweather allowed some interest in his voice, "Not pay anything?"

He took the leaflet, unfolded it further, and poured the pocket detritus it had gathered into an ashtray—his distaste only momentary.

"The employer pays nothing at all?"

"Mr Green says you can only apply for a programme."

He was reading, skimming through, looking for the part that explained about employers being able to get free labour. He asked, "This Mr Green, who is he?"

"At the careers office," Errol said. He decided that Bonnyweather was interested, so after a glance at Beatrice and a kindly smile from her, he sat down again.

"He says the government is very interested in people of my age who are unemployed because I represent the future."

"Oh he said that, did he?"

Bonnyweather was interested in what he was reading. He wasn't entirely unaware of the fact that, for the past few years, the government had been worrying about unemployment and thinking up a number of special measures, particularly for young people. He bought newspapers every day, of course, but really only read the front page—they were bought for the classifieds, and that was Beatrice's area. Although he had attended now and then at the department of Social Security. And there he had leaflets about something called "a right to work" thrust at him by attractively breasted (if otherwise scruffy-looking) students or some such.

He quite honestly hadn't read anything that was printed in anything less than one-inch type. He certainly hadn't been aware of any scheme that paid an employee's wages. It was very interesting. He thought, And it's yet another attempt to dull the incentives and motivations of modern society. If a man couldn't stand on his own two feet and have the right to starve if that was what he elected to do, then the bloody country was going to the dogs. But if there was free labour being pushed about, then he wanted it pushed in his direction.

Errol was trying to remember more of what he'd been told.

At the time, yesterday morning, it had seemed like the usual bullshit he got from career advisers when he told them he wanted to be a private investigator. But now he could see the interest from Bonnyweather.

"Even the unions are interested," he said, "Although they want firms to make new jobs for people like me. He says everybody's interested in people like me."

"Oh did he?" Bonnyweather replied, rereading the part about how pleased Manpower Services Commission would be to help anyone who wished to participate.

"He says the scheme is a boon to an employer. Even some places like solicitors and dentists are interested, but big firms like supermarkets are abusing it."

Bonnyweather looked up. He had been only half listening, but Beatrice thought it all sounded terribly interesting and wondered if it only applied to those from a state school.

"Now this is interesting, very interesting. Nothing at all, eh?"

Errol was quite relaxed now, enjoying the feeling that he was telling someone something he didn't know.

"He says, of course, it will bring out the worst in money-grabbing employers, but it will keep the unemployment figures down for this year."

Bonnyweather's sense of belonging to those who are playing a responsible part in the country's economy—albeit, the CBI didn't speak for entrepreneurs like himself—was irked by this comment.

"This Mr Green . . . he's a communist, then, is he?"

"He's a careers officer."

"And he sent you to see me?"

There was scorn in Errol's voice: "No." He continued his sort of amused scorn, "They don't know about jobs. They just talk to you."

The telephone came to life, shattering the intimacy.

"Telephone, Miss Billings," Bonnyweather said, sitting back in his chair, watching the phone making its noise.

"Oh you really are . . ." Beatrice went to the phone and said, "I'm awfully sorry, Mr Billington." Errol looked at her wondering what she was sorry about.

"Perry Ironside Agency, Beatrice Thompson speaking," she intoned, turning her back to Bonnyweather and smiling at Errol. "Yes, yes, oh how awful," she said.

"How did you find me, then?" Bonnyweather asked.

"It was your advert, and I went through the telephone book to look up the number and find the address."

He ran a small, inexpensive ad in the *Standard* twice a week: "Private investigator available for tracing loved ones," and it provided his telephone number.

"Can I have the details," Beatrice was asking, "Name—no, your name first . . ."

"Went through the book, did you? All the London directories?" Bonnyweather was impressed.

"Well you were the first one: art gallery chambers. It didn't take long."

Beatrice had lost her smile and was holding her free ear. "Leave it with us, Mrs Hanson. Our duty officer . . ." She had to pause because Mrs Hanson was speaking again.

"It didn't say you were an investigator in the telephone book, I just put two and two together."

"Two and two together, eh?" Bonnyweather wasn't too sure now: if the kid could do it, anybody could—even the Inland Revenue. He'd have to think about going ex-directory.

"Right," Beatrice was saying, "About four. You mustn't worry. She turned back toward Bonnyweather, concentrating on the caller, "Of course, of course, we will. Thank you. Bye, byeee." She put the phone down.

"Seems emotional. Cat. You have to be there at four o'clock," she said and went back to her table to write down Mrs Hanson's address.

"Excuse me," Errol interrupted Bonnyweather's thinking. He was watching Beatrice and noting the way her breasts pressed at the table as she wrote. And he was thinking about free labour.

"Will I be able to start?"

"Well that remains to be seen. These schemes, as you well know, need pursuing . . ."

"Would you like to come in voluntarily for a few days?" Beatrice cut short his word searching, "To see whether you'd like it?"

"Yes," Errol replied and looked at his ally. "Can I start now?"

"Now?" Bonnyweather hadn't met keenness for some time.

"I could do tailing for you, even suss out somewhere."

Bonnyweather stood up and said, "Ah-ah." Then he turned quickly to Errol and snapped, "Memorize that picture." He had pointed to the goldfish on the wall behind the desk.

He bent to Beatrice and said quietly "Suss out?"

"Have a look round."

"Oh," he said and straightened. He looked approvingly at Errol searching the goldfish picture for details and went to the window. "Well, well then, Mr Billings, we'll have to think of something."

Errol was certain that he would only be asked catch questions. He felt he needed more information.

"Is it important? You know, like a code?"

Bonnyweather had already forgotten that he'd commended the goldfish and was standing at the window.

"Of course it's important: organisation plus initiative . . . that equals intelligence."

Errol couldn't see why memorising a picture of a goldfish should be so important—or indeed had anything to do with organisation and initiative.

"There are many tracks down which a tiger can walk, as the Turks say, Mr Billington. Of course it's important. You have to have things to do."

"Stalk," Beatrice said like a tennis spectator thinking aloud.

"What?" Bonnyweather turned from his window.

"Tigers stalk; they don't walk," Beatrice was definite.

Errol thought he'd memorised enough and twisted round in his chair before saying, "No, I mean, is it our symbol?"

Beatrice sounded kindly, "No, we've never had a client with a tiger, Mr Bonnyweather." She gave her employer a look that caused him to turn back to the window. "He was being literary . . . or something."

"Tigers, Miss Thomas," Bonnyweather said to Percy Mews "are cats."

"No, I mean this picture," Errol said. But Bonnyweather didn't turn to him or answer, so he looked at Beatrice and she merely lifted her shoulders. There was a lull in the conversation, and Errol felt vaguely that some sort of initiative was slipping away from him. His eyes were caught by Beatrice's boots.

"Are they riding boots?"

"Yes, I've just had them sewn; he's done them rather well."

They both gazed interestedly at the boots for a pause.

"Were they split?"

"Wear and tear," she said and smiled. "They've had quite a bit of attention." She was delighted with his interest.

"Do you ride?"

"Ride what?" He was wondering why Bonnyweather wasn't saying anything.

"Horses, of course," she laughed.

"Oh, them. Yes."

Bonnyweather said without turning, "And I suppose you vent as well?"

"Eh?"

He turned to the window saying, "No, of course, you're one of Harvey's lot, aren't you?"

Errol just looked at him, puzzled.

Beatrice couldn't understand why he was being so rude. There was no reason why he should be so unpleasant, and her voice was sharp to stop this silliness.

"You're being a little less than adult, you know," she said and smiled at Errol. "Gymkhanas?"

Before he could answer, Bonnyweather was briskly on his way to the desk.

"Right, what can you do?"

Errol just looked at him.

"It's no good. You'll have to fix that bloody tap; it's affecting my bladder."

"I can do it," Errol said eagerly, "if you have a spanner and a washer."

"Do you have the equipment, Mrs Thompson?"

"Miss," she corrected. She disliked being thought a plumber and said, "It's in the transit department."

"Right," Bonnyweather said, brisk like an employer should be, "Well I have work to do. Fix him up, show him the ropes, and I expect that tap to be perfect within an hour." He took his hat and put it on. "Ties, a good hat, and this," he waved his stick at Errol, "are important in our game, Mr Flynn. Very important."

"Why?" Errol asked.

Bonnyweather looked at him as if deciding whether it could damage security to explain something. He decided. "Come here," he commanded, then he turned his back to Beatrice and pulled Errol close to him. He surreptitiously showed him that the stick was in fact a sword stick. Beatrice had picked up a newspaper and showed no interest, but Errol was agog.

"I've never seen one of them before. Do we all have one?"

"Ah-ah," he said slipping the blade back into its sheath on the third try, "Appearances. That's what people notice. Look, listen, think, and then act—that's the secret of detection, my lad." He went to the door, leaving Errol excited at the thought of the sword stick. He'd never even seen a private eye on telly with one.

"*Ceteris paribus,* you know what I mean?" He paused on his way to the door and lowered his voice, "*Ceteris paribus,* and the obvious stands out."

As if satisfied by Errol's attentive look, he turned to Beatrice who was immersed in her newspaper and said, "An hour. No more, no less."

"If he comes in, I'm going," she said and didn't even lower her paper.

CHAPTER 4

Outside in the corridor, as was his habit if only a few punters were in the building, Roy Jenkins was continuing his desperate search for names and addresses of Bonnyweather's clients—or for anything that could be of interest to his ambitions. He had his full range of equipment with him: the camera and a transistor tape recorder that he carried in a wire supermarket basket hung over one arm. He also carried a small microphone. In his free hand he held a glass tumbler, which he placed between his ear and the door, ready to record anything useful he heard by quickly whipping the microphone into position beside the tumbler. He'd seen this system of eavesdropping used on a television series called *The Man from Uncle* years ago, but so far his recordings were mainly crackling and exceptionally low rumbling noises not dissimilar to the recordings made underwater by marine linguists. He was bent to the door, ear pressed to the tumbler, both pressed to the door, and he moved quickly back a pace when he heard Bonnyweather clearly say "Tell him about the elementary techniques. It'll be a start, *schlom.*"

The door opened and Bonnyweather was the most assured in their sudden meeting.

"Ah, Bernard, busy?" He held the door wide open. Something in Jenkins's guilty face made him pause. Jenkins realised that the tumbler looked obvious in his hand.

"Hello, Ambrose. Out on a case?"

"Got it in one, Bernard. What's the glass for?"

Jenkins decided that honesty was dignified, "I was listening," he said, looking resolutely at Bonnyweather.

"Is it like a shell? Can you hear the sea?"

Ambrose could be innocent at times, and because he was still a pace into the room holding the door open, Jenkins couldn't resist a peep to

52

see if the adorable Beatrice was in. He came close to Bonnyweather and peered into the office.

"I was listening because you refuse to cooperate. Hello, Miss Beatrice."

"Hello" she was cold.

"Well go on," Bonnyweather urged.

"You're perfectly aware of why I want information. One of these days the assistant director is going to find out about this. Only this morning he was asking . . ."

Bonnyweather flourished his wristwatch, "By Jove, look at the time. Do you want to chat with Mrs Thompson?"

"Miss," Beatrice said, automatically.

"Eh?" Jenkins was taken by surprise, "I mean, well I don't mind. Would you like to come outside, Beatrice?"

"No," she was emphatic.

He didn't have an answer, and his eye caught sight of Errol at ease in the armchair.

"Morning," Errol said, wanting to be pleasant.

"Morning," Jenkins said as he stole another look at Beatrice, who was looking stonily at him. He shifted the wire basket from his arm to his hand and said, "Well I must get on."

"That's true, Bernard. That's true."

"Why do you keep calling me Bernard? My name's Roy."

Ambrose put a matey hand on his shoulder to wheel him into the corridor, "I don't mind. It's the old dualism—a metaphorical bifurcation one is prone to in an affectionate relationship."

As he closed the door after them, Jenkins voice sounded mollified.

"But I prefer Roy. I mean, it is my . . ."

Errol and Beatrice looked at the door for a pause, and then she smiled at him.

"What does *schlom* mean?" He asked.

"Oh that. He thinks it's Israeli for 'cheerio.'"

"Oh."

He was going to like working here. It was sort of relaxed and, well, professional—just like he thought an investigator's office would be.

"It's a funny place to have an office—in an art gallery," he ventured.

She was more than ready to explain things now that he'd joined the team.

"He doesn't like callers, and he says it's a good front."

He looked at her as if the significance had escaped him.

"He's really supposed to be unemployed, you see," she explained, "He's registered as a philharmonic trumpeter with Per."

"Per?"

"It means professional and something. He's not claiming social security, though. He thinks quite rightly that that would be awful. In fact, it would be immoral."

Errol wasn't really listening. He was gazing around the room; he knew it was important to familiarise himself.

"Where does that door lead to?"

"The transit department."

He went to the door and looked in the other room.

"There's budgies and cats in cages."

"Lost," she said and picked up a newspaper. This was the time when she could relax, when Bonnyweather was out. "Ambrose finds them and waits until they're advertised."

He closed the transit department door and went to the window.

"I've always wanted to be an investigator," he said as he looked down into the small strip of Percy Mews, "Does he get caught up, you know, with women who hire him?"

"What?" she asked. That was a thought that had never occurred to her. "Hey, there's a girl from tech, Arabella Weisman."

Beatrice put her paper down. Anything interesting, any indication that there might be life in Percy Mews was worth seeing. She went to the window, but the girl had gone.

"Girlfriend?"

Errol was scathing, "Her? No. Too young, too immature."

Beatrice smiled at what she thought was youthful embarrassment.

"Oh," she said "Immature."

"I mean understanding, you know," he looked at her very seriously, "The relationship between men and women, the biological drives and needs of the adult human." He turned to the window again, and she thought, *What a surprise this boy was, so strange and yet so articulate*

Considering that he was so obviously underprivileged.

"She can't titillate like an adult female."

"Oh," there seemed to be something more than clinical biology in the matter-of-fact, knowledgeable way he said it. He really was awfully interesting. She noticed his as-yet unshaven face—quite good looking. And after all, he was young enough to learn better ways.

"I'm not sure I can either."

It was half-truth—and half a response to the strange feeling he gave her, a sort of dimly exciting sexuality.

He turned to look at her, his face serious because they were discussing serious things.

"You're all right," he said, reassuring her. And he looked her up and down appraisingly. For some reason the shock of his insolence made her tingle, not cross. He summed her up: "Small, neat build. Shoulders matching hips, not bad legs," he said before taking hold of her shoulders and turning her round.

She turned willingly with her back to him, and she was amazed to feel that she almost enjoyed being inspected. He turned her back round to face him, "Nice, small tits. You could be all right," he decided.

It was a moment before she could speak.

"Well," she said with a little part of a nervous giggle, "thank you." He folded his arms and stood with his legs apart—*Masculine, like Horatio,* she thought. Horatio was a wrestler who'd stood like that the one and only time she had been to a wrestling match, and she'd often thought about the way the wrestler stood. Horatio.

"I suppose you're his doll?" he asked as if the answer was obvious—and because she just stood looking at him because she couldn't think of anything to say. He went to sit on the desk.

"I'll have to find my own, I suppose," he said and sat thoughtfully swinging his leg. He sat as if he were going through a filing system of passport photographs in his head.

She'd never met an Errol before. It wasn't just that he was interesting to her as an object, as someone who could be thought sociologically interesting to know about, but he was interesting to her because he was an original. She'd never met an Errol before.

Errol was unaware of his impact on Beatrice's thinking.

"Errol, will you call me Beatrice?"

"Yes," he said.

"I don't think I am a doll," she said as she went slowly to him at the desk. Her voice had the tone of someone who wished to explain something, "In fact, you could almost say, I'm a free agent."

"He's probably testing you. Seeing how much you can take before you crack." He knew all about this sort of situation, and he felt a tinge of being sorry for her. He slipped off the desk and went to the washbasin.

"Get me the things, Beatrice, and I'll try and fix this tap." And because she was still standing by the desk, looking at him seriously, he added to reassure her, "You'd make a good doll. You just need the right clothes."

She didn't answer.

He bent to examine the tap and said, "In fact, if you weren't his, you could have been mine. I'll probably need a doll when I really start—you know, somebody I can discuss things with, discuss a case with . . . in bed or in my sports car"

After a pause, she walked slowly to him and the washbasin.

"Can I be any help?"

He straightened, looked at her, and then went to the door of the other room.

"Do you know where the stopcock is?" he asked, "Is it in here?"

Her eyes were round and bright as she stood looking at the open doorway through which he had gone.

CHAPTER 5

Bonnyweather rarely used his car, and that was possibly the reason why the old rover, which first saw the light of day in 1966, looked so new in an old-fashioned way. It was big and smelled like leather, petrol, and the warm atmosphere of closed windows—like the private car it used to be called.

Errol was in the passenger seat, surprised by the height of the windows and the lowness of the seat. His head, like Bonnyweather's, was the only part of his body visible to anyone outside of the car.

In the 1960s, one sat on a cushion if one wished to travel with an elbow protruding. He'd used the car because the client who had rung that morning, Mrs Hanson, lived in Raynes Park. He felt it would give a better image in suburbia (being decently mounted), and also, he never felt quite at ease on a London transport bus. Bonnyweather had no egalitarian principles. They had discovered Kipling Road, and with the speed of a milk float—but with more dignity—they had rolled along until they spotted number twenty-seven. Errol had to kneel on his seat to guide his employer during the reversing stages of his parking, and he'd enjoyed barking out the commands. The rover wasn't easy to park; it was cumbersome, as befitted its age.

Bonnyweather put the handbrake on and switched off the engine. They were outside a semi-detached house built some time ago judging by the height of the box hedge and the gnarled laburnums.

"Park View" read a sign on the double gates—put there presumably before the house opposite and the ones behind them were built. Perhaps there was a view of the park from a bedroom window? Bonnyweather had parked the car in front of the double wooden gates.

In the living room of Park View, a room with French windows that was furnished comfortably if solidly, there was a large, folded, and polished dining table used perhaps for more formal meals. Josephine

Hanson was standing at the open French windows, looking out across the rockery and well-mowed square of lawn toward the creosoted black shed beneath the apple tree. Behind the shed, and out of view from the French windows, was a small lean-to greenhouse where her husband grew tomatoes and kept his pile of girlie magazines. It was a secret he thought was safe, believing as he did that his wife never went to the greenhouse. She was also aware, just as he was that the provocative if rather common Mrs McCardle lived in the house facing the greenhouse—and in the summer she sunbathed topless. Mrs Hanson was not impressed by Mrs McCardle's figure, but Mr Hanson was. Josephine Hanson did not look provocative, but in spite of her forty-eight years, she was slim enough not to be plump.

She was attractive enough (and certainly feminine enough) to compete favourably with her age group, and she was a woman whose emotions were only displayed in emotional circumstances, at times of sentimentality or sensitivity. Her relationship with her husband was normal for a wife who had been married twenty years. She was interested in her husband's promotions, some of his family, and the idea of manoeuvring him into a position to achieve some given end. She even allowed herself to be dutiful over and above normal needs if the end was something like a new washing machine. Her great love—the object to which she could unashamedly communicate her emotions and be openly sentimental or gush—was her cat, Norma.

But Norma had been missing for two days, and this was the reason why Perry Ironside Agency had been called in.

She looked out at the garden and called her cat. She called it with that long stress of the last syllable that mothers use when calling a child.

"Norma, Norma love."

But there was no response.

For a pause, her eyes again searched every corner of the garden before she went back into the room. On the record player by the television was a record, and the upturned transparent plastic cover of the turntable gave the impression that the record had been played regularly. And it was to the record player she went and stood looking at the record, wondering whether to play it yet again. The record was an LP made by The Rolling Stones.

At the front of the house, Bonnyweather was moving to the front door. Suddenly, as if changing his plan, he moved to the bay window instead and looked in. His feet were planted firmly among the lilies of the valley as he peered. Errol was a few paces behind. He had been delayed because he was donning the old mac he usually carried. This was his version of a uniform.

"Shall I ring?" he asked.

Bonnyweather put a finger to his mouth to signal silence, and he frowned when he saw the way Errol was dressed. He moved quickly to the side of the house and indicated brusquely that the young man was to come with him. Undoing the trellis gate with great care, they went down the path to the side and rear of the house.

She was standing by the record player, undecided. When she shot another worrying glance toward the garden, she was startled to see a burly man and a youth looking at her through the open French windows. Bonnyweather was smiling.

"Good afternoon, Mrs Hanson?"

"Oh you made me jump."

"Perry Ironside Agency. May we come in?"

She went to them at the open door for no clear reason. "You gave me such a surprise. How did you get round?"

He looked at her seriously, ignoring her question, "Always use the back door, Mrs Hanson. Always starts a case intimately—that's our maxim."

She looked at his face and smiled uncomprehendingly before taking a pace back to let them in.

"Lovely day, isn't it?" Bonnyweather said. He liked to try to be cheerful at the start of a consultation, "This is my associate, Mr Billings," he added with a scathing look at Errol's mac.

Errol gave her a swift smile and she returned one. She watched him follow Bonnyweather to the centre of the room then take up a position alongside him before she yet again looked out at the garden for Norma.

"I am Bonnyweather, Ambrose Bonnyweather."

Mrs Hanson realised that she was being spoken to and reluctantly took her eyes from the garden.

"I'm sorry, what?"

"Bonnyweather."

"Yes, it is nice, isn't it?" She went back to the record player, "Would you like to sit down?"

Ambrose sat on the settee, and like his shadow, Errol moved with him and sat with him. His whisper to Errol was fierce.

"You can take that old coat off now."

"Columbo doesn't," Errol said defiantly, "Anyway, you should take your hat off."

It was insufferable. He'd been so incensed at the sight of the old mac that he'd actually forgotten the civilities he'd taught himself. He took off his hat and placed it carefully on the arm of the settee. The music came on suddenly and fairly loudly; it was a track called "Satisfaction." Mrs Hanson sat herself in an armchair and looked at them soulfully as if she were prepared to sit and listen, and Bonnyweather wondered if she realised why they'd come. Surely they weren't just going to sit there and listen to that bloody noise?

"A little light music, eh?" he said after a few bars and tried to smile.

"Rock," Errol said as he leaned toward him to explain, "Old rock."

Mrs Hanson said, "Do you think you can find her?"

Errol didn't quite hear her and asked loudly, "Have you got *Goats Head Soup*?"

Both Bonnyweather and Mrs Hanson said, "Pardon?"

"It's got some great tracks," he noted, and he raised his voice again to her, "My cousin has it."

"We're not here to talk about soup," Bonnyweather said severely.

She had picked up her handbag and was rummaging through it.

"I have a picture. She said you'd need one."

Bonnyweather had only heard a couple of her words because Mick Jagger was singing "I can't get no satisfaction," so he said very loudly, "Do you think we could have the gramophone a little softer?"

"Oh I'm sorry," she said and went to the player, "I suppose I'd better turn it off." But she seemed unsure. She paused and looked at the spinning record.

Bonnyweather was saying, "We'll need a picture. Have you got a picture?" And as she turned the record off halfway through his request, his voice was a shout in the sudden silence. There was a pause until she said rather coolly, "Yes, I said I've got it here." She offered him the snapshot she had in her hand, "Although she was never photographic, she wouldn't sit still long enough."

There were tears of regret very near in her voice, and she looked at him as if she had given him something very special. She walked to the open French windows, and even her walk had an air of tragedy about it.

"I was playing that music because it's her favourite. She always wanted that on."

She looked back at them sorrowfully, apologetically. It was difficult to just sit. At least she felt she was trying by going into the garden. *Surely that's the way Norma would come home,* she thought. She must be there to greet her, welcome her.

"Excuse me, I must go and have another look," she blurted out. She couldn't help it: she went out into the garden, and they both watched her go.

He just said, "Aha." Grief took his lady clients in different ways, and he said, "Aha" again when he looked at the photograph in his hand. It was a picture of a rather large young woman in a bikini, sitting (it seemed) on one large leg and looking sun dazzled at the camera.

"What's she given me a photo of a fat daughter for?"

Errol was leaning on him, straining to see as Mrs Hanson came back into the room. She went to her chair and sighed, "Oh I miss her. I miss Norma."

Errol tried to take the picture from Bonnyweather's hand. "Let's have a look," he begged, but Bonnyweather deliberately held it face down on his leg. "All in good time," he said.

"Mrs Hanson, do you think we could talk about a cat?"

But before she could answer, the front door chimes rang to the tune of "Three Blind Mice."

"Excuse me," she said and stood. And this time he remembered his manners and made a half-hearted attempt to stand.

"No, I'll go," she said and went into the hall.

He looked at Errol and said almost as if he was saying it to himself, "This is going to be a difficult case," and he sighed before he sat down again.

"Why?" It all seemed incredibly interesting to Errol.

"Watch," he was told, "Just watch, listen, and learn."

There was a rumble of voices at the front door.

"It seems open and shut to me," Errol said. And it did—he couldn't understand his employer's doubts.

"Well it was nice of you to call," Mrs Hanson was saying as she came back from the hall, "They didn't seem very interested on the phone."

A policeman followed her into the room and paused when he saw Bonnyweather and Errol on the settee.

"Afternoon. Afternoon, sir. Mr Hanson?"

"Afternoon," Errol said and smiled. Now that he was in the same sort of game—only higher up the ladder, as it were—he didn't mind hobnobbing with the law.

"No, Mr Hanson is at his office. This is Mr Perry . . . Errr?"

They all looked at her as her voice tailed off.

The policeman took the smile off his face to look at Bonnyweather. "Just visiting, sir?"

"Just a call," he replied and put a sort of smile on his face. Policemen bothered him, and he couldn't remember whether he'd done anything about the tax disc on the car, "A little business."

It wasn't wise to tell them much. The policeman seemed satisfied and turned back to Mrs Hanson.

"We thought you were having a party," he said.

Mrs Hanson had thought he was going to say something that she would understand, so she just said, "Oh." She sat down in the armchair again, looking at him.

"Nobody minds a party," the policeman was saying, "Well depending on the area—the residential area, you know—but it seems to have gone on a bit."

The three of them looked at him uncomprehending. Perhaps it was a police warning, and he was visiting every house?

"Well," he said half apologetically, "You know what it's like in an area like this."

There was a pause for a silent whirring of thinking. Mrs Hanson thought, why couldn't Joan have married a fine-looking young man instead of Henry.

"You haven't found her?" she asked.

"Who?"

"Isn't it about Norma?"

"What is it like," Bonnyweather said as he studied the young man, "in an area like this, officer?"

"Well you know, sir. You either like pop music or you don't, don't you?"

"True," Bonnyweather said. It was a fair statement.

"The last call said there seemed to be a party this morning," and because he was looking at her, Mrs Hanson said unsurely, "You mean someone's seen her?"

"They telephoned," he said and took his hat off. There was no need to be official, they seemed to be a group of decent ratepayers. "I thought I'd come straight here," he added and he smiled at Bonnyweather, who gave him a quick flash of teeth as an automatic response. "You never know. It could be quite innocent, something quite innocent like learning to dance." He beamed round at them, "Is that what it was then?"

Mrs Hanson was struggling to relate what he was saying to Norma's disappearance. Errol and Bonnyweather were not struggling; they didn't know what he was talking about and knew they didn't.

They gazed at the constable like Orientals would at a customs inspector. Errol broke the lull, "Are you learning to dance?"

"No," he chuckled at the thought, "I enjoy dancing. Been doing it since—oh since I was fifteen."

Bonnyweather thought that couldn't have been long ago.

"This is number twenty-seven, isn't it?"

"Yes," Mrs Hanson agreed, again because he'd spoken directly to her. "I wasn't sure he'd got it down—he didn't read it back like they usually do."

It was the policeman's turn to look puzzled. PC Bauer had been a constable for three and a half years, and it was the only job he'd done since he left St. Phillip and St. James Comprehensive School. Three and a half years he'd been a policeman—and for the last year, a Panda Patrolman with his own area—but at the moment he was thinking that it seemed to be a very odd inquiry to undertake. He had met some nuts in his time.

"Oh," he said to her.

"It's not illegal, is it? Dancing?" Bonnyweather asked because he hadn't heard of any new legislation—not that it was in his field, but it could be useful to know.

"Well it could be," Bauer replied, glad he'd been asked an intelligent question, "if you're charging admission and using a public place. It has to have a licence then, but not in a private house." And he added in an even more official tone, "Unless, of course, it is causing a public nuisance."

Again they listened to him respectfully.

"Oh," Bonnyweather felt constrained to say, after a pause.

"Have you been here for the last few days, Mr Hanson?" he asked Bonnyweather.

"No, I'm not Mr Hanson. He's at work," he replied, putting his smile on again and explaining, "I'm just calling on Mrs Hanson."

"Oh I see," the policeman moved to look at Mrs Hanson, but she didn't look embarrassed.

"Mr Hanson doesn't know he's here—they're here. He will when he gets home, though." She looked at him more seriously and said, "I'm very worried. It's been nearly three days now."

"Hasn't he been home?"

"It's a she," she said, gently reproachful.

"Oh," it dawned on him: they were waiting to give her old man a bollocking when he came back. But he doubted it would have any effect—they really go over the top when they find a chick at the age her old man must be. He felt sorry for her. "And you're waiting for him?" Was all he could think of saying, and he said it to Bonnyweather.

"Well yes," he said unsure, "If he comes before we go."

There seemed no point in pursuing this particular avenue, PC Bauer thought, *Better stick to the complaint call.*

"Well," he wanted to sound cheerful, "it doesn't look as if there's been a party here for the last two or three days."

"Here?" Bonnyweather was the first to give voice to surprise.

"A party here?" Mrs Hanson questioned, a close second with her surprise.

"Yes," the constable smiled at her, "Music—loud music—dancing. You know the sort of thing."

"What time did they tell you to come?" she asked.

"About 1:30."

"Last night? I mean, this morning?"

"No, this afternoon."

"This afternoon?" she looked at Bonnyweather for support, but he was looking at the constable, "At number twenty-seven? What did the invitation say?"

"No, I haven't been invited to a party," he replied and smiled at the thought behind the error, "I came to quieten it down."

"Oh," she was a little lost now, "So you weren't invited?"

It all seemed to have very little to do with Norma.

It dawned on the constable that there might be some wires crossed somewhere. He'd seen lots of people trying to play innocent, but this was ridiculous.

"Maybe if you two had been out, maybe gone away for a couple of days—you know, the coast or somewhere. Maybe your son here has had a few friends in?" He smiled at Errol knowingly, "That's often the reason if there isn't a party." He turned his smile to Ambrose.

"My son?" there was some shock in his voice.

Errol was the first to understand: "I know what's happened," he said looking conspiratorially at Bonnyweather and Mrs Hanson, "No, I've been with them all the time."

"To the coast?" Josephine Hanson felt completely lost and said, "With Mr errr . . ."

"Bonnyweather."

"I don't understand," she said to the policeman and then to Bonnyweather remarked, "Yes, it is nice." She was wondering why on Earth he'd mentioned it.

"It's all right," Errol said and winked at her. He then leaned across to pat her knee and said, "The policeman is looking for someone who's been playing records too loud. You know, like 'Satisfaction.'"

"Yes, that's it," Bauer beamed at Errol as if some very clever interpreting had been done, "Perhaps you've been upstairs and not heard it? They said it's been going on a couple of days."

Bonnyweather was still uncertain about what Errol had said, and the informal knee tapping bothered him. "Satisfaction?" he asked him.

Errol winked at him and said, "That's right, Dad." And before there could be any remonstration, the penny—as they say—dropped to Mrs Hanson, "Oh of course. No, we've been away . . . and upstairs. We haven't heard anything."

PC Bauer smiled happily at her before explaining his plans to Bonnyweather.

"Right. I'll go back and check. We often get these wild geese chases," he said and put his hat on. "You see, we're bound to act if a member of the public complains," he explained.

"Oh," Ambrose said bemusedly, "Oh yes."

"Public accountability, isn't it?" Errol said.

The constable looked at him, and Errol continued to explain what he meant, "You know, helping the public. It's like being unemployed, isn't it? I mean, somebody, some setup has to do something if some other setup—you know, like the government—says it's wrong. Don't they?"

The constable hadn't understood all Errol had said, but he thought he'd caught the gist and paused at the settee.

"You've got a bright lad there," he said, patting Bonnyweather's shoulder in the way that younger men have of congratulating much older men.

"Oh," Bonnyweather didn't feel he was being patronised, he had given up on the conversation some time ago, "Oh yes."

"Well I'll be off," PC Bauer said before heading to the door and looking at them cheerfully, like a salesman. "I hope Mr Hanson comes back," he said and then he lowered his voice and looked at Bonnyweather, "And if there's any trouble, get in touch right away."

"You will keep a lookout, though?" Mrs Hanson said as she stood up. He was going, and her anxiety was coming back.

"Oh yes," the constable said sympathetically, not that the police could do anything if no incident was reported. But he felt sorry for her and said gently, "Bye then."

Bonnyweather said, "Bye," and Mrs Hanson followed the constable into the hall.

"My husband will be sorry to have missed you," she said as she went out.

Bonnyweather leaned back on the settee and thought, *you couldn't have a conversation like that in a play because nobody would believe it*. He was still unclear why the policeman should have called and she, Mrs Hanson, was clearly as queer as a coot: playing records for cats and showing photos of fat girls.

He leaned back and told himself that, at least in his job, he saw the full, rich tapestry of life. He said to nobody in particular, "*Existential,* that's the word. Bloody existential."

Errol joined him in lying back, but he thought that the last ten minutes had been very interesting. It was good to feel that he could take part in those sorts of discussions.

"If you say so, boss."

"Don't be so insolent."

CHAPTER 6

There were no limits, even in a master apprentice situation, to the extent to which thought sharing could be pushed.

Errol showed no sign that he had been put in his place.

"Well that was a surprise, wasn't it?" Mrs Hanson said as she returned. She stood smiling down at Bonnyweather who said, "Yes."

"I'm still a little confused about some of the things he was saying, but if it hadn't been for your son, I'd be completely in the dark." She had a grateful look on her face.

"My son?" Bonnyweather asked, genuinely surprised. Two people in ten minutes thinking that his employee (well . . . almost) in a filthy mac was a relative. He scowled at Errol who smiled amiably back at him, and before he could think of a suitable riposte, there was the distant crash of the front door closing.

A voice from the door's direction called "You in, dear?" And Mrs Hanson's face lit up. It was her husband. And although his arrival was not usually a signal for joy, his entry now made her feel hugely relieved. He could take over this interview, and perhaps there wouldn't be all this confusion.

"Oh he's here. I didn't think he would have time."

Bonnyweather looked at the door into the hall, then he looked back at her. He was impressed by the effect her husband's arrival was having on her.

"Would you like a drink? Whisky? Arthur can tell you about it all much better than me. I'll tell him you're here."

She rushed out like a twittering bride to greet and inform her man.

After watching her go and edging to the edge of his seat in unconscious awareness that the man of the house was in the offing, about to enter, Bonnyweather allowed himself a comment, "This one is a nut."

"What?" Errol asked. He had been thinking that it might be a good idea to have one of those blue lights that you can put on top of the car in an emergency like Kojak does, and he had missed Bonnyweather's remark.

"I said—" but he cut himself short and stood up quickly when a large man with a pale face came into the living room saying, "Ah good morning."

It was Arthur Hanson, and he paused just in front of the door to look first at Bonnyweather and then more sternly at Errol who sat on the edge of the settee in his mac, smiling.

"Good afternoon," he said, and he emphasised it to show a correction, "You're from the agency, aren't you?"

Bonnyweather held out his hand—he was urbane, suave, and used to meeting men in their castles. "Right. Ambrose Bonnyweather, specialist." They shook hands—Arthur Hanson rather awkwardly, as if unused to the habit. Errol had stood and Bonnyweather nodded at him, "This is Mr Billings."

"Billington," Errol said and held out his hand, but Bonnyweather had taken Hanson's arm—friendly, American in its familiarity—and he was leading him into the room.

"Now as I was just saying to your good lady, Mr Harrison, I think we have a misconception . . ."

Hanson almost broke away from Ambrose in an effort to show the importance he attached to the situation and interrupted, "Impossible. Mr Campari assured us. Point is: can you find her?"

Errol sat down again and watched. If the two men's voices had not been assertive and resonant, one could have imagined that they were close friends, standing close, one holding the others arm—like Italian brothers.

"She means a lot to my wife, and I'm a very busy man. It isn't that I can't get time off—I can get plenty of time off—but in my position I have responsibilities, people to see, appointments, arrangements to be made."

Bonnyweather had been nodding vigorously, fully supporting Mr Hanson's contribution, and now he patted the other man's arm as he spoke.

"Precisely, precisely. Exactly as you say it. You don't have to spell it out to me," he said, and he flashed an understanding grin at Hanson's increasingly pink face. Then he became serious as he said, "Every man's task is his life preserver, Mr Hanson, as a famous American once said. Our business is quick results. Now what I couldn't get your wife to understand . . ."

"Can I have another look at that picture?" Errol asked. He had just had a thought.

"No," Bonnyweather said and took the opportunity to release Hanson and go to sit in an easy chair, "I think she thinks that I have some sort of specialisation in people, whereas . . ."

This time Hanson interrupted. His eyes strayed from Bonnyweather's talking face and he asked, "Is that record player switched on?" He went over to it to check. His wife came in with a tray.

"Oh you're not putting the television on, are you, dear?"

He was terse, "Of course I'm not. This record player's on."

She gave Errol a smile and went to sit next to him and put the tray on the coffee table.

"Now I'm sorry, I've forgotten your name."

"Errol."

"How nice," she said and took a glass from the tray for him.

Hanson switched the player off, and as usual, it irritated him that his wife had such slipshod ways with expensive equipment: record player on and pushing whisky as if it grew on trees.

"Some idiot's parked outside the gates again. I had to leave the car miles down the street," he said to her as if it were her fault.

She merely gave him a look and then returned her attention to Errol, "Well Errol, would you like water?"

She handed Errol the glass and said, "I'm afraid we haven't anything else."

He was unsure. He looked suspiciously at the small glass in his hand and asked, "Water?"

She gave him a smile and then moved her look to Bonnyweather and said, "Mr Ironside?"

"Just a wee *drappie,*" he said, trying to use his Doric in the way an Englishman does when faced with whisky in a living room in suburbia. As he went to her, he watched her drown the remaining two glasses with water from the jug.

Mr Hanson followed for his share and said, "Right. Well I'm sorry if I seem brusque, but time is precious to me."

Bonnyweather had returned to his chair and replied, "Absolutely, absolutely right, Mr . . ." He hadn't forgotten the man's name, he'd forgotten that the easy chair had no arms. And when he had leaned back sideways to cross his legs and enjoy a civilised chat, he had moved quickly down to the carpet. He avoided a complete topple by thrusting out a hand, but some of his whisky was spilt.

"Whoops! Thought the chair had arms," he said as he straightened and pushed at the spill on his jacket to flick droplets onto his trousers. Hanson was suspicious. Bonnyweather's involuntary explanation had reverted to his native dialect, and Mr Hanson knew all about Scotsmen.

"How long have you been here?" he asked.

Errol said, "Oh ages," and he beamed at Hanson. "In fact, somebody thought we'd all been away for a couple of days, didn't they?" he asked Mrs Hanson, who laughed.

"Oh yes: your father and me away on the loose," she answered, and her laugh had a little shriek as a sort of apex.

Apart from not having heard his wife laughing like that for some time, Mr Hanson was rather shocked by the intimacy implied in what she said.

"You what?" he enquired brusquely.

Bonnyweather gave Errol a glare before switching on his strange grin for Hanson.

"What sort of work do you do, Mr Hackney?"

"Thought we were away at the coast and upstairs," Josie said, relieved to be able to laugh about it all.

"Hanson," he corrected, and he was frowning at his wife's merriment and wondering what the hell she was talking about. He wondered, *Had she been at the whisky as well?*

Errol took a swig of his drink and it surprised him. He coughed as if he were having a paroxysm, and Mrs Hanson moved quickly to his aid, patting then thumping his back as she explained proudly to Bonnyweather, "He's an acting higher executive officer."

"Oh," Bonnyweather said and tried to look impressed. "Nice."

"Have you heard of the youth training scheme?" Hanson asked him, confident that he had and confident that Bonnyweather wouldn't perceive him as a nobody.

Errol gave his coughing a final burst, and Hanson glared at him for interrupting—that being more irritating to him than the fact that his wife was almost embracing the young man in her efforts to relieve his spasm.

"Well I run it here," he said, raising his voice to Bonnyweather, "I'm the area officer."

"Oh how interesting," he replied. *This is extremely interesting,* Bonnyweather thought before saying, "I'm thinking of . . ."

"Now about Norma," Hanson interrupted. He had made his point, and you don't carry a title like area officer without keeping to the business in hand. "Can you find her?"

Mrs Hanson left Errol to occasional hiccups, a tickling throat, and his own devices when she heard Norma mentioned.

"Oh I'd be grateful," she said and looked at Bonnyweather with abject promise, "It just isn't the same without Norma."

He took his eyes from her and looked at her husband, whom he thought was looking at his wife with a sort of distaste. "And do you make the decisions?" he asked, "Or is it a sort of civil service committee?"

"What?" he asked. He'd been looking at the promise in his wife's face, and for some reason, his mind flew back to their first years of marriage. "Oh the scheme." He came back to today and spoke like a modest man who'd been given more power. "I have the normal discretion of an area officer."

Bonnyweather sounded impressed (as he intended himself to sound), "You sit in judgement, so to speak, on each application?"

"More or less," he responded, but that wasn't what he was paying for. "At the moment, I'm more interested in Norma. She means a great deal to my wife . . ."

"If I wished to participate, could you put me on your programme or whatever it's called?"

Hanson was surprised; it had never occurred to him that this man could be a possible applicant.

"You? Well yes. Just outline a range of tasks that last for twelve months, and providing there is training and honest experience, well it's just a matter of submitting it."

"To you?"

"To my office," he said and gave him a card, "Here, this is the address."

"Will it take long to find her?" Mrs Hanson asked, just a little put out—all the talk about experiences and offices when Norma could be anywhere . . . even trapped, in pain, lost, waiting for her. "Oh can't you start now?" she pleaded.

"Well if we had a photograph . . ." Bonnyweather replied. He was prepared to digress for a moment in his discussion.

"But I gave you one."

"That was a lady, not a cat," he intoned in a prim voice.

"I think the cat was with her," Errol said. He was in agreement with Mrs Hanson: they ought to be getting on, tracking Norma down. "Couldn't we have it blown up?"

"Oh no!" she said, aghast.

"Blown up?" Even to Arthur Hanson this seemed an extreme measure.

"I mean," said Errol with the authority of someone who is the only one paying attention, "I mean made bigger."

There was a pause during which Bonnyweather took the photo from his pocket and gazed at it. He hadn't seen a bloody cat.

"Possible, possible. Difficult but possible."

Ah there it was: near the lawnmower, behind the female.

However there were more important things: Hanson was on his feet, and an opportunity might be rushing off.

"It's straightforward then, is it? The government pays, and it doesn't cost the employer a ha'penny?"

Typically bloody Scotch, Hanson thought. And anyway, this was certainly not the attitude he wanted to see in an employer.

"Yes," he said shortly. He had things to do—he'd done his bit by wasting time coming home. He had left more important things to see about than her stupid cat, and he didn't think these loonies could find a camel in a herd of cows. And Josie . . . fluttering about as if it were him who'd gone missing. If the cat had any bloody sense, which he doubted, she'd be off looking for a tom.

He turned to her and put a worried look on before saying, "Well my dear, I must fly. There are people waiting."

His new secretarial assistant, Miss Anstead, would be waiting. It was the first time in his career that he'd had a personal secretarial assistant.

"You ought to have a word with Mr Green," Errol was saying to him, "He says that you are only bothering with big places, you're not interested in the small employer."

Mr Hanson thought *Cheeky young sod. Who does he think he's talking to? And who's this Mr Green? And what on Earth is a little scruff like that doing in the house?*

"Rubbish," he snorted as he went into the hall.

"Oh I do hope you find her soon," Mrs Hanson said, struggling to bring back the conversation to where she thought it should be.

Errol looked at Bonnyweather, but he was draining his whisky. He felt it was up to him to reassure her, "Don't worry, madam, we'll get our grasses to suss it all out." She looked at him and realised that he was reassuring her, but she was mystified by his words.

"What do you mean, *grasses*?"

Errol lowered his voice as if letting her into a big secret: "Narks," he said, "Every moggie in the manner will be checked—that so boss?"

Bonnyweather stood up and said, "Shut up." Then he raised his voice to call out to Hanson in the hall, "You can stop worrying. I'll have the application in by tomorrow." The front door was heard being banged shut. He clapped his hands together as if the first hurdle was over and sounded brisk: "Well we must press on. Don't you worry, we'll have your Norman home as quick as is humanly possible." He picked up Errol's unfinished drink and asked, "Are you leaving this?" He didn't wait for a reply before downing it. That done—and ready for the road—he wiped his mouth with the back of his hand.

"It likes that noisy tune, eh?" he asked.

She didn't say anything. She nodded at him, but she was thinking how different this man was from Arthur. And she wondered whether he would waste his time in a greenhouse looking at pictures of those silly girls, or whether he would be even remotely interested in Mrs McCardle. He looked strange, he seemed strange—but there was something about him and the Scottish accent that made her trust him. And she felt that if she gave him half a chance, he wouldn't be like Arthur.

Errol was asking something. "Satisfaction? She liked that?"

"Don't be crude," Bonnyweather said. Then he went to her, and she was looking at his eyes—blue eyes under black eyebrows. "Right then, ma'am. We'll be in touch."

He gave her his wide-open, charming smile, took her unresisting hand, turned it palm down, and kissed it.

"Thank you for your hospitality. You have a beautiful home."

He knew what women clients liked—anybody who was different than their husband. He turned quickly from her and went into the hall. Errol gave her a nice smile; he was very impressed by Bonnyweather's adieu—he'd never seen anyone kiss a woman's hand in real life before. He followed him into the hall.

Mrs Hanson watched them from the living room doorway.

"Will you ring?" she called.

But they merely gave her a smile before closing the front door.

For the first time in a long time, she felt a sort of uncertainty—like what to cook for supper, but it was applied to her life, the way she lived. She contemplated her life in the house among the furniture with only Norma to be a lover to. It was a strange feeling. She'd never compared anyone to Arthur before—not in the house anyway.

Outside, they were going to the car, and Errol was taking his mac off. He said, "Why don't we use a flasher on the car. You know, like Kojak?" Bonnyweather ignored him.

CHAPTER 7
_____

The gallery had been fairly busy. In fact, it was doing good business considering it was midweek. The morning had seen a party of six puzzled Japanese who appeared to be undertaking some sort of terminal mission; an elderly couple that didn't say a word to each other and were probably English, a woman who shrieked at the sculptures with three children (who were unmoved by their mother's noise); a young German couple that spoke to each other loudly to practice their English; and the usual older man who sat for an hour looking at "The Slave Market" in the style of Alma-Tadema. Roy Jenkins had been kept fairly busy. He had to look important in the foyer, nodding in greeting or looking stern if people were laughing. How he wished he could search bags like they did in the national. The afternoon had been slower moving, but every time he had gathered his equipment together for wall listening outside Bonnyweather's office, there had been a visitor whom he thought might need some supervision. He even sold four postcards to a Swedish couple who wouldn't take the change he offered them. At the end of a protracted conversation, they gave him a postcard of a street in Uppsala where they said they had a small gallery.

At the moment, there were only a boy and girl—dressed quite unsuitably, Jenkins thought. Why was everybody so bloody scruffy these days? Well to be fair, she wasn't scruffy—just unsuitably dressed for serious gallery visiting.

He stood in Modern Works & Exhibitions and watched them. Her lissom, youthful body was so obvious in its jeans and singlet, and the coolness of the gallery gave her singlet button points. And as usual, his thinking moved without deliberation to the boy. And not without sneering.

He just knew that this youth was quite unaware of the incredible allure of her firm, desirable body. He knew that he was totally inadequate for the passion and appreciation such a body deserved. That's what it is today: the system—the whole system—of organised life that entails killing off red-bloodedness. They had too much these days—too much done for them, too much offered on a plate. Everything was always there, and it was too obvious to be wanted. No, it was a kid's world, all right, and they treated it like kids. He wished for a moment that he was the boy. What he would do to show the girl that she was a woman. God they hadn't looked like her—girls—when he was sixteen.

Maybe that was it: they didn't have to be red-blooded anymore, didn't have to search, explore. Everything was obvious—there was no passion, no discovery any more. They probably asked now, didn't have to grope. He pulled his thinking back to business and took his eyes from the singlet. Those two looked safe enough—they were probably doing A-levels or filling in time until some film started. God, the way kids wasted their lives. They were discussing a painting in serious whispers when he left to go to the office.

He was still smarting from the morning's faux pas when he'd been caught red-handed with his listening equipment in his hand. The professionalism he'd built up in his eavesdropping had been hurt, but he was going to be too clever to be caught again. Bonnyweather and the boy were out, he knew that, so there would only be Beatrice in there. But there could be telephone calls. She might have to repeat a name and address. He gave the young couple—and particularly the girl—a last look as he replaced the rope at the end of the corridor and took his basket of equipment down to Bonnyweather's office.

In the office, Beatrice had a newspaper spread before her on the table. She was looking at it but not seeing it; her mind was elsewhere. She had been thinking about The Boy and that she must get home as early as she could that weekend to concentrate on his dressage. After all, she couldn't really see Audrey doing much with him, even though she promised. Audrey was always promising to do things for her, and quite a lot of times, she just didn't. Daddy had told her that Audrey had to look after the horses and that there was no question about her not handling Beatrice's two. And he'd sort of told her off in that quiet way he had of not looking at her when he was cross. He told her quite plainly that she was being less than honest by suggesting that Audrey was only interested in his hunters. It was her time more than anything he explained—she was only a girl, and she couldn't be expected to do the sort of hours old Bedworthy had done.

She remembered how cross she'd felt. She'd blurted out that it was all jolly fine talking like that, but if Audrey didn't spend so much time in the tack room and going with him to look for new hounds, she'd be able to do just as much as Bedworthy had. It was ages after Daddy had gone (after looking absolutely livid and saying that she had a mind like a sewer and Gloucestershire wasn't like London) that it dawned on her what he meant. She still couldn't believe it—surely not. Daddy and a groom? He wouldn't be so silly.

Gosh, Mummy would be cross if she knew. But even she seemed to be so jolly busy these days since she'd started studding with the obnoxious Weston-Green family. How she loathed that awful Nigel and his coarseness. He actually said to her—in front of Audrey—he'd actually asked her with a roaring, beery laugh whether she was being covered enough in London. She honestly could not see how Mummy put up with him. But Daddy and that little bitch of a groom—it was awful. She couldn't really believe it.

Maybe she had a mind like a sewer? No, she was sure there must be something odd going on. She could tell by the way Audrey was so sure of herself whenever Beatrice found one of her martingales missing, or when she pointed out that Annabella hadn't been mucked out properly. She certainly seemed jolly sure of herself with all her denials. And coming into the tack room in a bathing suit—that bikini—when she and Daddy and the vet were talking to The Boy. The vet she could understand, but she remembered vividly Daddy's eyes and what they were looking at. It was disgusting at his age—and her father, too.

It was via a natural progression of thought (and possibly a tiny tinge of guilt) that Bonnyweather swam into her mind. But he wasn't as old as Daddy, and he was different. And so was Errol.

He was only a boy, though. She couldn't say she was old enough to be his mother because she wasn't, but there seemed to be something strangely naughty in being attracted by such a working-class boy.

Perhaps, if Daddy had seen more of real life, he could enjoy life as a lot of experiences and not be bamboozled into wallowing about like a sex-starved, dirty, old man with Audrey Sykes-Kahn. Even if her mother was Lady Townend's sister. Of course, Daddy could be sex starved, she supposed. Mummy did seem awfully busy all the time. They would have been much wiser giving a chance to a horse-loving, working-class girl who could have lived in the village. But Bonnyweather and Errol were quite different. In fact, she was only amused by them and interested in them because they were so different from all the run-of-the-mill people.

Jenkins, on the other hand—caretaker Jenkins—was just like Nigel Weston-Green without the noise, coarseness, and unpleasantness of a middle-class oaf. At least Jenkins was obsequious, knew that she wasn't a tart like Tanyia Smythe at school—she used to flaunt about her bricklayers and things. At least Jenkins was respectful in his lust. Men really were odd creatures, and it occurred to her that she'd never thought so much and for so long about them as she did now. She folded the newspaper and concluded that men were fairly exciting to have in the offing, but they were not terribly interesting to know. Except, possibly, rare ones such as Bonnyweather and Errol. But she did hope Audrey would remember to exercise The Boy.

She put the paper on top of the pile on the floor and wondered whether they would come back to the office from Raynes Park. She ought to make something rather special and tempt Ambrose to come round tomorrow night. Ratatouille—that would be easy—and she could make some of those prawn and anchovy things. She'd need aubergines . . . she had a courgette, but she'd need aubergines. She could go out and get them now. It was boring just looking at wretched newspapers; she'd go now, leave early. Putting her coat on and wondering whether to invite Errol if Ambrose dropped out, she opened the door with her free hand.

Jenkins barely had time to move his ear from the glass tumbler as the door flew open to expose him. Beatrice for her part was startled to see Jenkins leaning forward, glass in hand, as if bending to fill it at a tap. There was a moment's statue-like stillness before he straightened himself.

"Oh," he said, "Hello, Beatrice."

Her first impulse was to slam the door shut, obliterate the sight before her, but she recalled how easy it was if she kept her wits about her.

"What on Earth do *you* want?" she demanded with heavy emphasis on the word *you*—as if it were outrageous for him to want anything.

"I was just passing . . ." his voice trailed off to surge once again upwards, "Are you leaving early?"

"It's none of your business," she said, still holding the door and making no move to go in or out.

Maybe he sensed some indecision in her and defined it as being happily surprised at seeing him.

"You look lovely, Beatrice. Totally," he began and (again) had to think quickly, "lovely."

"Don't be such an ass," she answered curtly. She wasn't smiling, but she was a little pleased. "What on Earth are you doing in this corridor?"

"This corridor?" Even love could not control an affront to his sense of professional responsibility. He replied, "What am I doing in this corridor? It's my corridor."

He was plaintively assertive, like someone hurt. She just looked at him.

"Beatrice," there was a pleading in his voice, "Just wait five minutes. I'll lock up; we can go somewhere," he said, just thinking desperately and quickly, "to the pictures. How about that? To the pictures or maybe for a sandwich, eh, Beatrice?"

"Oh do stop being ridiculous. Can't you think of anything but sandwiches?"

Talking of food brought to her mind the aubergines, and although she knew it would require very little courage to push past him, there was an urge to dominate for just a little longer. She looked at his pleading face, creased in a smile because he thought he was winning.

"Now you must really stop harassing me, Mr Jenkins. I'm . . ."

"You're adorable, and I worship you."

"Oh shut up, can't you?"

It was embarrassing. Of course it was flattering—even having an idiot saying nice things was flattering—but the whole thing was totally impracticable, it was obscene.

"Beatrice," he said, throwing control to the winds, "Beatrice, love, can't you see I want you?" He moved to her.

It was a sort of fright reaction that made her move forward, go to meet his nearer moving passion. She pushed at his chest to move him out of her way. She was amazed to be stopped—her arms held, his face close—even surprised by the strength of his grip. And she became aware of the buttons on his tunic and his aftershave—and a not unpleasant smell that reminded her inexplicably of her doctor.

"Please, Beatrice . . ."

It was all very well (and rather frightening in a flattering sort of way), but one had to make oneself clear. She shrugged her way rather violently out of his arms and moved a pace to pass him.

"Please do not be so ridiculous, Mr Jenkins."

"Roy. You must call me Roy," he said, still hanging on her arm.

Because just a tiny bit of panic was surging into her thinking, she felt that some minimal humouring would help her break away from him. She said, "Well stop it, Roy. Leave me alone. Don't be so foolish."

"Don't go if I let go, love," he said and loosened the hold on her arm, only leaving his hand near to the warm excitement of her coat. "You called me Roy," he said simply but with such great pleasure. He moved close to her, and he seemed about to hold her again—kiss her, even—so she slapped him hard across the face, knocking him sideways away from her and against the wall. Using double reins on spirited stallions had given her a strength she'd been unaware of.

There was a jerky cough summoning attention from the end of the corridor, and Barrymore Pugh was reacting as he thought fit given what he'd seen in the last couple of minutes. Caretakers and their cleaners was one thing, but not when people were in the gallery—he should have been on duty in the foyer or somewhere.

"Could I have a word, Mr . . . Errr?" It was the least he could say, the whole thing was embarrassing.

"What are you doing here?" Jenkins demanded.

He was holding his burning face, still in a state of shock, and his response was instinctive rather than respectful.

"Well," Pugh began, not liking Jenkins's tone, "I think I ought . . ."

"Go away. Go away both of you," Beatrice said as she looked at the hurt Jenkins, "I'm sorry, but this is too much. Go away." She went back into the office, slammed shut the door, and locked it.

"What's happening, Mr . . . errr . . . what is your name? I'm sorry, I've forgotten."

"Jenkins, Roy Jenkins. You didn't say you were coming back."

"It's a good thing I did, Mr Jenkins," he said as he headed down the corridor to a still-abashed caretaker. "I was quite unaware of the situation, quite unaware"

"It isn't what it seems to be," Jenkins remarked. He had just realised that Pugh had discovered the corridor and said, "It was just a difference of opinion sort of thing."

"I could see that," Pugh replied, allowing his look to lighten for a second. "Now look here: I'm a fair man, and obviously this is more serious than I thought. You know very well they should be out of the building by nine o'clock."

"Who?" he asked as he looked at the assistant director, puzzled.

Pugh wasn't falling for innocence, particularly in someone of Jenkins's age and looks.

"You're going to make some other arrangements if it's as bad as all that," he said, again flashing a quick, sympathetic smile. "Although she does seem to have a different point of view than yours, doesn't she?" he added.

Pugh, because he had his own longings, had some sort of sympathy for this caretaker. But from what he'd seen of the woman, she was quite reasonable as cleaners go. As he remembered he used to see them (cleaners) on odd occasions when he was doing overtime in the early days. But regulations were regulations, and if it was affecting efficiency—and those sorts of things had a habit of becoming heated and obsessive—then it must be stamped on. It might be easier if he did the stamping rather than Mr Murphy.

He wanted to be an understanding boss, a man-to-man sort of man.

"Now look here," he said fatherly before adding, "I'm sure it all seems so easy: a quiet gallery and all that sort of thing—and particularly if she's willing to come back." He offered up a big, matey grin and said, "Although she didn't seem too keen a few minutes ago, did she?"

He looked at Jenkins, who was wondering what the hell he was talking about and how he could get him out of the corridor, away from Bonnyweather's office.

"I mean, there's the public to consider, isn't there?" He seemed to need an answer.

"Well yes," Jenkins replied, thinking hard, "You see, it wasn't what you might have thought. We're really good friends . . ."

"Please," Pugh stated and held up his hand, "I don't want to know details. It's the principle I'm concerned about." He looked seriously at Jenkins as if he were a recalcitrant pupil and said, "I'm afraid she'll have to leave. As I say, nine o'clock is the time, and nine o'clock it must be."

"Leave?" He had pulled himself together and decided he must make the man leave. He said, "I'm afraid that's impossible, sir."

"Now I think we've got to be sensible . . ."

"Why don't we talk in the foyer, sir?" he said and took Pugh's arm to lead him away.

This one really had it bad. Perhaps he ought to have torn him off a strip? He shook off the caretaker's hand and said, "I don't think there's any need for that. I'll have a word with her."

"No," Jenkins was quick to respond, horrified at the thought. He grabbed his arm again and said, "No, don't do that. She wouldn't understand—it would only, well, confuse her." He tried to smile and continued, "Come on, sir, into the *fwayer,*" and he pulled him a couple of paces before his hand was shaken off again.

"Now just stop this!" Pugh interjected. He didn't like being a boss, but this was ridiculous. "I'll have a word with her. We'll sort it all out."

The bell rang in the foyer and Jenkins cursed at forgetting to put it on the floor.

"There," Pugh said, "you're wanted. Now off you go."

"No," Jenkins said, totally unsure, "you go."

"Me?"

"Yes, you go, sir. I'll see to things here."

Pugh thought this was too much, he looked serious. "I'm sorry," he said, "you must go. It's your job to deal with enquiries."

"Will you come with me, sir?" he asked, desperate, "It might be important; they might want to see you."

The bell rang again: three times, sharply.

"Go and see who is ringing, Mr . . . errr . . ."

"Jenkins."

"Go and see to it, Mr Jenkins," he said sternly.

Jenkins shot a worried look at Beatrice's door and reluctantly went.

Mr Pugh thought, *My God! Really got it bad, this one. I'd better have him up to the office and sort the whole thing out. We can't have this.*

He knocked at the door but didn't quite make out the muffled remark inside, so he knocked again. This time the response was clearer: Beatrice was on the other side of the door, torn between the need for aubergines and safety.

"Go away."

"Can I have a word?"

It didn't sound like Jenkins, perhaps it was that other man—whoever he was.

"I said go away."

"I'm afraid it's not as easy as that. I would like to help."

He certainly sounded different than Jenkins.

"Who are you?"

"Mr Pugh."

"Who?"

"Pugh. Now come along, be sensible and open the door."

It was a name that meant nothing to her. Perhaps he was a gallery visitor, but he sounded sympathetic. She opened the door slowly and looked at him

She certainly looked a different sort of cleaner than the ones he'd known—no wonder Jenkins had fallen for her.

"I think we ought to talk about things," he said, "May I come in?"

"No," she said as she held on to the door, "no, I don't think you should."

She didn't talk like a cleaner—perhaps she was down on her luck, husband left her, and all that. Nevertheless, she had no right to refuse him entry.

"I think I ought to come in . . ."

She quickly pushed the door at him, and he had to put a hand out to stop it from being closed. She was obviously disturbed, and he must keep some dignity.

"Oh all right, very well," he said as he pushed the door open again, "very well, we'll talk here."

"I have a gun, and I'll use it if I have to," she said, and it even surprised her. It was a sort of reflex thing to say.

Barrymore Pugh was startled—even frightened—at the seriousness of the situation. He really had been pushed into deep water.

"Now please," he said and held up his hand like a priest, "please keep calm. It's just that I have to say what I'm going to say."

He paused, not really sure how to go on. She was looking at him with a very uncooperative face—and if she had a gun . . . my God!

"I'm sure there are two sides to this. I mean, there has to be. But regulations, well they're regulations, aren't they?"

She nodded, wondering who on Earth he was and what on Earth he was talking about.

He interrupted her thinking, "I'm sure you were encouraged—it would be less than, well, human to think otherwise." He paused again and smiled at her. Because he looked so ill at ease, she gave him a quick smile back. This encouraged him.

"I have to think of efficiency though, haven't I? Private affairs are private affairs, things for outside of working hours."

He felt he was developing just the right line, "You will no doubt say that he's encouraged—urged you—to come in, but it's just as likely that Mr Jenkins will tell me that you insisted on seeing him. I don't pretend to know a good deal about relationships, but I do know that if two people wish to, well, have an affair . . ."

"Jenkins? Him and *me*?" She was appalled, horrified that anyone—even this man, whomever he was—could actually think that Jenkins and she were having an affair.

"Well yes, it's . . ."

"Go away," she said as coldly as she could, "go away." And she remembered something from her earlier thinking: "You have a mind like a sewer," she added with all the distaste she could muster.

"Now just a minute," he replied; he didn't like her tone. "Nine o'clock is the time when your duties finish, and you know it. Mr Jenkins has no right . . ."

She slammed the door shut.

"I will not allow these sorts of things to interfere with work," he almost shouted at the closed door, "Now be sensible, get along home, make some arrangements with him." He knocked at the door and asked, "Do you hear? Do you hear?"

As Roy Jenkins was going reluctantly to the foyer, the bell rang again, and he was not civil when he reached the ringer. He refused to look at the woman until he was properly behind his table, a table of postcards away from the general public.

"Well?" he asked when he was in position.

"Have you had far to come? I'm terribly sorry," the lady said, knowing it would mollify him. It did.

"It was just that I was occupied," he said, "Can I help you?"

"I certainly hope so. I would like to see the Caro piece that I'm told is here. I haven't a lot of time, so I don't want to spend hours looking for it. I hope you don't mind me asking?"

"Not at all," he said. She was the sort of visitor he liked, could do with more of. She knew what she wanted to see and knew that it was wise to ask his advice. He couldn't, however, call to mind the word *Caro.*

"Are we looking for a two-dimensional or three-dimensional work, madam?"

"I didn't know he'd done any two-dimensional."

"Who?" he asked, but she didn't seem to hear. She had turned from him and was looking through the doors into the street.

"Now that would be interesting to discover," she said to the doors.

"What would?"

"I didn't know he'd ever done any," she said as she turned back to him, smiling. It was the sort of smile that vicar's wives have. "Are you sure?"

"Who? Whom are we referring to?"

"Caro."

"Caro?"

"Antony Caro"

He realised it was a name he should have heard of. "Is it a piece or a painting, madam?"

"A sculpture, of course. I heard about it yesterday, and was told it was here." She hadn't lost her smile and continued, "You have some of his cartoons as well, have you?"

"Now let me think," he said, pretending to understand and thinking rapidly. He thought, *Caro, Caro? They all had such bloody strange names nowadays!* "I honestly think," he said slowly, thinking furiously, "that the Caro we had was transferred to one of our other galleries."

"Oh God! The person was quite definite, saw it here a couple of months ago."

He looked at her. The lady was obviously disappointed. He heard Pugh's voice in the distance shouting, "Do you hear?" and they both looked towards Modern Works & Exhibitions.

"I think it was last month or maybe the month before," he hazarded, then he had a brilliant notion and smiled smugly, "But you're in luck, our assistant director is in the building, and I'm sure he can help you. I'll tell him you're here."

"Oh," she replied, partly mollified, "that's very kind of you."

"Not at all," he said, "I won't be a minute," and he went off feeling triumphant into Modern Works & Exhibitions to get rid of Barrymore Pugh.

He joined Pugh, who was knocking at Bonnyweather's office door. "I don't think she'll open it, sir. She's very obstinate."

"She will open the damned thing! I can be just as obstinate," Pugh shouted and rattled the handle, calling, "Come along now. Be sensible."

They both heard her yell, "Go away."

Jenkins was smiling smugly at him.

"This is ridiculous. You should never have allowed a cleaner to get so uppity."

Jenkins lost his smile with surprise—he hadn't realised that Pugh might have thought Beatrice was a cleaner. "She's not a cleaner, sir, not Miss Thompson. Oh no," he said, sounding shocked at the suggestion.

"Oh?"

"Oh no, sir, Miss Thompson isn't a cleaner."

This put a different light on things, "Who the hell is she, then?"

Jenkins didn't like his tone, but he was thinking desperately and quickly.

"She's a . . ." he began. What could he think of? "She's a specialist in the unit, sir."

Pugh looked at him. He didn't like the way this man went about things: grappling with females, asking him—the assistant director—to answer bells, and now standing there looking at him with a wet smile on his ugly face.

"Unit? What bloody unit?" he asked, but he regretted the curse—it somehow brought him down to the caretaker's level.

"I mean this is a storeroom, isn't it? I've seen the plans, and I understand there are two rooms in there."

"Oh no, I mean, yes, sir," Jenkins stammered, in a fix. "But they're private. Yes, private, sir."

"Private? In one of our galleries?"

"Well not really private, sir," he lowered his voice confidentially, "It's a very special intelligence unit set up by the chief executive. He doesn't want anyone to know about it, you see."

Pugh looked dumbfounded.

"The chief executive? Mr Hedworth?"

"Yes."

"Intelligence unit? The director has never mentioned it," he said in a tone of a man who is privy to the director. "What sort of intelligence?"

"I don't really know. I think it's something to do with education—maybe gathering information. You know, research . . . to be able to reduce its size."

Quite unwittingly, Jenkins had stumbled on to a subject that any senior local government officer not in the education department would dearly love to hear about. Education was the largest, most powerful money spender in any local authority.

"Oh," Pugh said, and then asked, "What sort of research?" Not doubting it seemed that the caretaker would know.

"Well," Jenkins said, enjoying it now, "I think it's about the irrelevance of the A-levels and reducing the power of teachers and people to dictate the pieces of paper people need to go to college."

"Oh," Pugh said again, not wholly clear.

"But if I can leave that subject, sir—about these rooms being private . . . I mean, not usable as storerooms—there is a lady in the *fwayer* who wants to talk to you about a Caro piece."

"About a what?"

"Caro. Sculpture, you know," replied Jenkins, feeling gleeful because it was obvious that Pugh didn't know.

"Oh," Pugh said yet again, not knowing what a Caro was and irritated by the smile on the caretaker's face. "But what about this woman?" he asked, pointing to the door, "What are you going to do about her?"

Before Jenkins could answer, the woman from the foyer called from the end of the corridor.

"Hallo, hallo, are you there?"

"That's her," Jenkins said quickly, "I think you ought to see her, sir."

Pugh was rattled, he didn't want to see the woman, he didn't want to see anybody without an appointment—and it was plain he would have to do something soon about this caretaker . . . too bloody cocky by half.

"You see her. It's nothing to do with me," Jenkins said quietly, "I think it's the chief executive's wife, sir. I've seen a picture in the paper."

Pugh looked up to the end of the corridor as the woman cautiously peered round the corner at them. The chief executive was God—important to be in with and to be seen helping, particularly his wife (who might mention him in the privacy of a chief executive's home).

"Ah hello, madam," he said and beamed at the lady.

"Hallo," she said, "are you the man that can help me?"

"I shall try very hard."

"This gentleman," she indicated Jenkins, "said you might know what had happened to the Caro."

"Ah well," he said, looking to Jenkins for support but finding none. He beamed his way to her and intoned, "Well I'm not too sure, Mrs Hedworth. It is Mrs Hedworth, isn't it?"

"Hepworth. I have a *p*," she said and looked at him with her vicar's wife smile in a tolerant, amused way, "How did you know my name?"

"Shall we say a little bird?" he said fawning, then he turned quickly to Jenkins. "All right, Mr . . . errr . . . Jenkins, I think you can go back to the foyer now."

"You don't think I should stay here, sir?" he said and nodded at the door meaningfully, "Just in case?"

"No I don't," he said. Really, the man was flailing about with his cockiness, and he was determined to keep him and his woman apart whilst they were on council property.

"No, off you go. I'll handle this problem."

"Oh dear," the lady said with years of femininity behind her, "am I being a nuisance?"

"Of course not," Pugh said, sounding shocked, "No, of course not, Mrs Hepworth." He flicked his head to Jenkins to indicate that he should go. Jenkins went, again reluctantly.

"Well I'm flattered with your attention, Mr . . . errr . . . whom am I speaking to?"

"Pugh, Mrs Hepworth. Barrymore Pugh, assistant director, galleries.
"Oh," she simpered, "the top man, eh?"

"Well," he began, but modesty forbade more.

Beatrice was listening carefully, but she could only make out a
little. She'd heard Jenkins voice, and now he seemed to have gone. But
there was a woman there, she was sure. Perhaps now was the time?
Surely she could be brave enough to just storm past him. She'd never
get the aubergines if she didn't go soon. She went into the corridor,
locking the door behind

Mr Pugh and Mrs Hepworth turned to look at her.

"Oh hello," Beatrice said.

"Hallo," Mrs Hepworth said, curious but not wholly interested.

"Ah," Pugh said, and then spoke to Mrs Hepworth: "Excuse me a
moment." Then he went to Beatrice; she was standing unsure outside
the office.

He lowered his voice, "I'm sorry about earlier on—thinking you
were a cleaner. I didn't know."

"Oh," was all she could think of saying.

"But I am concerned about the other business," he said, feeling
unsure about the cool way she was looking at him. "As you can see, I
have Mrs Hepworth with me, so I can't discuss it fully now—but you
realise that I cannot approve of scenes like that earlier on."

"No, Mr Hepworth," Beatrice said as haughtily as her upbringing
dictated, "neither do I. And I would rather you didn't associate me with
that ridiculous man."

"Oh well fine," he said, sympathising with her, "I'll have a word
with him." Then he leaned closer, remembering the importance of what
he'd stumbled upon and said, "You can trust me to keep mum about
things. Your business here is safe with me," he added and leaned back
again, satisfied.

"Oh," Beatrice said, not clear.

"I'm sorry to be a bother," Mrs Hepworth said and smiled. "Shall
I go?"

"No," Pugh replied. He certainly didn't want to lose Mrs
Hepworth—no, there was no need."

"I insist that you come with me," Beatrice said authoritatively as
she walked to the end of the corridor.

"Now I'm sure there's no need . . ."

"There is every need; the man is a lecherous lunatic."

Barrymore Pugh smiled apologetically at Mrs Hepworth, and she was now looking at Beatrice with interest.

"Come along," Beatrice ordered, "it seems the least you can do."

"Do please excuse me, Mrs Hepworth," he said, thinking that the woman must have an awful lot of sway if she could talk to an assistant director like that. He'd certainly have something to say to Jenkins tomorrow. He caught up with Beatrice on her way to the foyer, only now and then glancing back to see if Mrs Hepworth was still safely there.

"Oh Beatrice, can I have a word?"

"No, you can't," she snapped.

"That'll be enough of that," Pugh said, and he held the door open for her. She said, "Thank you, thank you very much," as if to a doorman. He looked at Jenkins as menacingly as he could, and his voice was low, "I want to talk to you later about all this."

"It's easy to explain, sir: it's just that she's feeling a little out of sorts."

"So am I," said Pugh.

Jenkins was determined to beat him and in a low voice said, "Oh sir, I think I ought to tell you as you are new here—about Mrs Hedworth."

"Hepworth."

"Yes, sir, her. It's rather personal."

"What is?"

Jenkins leaned to him and spoke almost in a whisper, "Everyone in authority knows what she's like with new principal officers."

Pugh, who had been looking anxiously toward Modern Works & Exhibitions, now gave him full attention. "Eh?" he said.

"It's common knowledge."

"What is?"

Jenkins looked at him as if he were reluctant to worry him.

"What is she like to new principal officers?" There was curiosity and anxiety in his question.

"Well sir, she usually manages to, well, compromise them."

Pugh looked at him as if he'd said something in another language. "Compromise?"

Jenkins lowered his voice even further, "I think she's a bit whatsit, you know." He looked very serious, as if Pugh would understand his reluctance to be more explicit.

"You mean she's, well, sort of sexual?"

Jenkins nodded seriously.

"Oh," Pugh said, looking toward Modern Works & Exhibitions and disturbed by feelings of career safety and lust.

"I'm glad she's picked on you and not me, if I may be allowed to say so, sir."

Pugh gazed at Jenkins's serious face for a pause. "Rubbish," he then said and walked away a couple of paces before turning to look at the caretaker. Jenkins shrugged and moved his head sideways as if to say, "Well all right, be it on your own head."

Pugh turned and walked slowly and thoughtfully into Modern Works & Exhibitions. When he'd gone, Jenkins permitted himself a smile and thought yet again about clowns who get into high places.

CHAPTER 8

It was Tuesday, and on Tuesdays Ambrose Bonnyweather did not do any washing at the office. Mondays and Fridays were his washing days, and his habit was based upon tradition in his family, he said. Clean clothes for the weekends.

It was Tuesday, and clean shod under his suit, Bonnyweather was at the office earlier than usual. He'd gone straight to his desk, eager to discuss with himself the merits or otherwise of hiring Errol, regardless of what had been said yesterday about trials and such. Being able to hire staff and not pay anything was such an incredible and wishful notion that it demanded an immediate acceptance. And then—only then—could any arguments be found to gainsay it.

Ambrose liked the word *gainsay* and wished he could remember to use it more often in conversation. It was like *solipsism* or *recondite* or *atavistic*—all words he used quite often in his thinking. Well fairly often, and usually only after he'd had to look in the dictionary to check some other word. But *gainsay* was a word, and it should have been easier to extend its use, he thought. There was one argument, or at least a point of discussion, about the possibility of free labour: did he need any labour—free or otherwise? Was there sufficient work?

What would he do all day if he delegated more? His mind shot to Beatrice, and he closed his eyes for a moment at the deliciousness of thinking that he'd have all day and every day with Beatrice. But his Calvinistic background soon shook that off. A man's role was to do what he had to do—no more, no less. And he was a personal agent because that was his skill. It was totally immaterial what staff he had or needed—the whole essence of his success was the confidence his clients could place in him at a personal level.

But he need not delegate; he could give Errol some other role other than a junior investigator. Perhaps they could create a new avenue altogether, one which the boy could develop. He had some doubts about such a possibility, so the answer was that Errol should be a sort of trainee, an apprentice, who (over a period of time) could perform the more mundane tasks such as cleaning the car. He could help Beatrice maybe? A doubt swept into his thinking, but he dismissed it at once. It was ridiculous. There was a gap in everything that mattered—neither of them would know what to do with the other. Anyway, it was maturity and intelligence she liked, so he had nothing to worry about. But he'd keep an eye on things, just in case.

"So," he said aloud, "I have decided to accept the offer being made by this MSC," and he also decided to there and then get things down onto paper and get it off to Mr Hanson. Training, the leaflet had said, and a programme had to be offered that showed how the year could be used to give as wide a training area as was possible. This, thought Bonnyweather, was too simple.

Having searched for paper—and deciding to write it out in rough first—he settled down to create a new post in his establishment. But looking at the blank sheet of paper for some reason made him think of the night before.

He'd gone round to her place, to her flat in Elgin Avenue. And although it was the third or fourth time he'd been there, it was the first time he'd met her flatmate, Tweaker Carr-Hightly—at least that's how he thought he'd caught her name. Tweaker was a big girl who looked as if she could handle a stallion—Or a bull for that matter, he thought—and she dressed as if she'd just finished demolishing a house. She had apparently only recently returned from an evening class where she was learning plastering.

Beatrice was just a tiny bit put out that he'd come without warning. If he'd only mentioned it earlier that he was definitely going to come, she could have encouraged Tweaker to have supper with one of her friends. But she hadn't known, and he had had to meet her, and she was glad when he sat down because Tweaker was so tall. She was a brick, though, and she shot off as soon as she twigged that Beatrice was having a visitor. She said she was going out anyway, and Beatrice gave her a thankful and anxious smile, hoping she wasn't just going down to the pub.

When Tweaker went down to the pub she usually came back pretty late—and with two or three strange women who seemed to get a kick out of arguing like mad about women's consciousness or something. They kept her awake if she hadn't already gone to sleep. But there he was, and Tweaker had gone. There he was as she'd so often hoped: sitting in her armchair, looking ridiculous in his tight suit and glimpse of white leg above a mauve sock. He'd come voluntarily, and she was excited.

She fussed in and out of the kitchen and brought things into the living room to chop and mix so that he could lie back in the armchair proprietarily and explain the problem of modern society to her. "Good Lord" and "gosh, really?" Were her standard replies, and she enjoyed seeing him swanking with his knowledge as she got the meal together. She made a cheese and peppers omelette, and she found some pate in the fridge. Plus Tweaker said she could have her strawberry flan, so it was a passable meal.

They'd seen off the remains of the gin and half a bottle of Spanish she'd had since last week, and he seemed more at ease than usual. There was almost an air of eagerness about him. She'd never seen him quite like that before: so relaxed and eagerly explaining the philosophy of confidentiality within a free market economy. And she'd only interrupted her nodding head and trying to understand to stand up to go and make some coffee when he completely dumfounded her by grabbing her and pulling her down onto his knee. He was rougher than she'd ever known him to be before as he kissed her and pulled and pushed at her blouse.

And although it was jolly painful at first being pummelled and grasped so passionately, it was incredibly exciting. It was so like the dream last week when she'd woken up gasping. She had known it was a dream, but the reality of the motorcyclist with the leather jackets who had laid her on the table and couldn't get her tights off stayed with her. The men stood round grinning at her with enormous penises in their hands. It was a mixture of excitement and dismay as she took in the situation: their awful leathers and her ridiculous tights and the weight of their hands fondling her breasts. It had been so real that she'd been holding her breasts to protect them when she woke up.

She found her breath and pushed at his chest to sit up straight. She felt light-headed with promise.

"Gosh, you're jolly keen."

He looked at her in a sort of owning way, and with some pressure caressed her breast—or perhaps massaged it.

"I've never seen your bedroom, have I?" His voice was throaty, and she'd never noticed how big his eyes were before.

"It's there," she nodded toward the door, "that door."

He buried his head in her neck and said something.

"I can't hear you," she said and moved her neck away from his face. She thought his eyes looked like Bowser's—a lovely spaniel Daddy had given her ages ago—and her heart melted at his look.

"Is she coming back?"

"Who?"

"That tinker female."

It was a moment before her thinking could orient to what he was saying, and it was instinct that made her stand, grab his hand, and pull him to his feet. "We're alone, Ambrose," she said as softly as she could, "Only you and I." She undid his jacket and pulled it with difficulty off him. Then she looked up at him, smiling to be kissed.

"I've never been in your bedroom," he said, and his voice sounded hoarse because he was so tense. He didn't realise that she wanted to be kissed, so feeling terribly intimate and wanton, she coyly put her hands on his shoulders and slipped the narrow blue braces down from his shoulders. She wanted to show him her submission, and she could feel him trembling—and his excitement excited her. Like dumb play, she took off her blouse and let it fall to her feet. Then she undid her bra, bent slowly forward to release her breasts, and with deliberation, dropped their harness. She watched his eyes follow its descent then return to her uncovered breasts.

His breathing was the only sound she heard—a slight whistle as he pushed his breath down his nose. She smiled at him like a woman who was wanted, and she put her hands on his waist. She slowly moved them to the front of his trousers and her eyes had to leave his face. His trousers had no zip, they were buttoned. Like a very young man first encountering a bra, she struggled to undo the top button. It brought him to a slow motion life; he bent his head to her breast, and his mouth found her nipple. It was ungainly but magical. She had to extend her arms to stay in contact with his buttons, and the excitement that flowed up her increased her efforts. Soon she was wrenching at his flies, and neither of them knew she had pulled three buttons completely off in her zeal.

His trousers sagged but didn't fall. She held on to the unbuttoned cloth. They were free, almost unclothed. They were free of the dailyness of normality, free to excite each other, and she pulled him to the bedroom door by the cloth she held in her hand.

He stood with trousers at his knees unbuttoning his shirt as he watched her take off her skirt and hang it in the wardrobe. Her body blurred in high drawn tights, giving her the temporary anonymity of a bank robber, and then she turned to look at him. She promptly threw herself on the bed—her legs in the air, furling her tights down to her feet.

He pushed down his trousers, hopped, skipped, and fell on the bed. His shoes had to come off before the trousers—feet undressed before loins—so he sat on the bed, bending down to his feet. He felt her curled around him, her breasts pressed against his kidneys, hands under underpants waistband, fingers pushing. He felt dizzy with bending and excited and exciting as he threw himself back and rolled over onto her. She said, "Oooh" with an expulsion of breath at the weight of his presence. They lay for some moments: her closed eyes, his wild eyes; her waiting, him coming. Her awareness of some delay, some change of tempo stemming from his dead weight and a wetness that was waste came after about a minute of blood-bubbling expectancy.

"Oh Christ," he said, "Jesus Christ."

The bubbles in her were pricked and fizzled out of her like unconsumed seltzer.

"Oh Ambrose."

"Oh fuck," he said. Then he heard himself and quickly got up onto his hands to look down at her: "Sorry. Didn't mean that. But oh Christ, I'm sorry."

The sorrow in his look brought compassion, and she pulled him down onto her. Her arms were round him, holding him tight.

"Oh Ambrose, don't worry. We can try again."

His body in her arms shook with his head. He felt wretched, a failure—the stupidity and wretchedness of failure when nothing could fail. Only him, and not even really him: some bloody chemistry that seemed outside his command. He thought with dismal futility that, after all that time, he should have his orgasms organised.

"Just relax, dear," she said maternally, "Relax, don't worry."

But he did. He always worried about sex.

The surging longing feelings Beatrice had felt so vividly such a short time ago were cooling into a sort of vaguely detached contentment, sorry but optimistic. She lay with him limp upon her. She knew how disappointed he was, and yet somehow felt again she'd learned something new. All her affection for the man—all she wanted from him—was really about something bigger than Ambrose Bonnyweather. If he failed, it didn't matter—she hadn't. Her emotions were really for herself. Ambrose was a contributor; it could have been someone else, in fact.

It dawned on her that men were sexually expendable. It was brand-new thinking, and it was exciting to know you were exciting. She made coffee and didn't care that her dressing gown came open when she handed him his cup. Then they were laying on the bed, sipping and thinking. He was without trousers, and she was vaguely covered. They were together on the bed with their coffee in the intimacy of their post-coital privacy. He was being philosophical about letting himself down, and he couldn't understand how some men he'd heard of could do it more than once in a couple of hours. Now and then he would think, *she must be terribly disappointed.* The fact was that she felt so marvellously in charge.

She looked at him laying on her coverlet, exposed in the most ordinary way, and she was not really impressed with his body at rest. She had only seen parts of it before, and then they'd been part of romantic intimacies. At last she knew and understood the machinery that was sex. She knew it was her she had to satisfy from then on. The shape of men was immaterial. Of course, Ambrose was an interesting man—maybe one of only a few really interesting men who would come into her life. But it didn't matter whether they were interesting or not—men were things she needed in order to satisfy herself. She didn't have to worry about them any more if they failed. She could comfort them, of course, but it would be like comforting a child or a dog. Men were an abstract need she might have said if she used words like that. Bonnyweather blamed himself for trying too hard too soon.

They heard Tweaker come in loudly and rolled off the bed with quick guilt to search for clothes. He was standing with one leg in his trousers when she knocked and opened the door.

"Oh sorry, thought you'd have gone," she said to him then smiled at Beatrice and said, "Was the meal okay?"

"Yes," Beatrice said, looking at Ambrose's embarrassment, "it was super. The flan was gorgeous, wasn't it?" She stopped herself from saying "Ambrose" because it seemed too intimate and "Mr Bonnyweather" because it seemed silly when they were in the bedroom.

Ambrose looked at her to see whether she was going to say anything else, and then said, "Yes, oh yes. Yes it was nice."

Tweaker smiled at him, and her eyes and smile were sort of knowing. She said, "Glad you enjoyed it."

He couldn't think of a reply.

"Okay if I come back in now? I mean, you're not sort of . . ." she began and let her voice tail off.

"No," Beatrice replied hastily, "No, we're just . . . he's going now," and she looked at him, "Aren't you?"

"Yes, yes, I'd better get on. It's late, isn't it?"

Tweaker grinned at him and said, "Well you mustn't let me spoil anything."

She shut the door and opened it again to say, "We'll be fairly quiet, Bea."

Beatrice and Ambrose gazed at the door after she'd gone, and then they gazed at each other. She shrugged at him. He continued climbing into his trousers.

"Have you found everything?" she asked, "All your clothes and things?"

He merely looked at her before sitting on the bed to put his shoes on.

"I'm terribly sorry about Tweaker, but she's awfully sweet, really."

"I'm sure she is," he said, making his voice cheerful to cheer her up, "I don't mind."

When he was dressed and ready and feeling a sort of normalcy again, he gave her his full attention. She was sitting on the bed watching him with a very odd smile on her face.

"What's amusing you?" he asked.

"Nothing," she said, but she couldn't help herself and laughed. "Nothing," she said again, "It just seems funny, doesn't it?"

"If you say so." In spite of himself, her giggling made him smile.

He would never understand women. He supposed she was hiding her disappointment—he knew women were emotional.

It was embarrassing going into the other room and being gazed at with curiosity by the two women with Tweaker—women with lots of frizzy hair who wore sweaters and well-worn jeans. They were sitting on the floor in a haze of smoke.

"Hi, Bea," one of them said.

"Hello," Beatrice said, and she looked at her with the confidence that a woman with a man has.

"You going, then?" Tweaker asked Ambrose.

"Yes," he said and made it sound like a decision, "Yes, *tempus fugit* and all that."

The other woman let out a shriek of laughter for no reason. Tweaker shouted, "Don't be a pig, Miriam," but she was smiling all over her face at him. The other two didn't smile, they just looked wistfully at Beatrice and said, "I bet it was beautiful, wasn't it, Bea?"

Beatrice smiled at her with new confidence before she said to Ambrose, "I'll see you out."

He raised his voice above the laughing woman's noise and called as he went to the door, "Well bye, then. Thanks for the flan, Tinker." He turned to smile uncertainly at them before he went into the hall. Tweaker shouted, "Watch the old John Thomas doesn't get a chill, Mr Bonnyweather."

"That's not very nice, Tweaker," Beatrice said with a smile on her face before she followed Ambrose to the door.

"What did she say?" he asked at the front door.

"Nothing. She was being funny."

"Oh," he said and opened the door, "Well goodnight." He smiled at her and considerately added, "Don't worry."

"No," she said smiling and closed the door on him.

By the time he'd gone to bed that night he knew that, for his part, his failure to stay the course was but an insignificant aberration. She would be hurt far more than he was.

Three buttons missing from his flies had been a bit awkward in the tube. He would have to wear his winter suit tomorrow.

But now it was Tuesday, the next day, and winter suit or no winter suit there were things to do. Last night was last night, and life didn't go backwards. New vistas, new developments, and even new establishments were to be looked forward to. This young man, Errol, was a gift horse he couldn't look in the mouth.

The Perry Ironside Agency's protégée (and possible new employee) let the glass door close behind him to reduce the Tottenham Court Road roar to a loud snarling hum. For a moment he was sobered by the quiet emptiness of the gallery. All Errol's life had been lived among people and sounds. Quietness and emptiness meant that he was on his own, and that disturbed him a little. Quietness made him pause and stay close to the doorway to a noisy world and glance about, boosting his hearing and sight to pick up any signs of comfort. He did find comfort: in the distance was a voice, a male voice—he thought, *It must be the caretaker, Mr Jenkins.* He saw the bell on the floor underneath the table, and with a grin on his face, he crouched and rang it. The sharpness of the ring surprised him, and he moved swiftly to stand by the entrance to Modern Works & Exhibitions where he could not be seen by anyone entering the foyer quickly.

Errol guessed right: Jenkins had not been upstairs, and now he marched in, wondering who the hell was ringing the bell at that time in the morning. Errol let him march by, then he silently simulated the ease with which he could have felled him with a karate chop. He then fled with hardly a sound into Modern Works & Exhibitions, leaving the caretaker with his irritation in the empty foyer.

Bonnyweather was not finding it easy to put down on paper the plain facts of investigation that would, at the same time, indicate the nuances of the work. He needed to summarise without making it sound simple. He read back to himself yet again what he had written: "Weeks three to eight: learning professional techniques; Weeks eight to twelve: appraising the needs of a client via the use of the telephone." He liked that—liked the efficient sound of that—and he spoke to himself as he carried on writing, "Dealing with invoices—no, accounts—procedures, visiting informants, processing developments (another good phrase), assessing strategies, running errands . . ." There was a knock at the door: three spaced out, three sharp, and another three spaced out. In Morse they spelt *OSO.*

Bonnyweather didn't look up.

"*Et cetera, et cetera. Ontray.*"

Errol, who hadn't opened the door immediately after he had finished knocking, saw that his boss was busy, but he felt a need to make his presence known. "Shall I shut the door?"

Bonnyweather neither looked up nor spoke. He was rearranging words on his paper, so Errol hung up his mac and decided to make himself comfortable until he was given a mission.

"Any developments, boss?"

"What?" Bonnyweather asked as he looked up. He looked at the young man in the armchair as if he hadn't heard him enter.

"Ah Billings."

"Billington."

"This is a fine time to arrive."

"I haven't a watch yet," Errol said laying back, "I did have one, but it broke two weeks ago. I'll get another one now that I'm working."

Bonnyweather looked at him for a pause before going back to his writing, and he spoke with unusual patience.

"Flexibility. I expect there has to be flexibility—our work often goes far into the night."

"In clubs?"

Bonnyweather merely gave him a flick of a look before Errol continued, "You know, big-time discos, places like that?"

Errol's question was ignored, and it gave him time to think of a doubt.

"You don't have to dance, though, do you?"

"Flexibility: that's the byword," Bonnyweather said as he sat up and looked approvingly at what he had written. Then he gave his assistant his attention. "Flexibility and adaptability make a good agent."

"Oh," Errol said. He didn't have an answer, but Bonnyweather's pause had seemed to seek one.

"Consolidation," he said and smiled at Errol, "Consolidation of experience during weeks twelve to twenty, eh?"

He wrote quickly and muttered, "They'll like that. That should satisfy them."

"You writing to Mr Hanson?"

There was a pause before Bonnyweather sat up, breathed out, folded his paper, and looked for an envelope.

"I suppose I could take up dancing lessons," Errol said thoughtfully.

Bonnyweather found an envelope.

"Find his bloody cat, make his daft wife happy, and you're laughing, my boy. Thirty-five quid a week . . . and the chance of a lifetime." He finished writing on the envelope, put his letter in it with a flourish, licked it, and banged it and rubbed it to seal it before looking at the reason for his feeling of satisfaction.

"Right. Start while the iron is warm as they say in the north. Come on, on your feet. Agents can't be agents if they sit on their arses. Let's have a bit of action—move, lad, move."

He was enjoying this. It was just like he thought it would be. Errol stood up uncertainly.

"Get round to master Callaghan, pick up the pics, and spread them around. Usual places, okay?"

"You had them blown up already?" Errol was surprised and impressed.

"Of course," Bonnyweather said dismissing any other possibility, "Best man in the business. Jimmy Callaghan can enlarge anything."

He punched at the air to uncover his wrist to see his watch. "He said four o'clock, so get round there. Tell him it's vital."

"But it isn't four o'clock; it's only just gone nine."

His innocence showed.

"I know that," Bonnyweather said in the manner of a testy father, "I know that, you know that, he'll know that. Always head into the unknown—keep 'em guessing, on their toes—everybody has a price as they say in Wales."

"Oh," Errol said again as he went to the door, uncertain and perhaps reluctant, "I mean, do I have to wait for them if they're . . ."

"The obvious first. Always go for the obvious when you're on a fixed rate."

He stood up. This was the life: teacher and pupil. Satisfying. He'd never had anyone to say it to before, and he developed his training technique as he moved to gaze out at Percy Mews.

"Where do people who notice cats go? What sort of people notice cats? Who loves cats? Eh? Eh?"

There seemed to be some response needed, so Errol said, "Well there's . . ." But he had to give in and concluded, "I don't know."

"Women, older women." He swung round to stare at Errol and let that sink in before he went back to his desk saying, "Women in hairdressers, expensive cake shops, pottery exhibitions, art galleries. Leave some prints around—ask, my boy, and you will be rewarded." He was really warming to it now, "A big smile, tight trousers—they'll look for your cat. They've all got memories; they may say no they may say yes, but they all like to be asked as Jimmy Callaghan will tell you. Go on then," he said and waved imperiously, "off you go. Tempo, tempo lad. Tick, tick, tick: that's why time is important."

Errol turned to go, and reminded by the coat rack, turned back and said more eagerly, "Can I take the stick?"

"No," he was told, and Bonnyweather busied himself with some papers on his desk. Errol waited a moment to be sure there would be no point in pressing his request before he went.

"Okay, boss, see you," he said as he went out, banging the door shut and causing a draught which blew one of the papers off the desk.

Bonnyweather picked it up and sat back in the chair, beaming at the world in general. He felt that he'd enjoyed that. It had made him feel good; it was just what he needed to put his ego back into place. *That's how things should be done,* he thought, *Wasn't it China where the generation gap meant the difference between innocence and wisdom?* Not that he'd lost faith in himself last night, but it had been a niggle at his confidence. He was lucky that he was a man who knew that a man needed a few setbacks. Life could be too easy, and boys like Errol needed a wise and confident man to lead them.

CHAPTER 9

Beatrice was a new woman—she could feel it: there was a sort of interesting newness in her. After last night, she felt a strange sense of power; she knew that she had to do so little to be the magnet. From now on, men were like pins (or iron filings, as she remembered her science from school). They could be attracted because she was a woman. Mind you, she'd always known that, but the newness—the sort of biological confidence she now felt—came from the realisation that after having attracted them, she didn't have to feel a sort of responsibility for their comfort. She didn't have to get too bogged down with thoughts of letting them down. What she discovered, though she couldn't put it into so few words, was confidence in herself.

She pushed open the glass door totally uncaring whether Jenkins was at his table, and only a flicker of her old apprehension went through her mind when she saw that he, in fact, was standing there. She allowed the door to close itself and stood with an uncaring look on her face, before she moved to pass the caretaker and his table.

"Oh," he said. He was surprised because she didn't rush straight past him. "Good morning, Beatrice. Good morning," he was eager.

"Good morning, Mr Jenkins," she said and actually smiled at him.

"Beatrice, oh," he replied. Her smile had shaken him and he said, "Are you staying in for lunch? Can I get you a . . ."

"Oh do shut up, Mr Jenkins," she said as she passed him and raised her voice cheerily, "It's a lovely morning, isn't it?"

"Yes," he said, completely taken aback, "Yes, it is." She was out of sight before he moved from behind his table and called after her: "I can get you a sandwich any time you like—just say so. I'm a regular; I don't have to queue."

But she'd gone, and he couldn't really believe it, but he heard a sort of amused laugh as she moved into the recesses of Modern Works & Exhibitions.

Bonnyweather was trying to sort out his pending tray. He did so every week, but he was always surprised by what he found in it. He must have a word with her—or better still, evolve a new system. Things couldn't go into the pending tray until they had been discussed and had been given the chance to be assimilated into his thinking. The red setter notes, for example . . . he could hardly remember what she had said at the time.

There was a knock at the door: three spaced, three rapid, and three spaced.

He called out, "*ontray,*" and Beatrice came in.

"Ah Bridget."

She didn't mind. She knew it was only a game he played with himself, and she realised that now she didn't have to mind about his foibles. She put the newspapers on his desk with a smile.

"Good morning, Ambrose."

He looked up at her smiling down at him, and he had a strange feeling of being unsure before he looked at the newspapers.

"Not where I'm reading. You could see I'm trying to sort out the pending tray."

He sounded hurt—and in fact he was. For one thing, she had nothing to smile about. He'd been rehearsing in his head different ways of being considerate, letting her see that last night's little debacle wasn't the end of the world, and she came straight in and irritated him.

"You could see I was sorting out the pending tray, trying to make sense out of these notes."

She'd gone to her table to deposit her bag, and she talked as if he hadn't said anything at all.

"Tony and Stella are going to Menton again this year. It's a hoot really."

She beamed at him as she swept to the coat rack, taking off her coat in a way that made him feel a draught as she went to hang it.

"Stella thought she was going to do her thing with Poppy again in Provence, but Tony had apparently already met the Healeys and impressed Janie. Stella was furious."

"What about that bloody setter? Where are we up to?"

She paused long enough to look at him as she hung the coat on the rack and said, "I don't think it is—it's a spaniel or something." Then she went back to her table, her head full of what she wanted to think about. "They didn't have it last year when I was there. Janie got it for Miranda whilst she was doing her A-levels. I think they regret it now. It's really priceless: she says it never stops eating and insists on being terribly precocious at dinner parties."

Bonnyweather decided that she was prattling on to cover her embarrassment and thought he'd better show her that work had to be done, regardless. He stood up.

"I'd better get down and see Fred at the home, see if there's one in."

He walked to the window. He didn't really want to go out, to leave her just yet.

"Did it have a collar?"

She was at her table, rummaging in her bag.

"I thought you were talking about the Healeys, you know, their spaniel?" he asked, and she realised it may have been something she'd put in the pending tray. "Did you mean Kev?" she asked, but he didn't answer, so she went back to the search in her bag.

"It always seems odd to me, seeing a spaniel in Menton."

He was looking out of the window.

She continued, "They get terribly fat, don't they? When they're not sort of worked."

"It's a pity he knows its thirty-five quid," he said ruminatively, "I could have said it was fifteen or something if I'd known first."

She flicked a look at him but refused to be drawn. It was nice being aware that she needn't be drawn into discussion every time he said anything deliberately outrageous to get her annoyed by pretending not to hear what she said. She decided to play him at his own game and asked, "Did you sleep well last night?"

He didn't answer straight away, didn't turn round from the window. He was surprised and thought, *What a strange thing to ask.* Maybe she hadn't heard what he'd said?

"Maybe even twenty quid could have made ten profit—just like that."

"Tweaker thinks you're a jolly good sport for not being offended."

This time he did turn round. "What?"

"Your buttons. They laughed and you didn't mind."

"Didn't mind?"

"Well," she said and shrugged her shoulders, smiling as if it were up to him, "you didn't seem to."

He looked at her for a pause, looked at her smile, and dismissed the thought that she was being insolent. Maybe Tweaker had been impressed? Then it dawned on him that he'd allowed his conversation to be broken, taken over. He turned back to the window furiously thinking of a riposte until he found one: "*Verbum sat sapienti.* Oh yes, indeed—a word is enough to a wise man."

"I was going to come round and see you this evening."

He stiffened as he listened. Her reaction was quite different from what he thought it would be—quite unexpected.

"But Peter rang. He's back in England now—had a filthy time in the monastery."

She went back to his desk to bring a newspaper. He never read them until it was too late. "They ate nothing with meat in it. Fish and eggs, only fish and eggs," she said and spread the paper out on her table. He wasn't sure what to say.

"He says he came by bus from Salonika. It only cost forty pounds, but he had four miserably boring hours in Milan. You know what Milan can be like."

He turned round because she paused, and he looked at her reading the newspaper, totally unconcerned about what he might have been going to say.

"No, I don't know what Milan can be like," he said, and he meant it to be sarcastic.

"Incredibly boring," she said to the paper.

He was puzzled—frankly puzzled—she seemed almost offhand.

Again she spoke without looking up from her reading, "I was going to come round. I was going to make you a small ratatouille—you know, using up things—but Peter's coming."

She looked at him.

"Oh," he said.

She smiled and lowered her voice, "I would have loved to come round, but, well, there it is."

"Oh," he said again, but this time his speech was laced with some concern. He turned back to gazing at Percy Mews, and she went back to her paper. There was a pause, it was a long pause. He didn't speak as he struggled with his thinking, then he effortlessly moved into ruminating. When he spoke it was as if he were speaking to himself, to his reflection in the window: "*Verbum sat sapienti,*" he said quietly, and it made her look at him as he looked out of the window.

"Twenty-five pounds. I need never have told him."

She wasn't really listening. She was looking at the way he stood, the way his stocky, broad-shouldered shape fit into the frame made by the window. The manliness he exuded was always a promise, and she wondered whether it was only the promise that was exciting.

"You know, the one major, outstanding flaw in the education system is the total lack of preparation for decision-making it confers upon students."

She waited for more erudition.

"Not enough reasons, too many answers. And too few questions."

She was impressed but unclear. His voice went lower, as if thinking aloud. He was also thinking deeply as he intoned, "its breasts you miss. Nothing else—just breasts. Beautiful comforters."

She saw during the pause the connection between school, child, mother, and woman, and it made her voice warmer and reassuring, "I would have loved to come round. I was quite full of anticipation."

Newness or no newness, she was affected. Her womanliness seemed to scream for newness, and she said very quietly, willingly, "Do you want something?"

He didn't answer, but he turned and smiled at her smile.

"I still think I should have said twenty pounds. It's quite enough."

"Bye, bunny," she said. And he went as bidden to—so powerful was the gentle way she said it.

Beatrice didn't let the smile leave her face after he'd gone. She looked like she felt: sort of seraphic.

Everything seemed so, well, Turkish delight: sweet, squashy, and not sticky. It was like waking slowly, keeping one's eyes luxuriously closed, and turning to let the softness of the pillow support one's thinking. It was like waking up from a dream in which everything she'd done, everyone she'd met, had been nice. Nice was how she felt, and her smile was the outward expression.

Of course, she was fond of Ambrose. She was even fond of him now that she knew that was all she need offer—fondness. But Errol was a different thing altogether: uncaring and probably unaware that his innocent offhandedness was so attractive. Errol was interesting because he wasn't drawn by her magnet. He was so brutally honest—the honesty of a child, unconcerned with the effect of his words. Errol was today and direct, uncomplicated and part of the obvious world of Radio 1 and bookstall magazines. He didn't have to be attracted; he would be spontaneous. He belonged to the age of yes and no.

He interested her, and he was highly usable as a practice ground for her new confidence.

She thought of the magazines she saw every morning in the newsagent's shop. How lurid they seemed: girls sprawling, astride, lying, clothed, unclothed. They had big eyes that were simple and asking. Stupidly submissive, cow-like creatures for rapacious men, she'd thought. But no, she understood now. Errol was at school with girls who were girlish because they didn't have to be anything else. He wouldn't think of them as playgrounds like the men she knew who hadn't discovered girls until they were seventeen—those men had been locked into a world of penises.

She went off to feed the cats. She spread the disgusting meal onto plates and put fresh sand in their trays. She did so automatically, her head full of pictures of herself.

At the washbasin, washing her fingers, she looked up into the mirror and made her eyes big. She pushed her hair up and tried to make her face look simple and asking. She undid the buttons of her shirt, pulled it down to expose her shoulders, took the slide out of her hair, and shook it to hang fluffy round her face. She smiled; she was enjoying herself. She walked to the armchair like she thought the women she'd seen in the magazines would walk—slinkily moving shoulders opposite to hips—and she said aloud in a sort of American accent, "Well Errol, baby, course I'm your doll. You just play with me how you like."

She knew Ambrose had cigarettes in his desk, and she took one, searched for a match, and lit the cigarette (which she'd stuck like a candle into her pursed mouth). She puffed in and out because she didn't smoke and wasn't sure really how to light one. She had to take it out of her mouth as she went back to the armchair, because it was making her cough and stinging her eyes. Holding the cigarette out from her like a character in a Coward play, she sat and then flopped back dramatically. She was at ease, and she threw her leg over the arm in what she felt was a wanton way. Her shirt, unbuttoned, freely hung from her bared shoulders and was held in place only by sleeves filled with her arms. It hung open to expose her navy blue bra. She was enjoying herself, and she could even pretend that Errol was in the room, standing there watching with admiration. She sucked in smoke from the cigarette and blew it out in a cloud. It hung in the air, hiding the place where she pretended Errol was standing.

"Yeah, baby. Rock me, man. I'm just a living doll. It's a gas man."

She paused, it didn't sound right. She tried again, "I mean, it's a real gas, man. You need a doll."

She smiled, amused at her play-acting, and took another pull at her cigarette. It made her cough. She didn't let the coughing affect her act, though. She flung her arms wide then offered them in submissive welcome. She said in what she thought was a sexy growl, "Yeah, come on. Rock me, man," and she coughed again. She didn't notice Jenkins standing in the open doorway.

He'd thought the office was empty. Like most of the times when he'd come to the corridor with his recorder, wire basket, and tumbler, he'd tried the knob. This time, to his amazement and joy, the door had opened. His amazement was complete when he saw Beatrice in the chair. At first he thought she was perhaps ill. And then, ill or not, he was aware of her disarranged clothing, the glimpse of bra, her bare shoulders, and her long, tights-clad, exposed leg draped over the arm of the chair. His excitement made him speak. It wouldn't let him savour the wonderful sight.

"I didn't know you smoked."

It was an intimate response, nothing to do with the lust that was warming him. He took his basket to the desk as Beatrice hurriedly put her leg to the floor, clutched her open shirt, and looked at him with horror on her face.

"What are you doing in here?" she demanded.

He didn't answer, just stood by the desk with a smile on his face. He probably didn't know he was smiling, it was just a visible expression of everything he felt inside. Seeing Beatrice—parts of Beatrice—was one of his wildest dreams, and here he was, here she was.

She was startled and annoyed by his intrusion into her privacy as well as the fact that he was in the office again, a place that Ambrose had insisted he had no right to be. She took another pull at the cigarette because she felt it between her fingers, and she looked at him haughtily and said, "You startled me."

Talking through the smoke made her cough again. It was an irritating tickling in her throat that made her put both hands to her mouth.

The coughing stopped magically, though, when she became aware that he was coming toward her. Her hands still at her mouth, one shoulder bare, she sat quite still watching his approach.

He stopped a couple of paces away and looked down at her, determined to stay as cool and controlled as he could be.

"Does your father have dogs and horses and things at his place in the country?"

The question was unexpected; he had gone down an avenue she'd never thought of. Curiously, it made her stiffen with apprehension more than if he'd pursued his usual pleas about sandwiches.

"Well yes," she replied. She was unsure and looked it. "Yes, of course."

"Tell me where he lives." His voice was now becoming warmer despite his resolve, and he asked, "Does he come down to London?"

"Well," Beatrice began, not sure what her reaction should be to prying into her family life, "sometimes. Why?"

He didn't answer for a pause. He just stood there, staring at her with a smile on his face, slightly pinker than when he came in.

There was a struggle going on in Roy Jenkins's head. His conviction that professional status would be a salvation, would give him an acceptability to her; impress her, and the urgency of the urge coming from his loins. His mind resolved itself without waiting for finesse, and he took a pace towards her.

"I worship you, Beatrice," he said with quiet passion. He was leaning down to her, his hands on the arm of the chair.

She said, "Don't be silly," and she pressed herself into the back of the chair. She heard herself trying to put authority into her voice: "You're just being silly."

He took the cigarette from her unresisting fingers and dropped it on the floor, on the carpet. He ground it in with his boot to extinguish it. She watched the operation like someone fascinated, hypnotised. He leaned closer to her, and she felt a sort of heat coming from him. His face, now close to hers, was disturbing, and when he spoke his breath blew at her. His voice was throaty and passionate, "Give me, give me, Beatrice," he quietly but urgently demanded.

"What?" she asked weakly.

"I want you," he said, and there was a choke in his voice. He couldn't help the drama. He said again, "I want you."

He paused as he leaned down to her. God, it was everything he'd ever dreamed of. He could smell her—could feel her warmth—and she had her eyes wide, looking simple and asking. But in her head she was shocked. She was not wholly fearful; she was excited by the danger in the intensity of the nearness. She held her arms wide outstretched and back like a captured soldier. This pause could have lasted five seconds, maybe ten. And then, like a whiplash, he moved from leaning to her. He straightened and dropped himself onto her lap, pulling her head forward to put his arm round her neck and his face into her hair. It was dramatic and sudden, and it took the breath from her.

The warm tickling perfume of her hair, the softness of her body, and the closeness of her were tremendously exciting. His tongue sought frenziedly for her ear.

She said, "No. No, don't," in gasps.

He had no control now. it was a moment to be grasped, and unable to find her ear, he kissed her neck. She felt the bigness of his hand on her breast, massaging in an anticlockwise direction. He was bursting. He wanted her, wanted her to want him. She sat there breathless for some moments, her arms still wide and his hip digging into her thigh as he passionately and wetly kissed her neck and throat.

"No, stop it, Mr Jenkins."

"Oh darling, darling, darling," he was saying to her throat, "Darling, Beatrice, let me be your lover."

The only resistance she could offer was her grip on his wrist, the wrist of the hand that was clutching her breast. He slid from her, backwards to the floor, and he pulled her by her arms down with him. He was loving his madness, and the split-second thought flashed through her bemused mind that he seemed to be terribly strong.

"I want you. I want you, Beatrice," he was panting, "I want to meet your friends."

She was kneeling, and he had his arm round her neck. Then he'd rolled over, and she gave a little squeal. Again, she had to gasp as he threw himself onto her, his face touching hers.

"Kiss me, kiss me, Beatrice," his words blew at her hair, and he put his mouth to hers. He pushed his tongue into her. Again, there was lightning clarity in her thinking that his tongue was pleasant and tasted slightly of peppermint before she twisted her head and struggled to roll him off her.

"Stop it," she said as she threw him with all the energy needed to make a stallion turn, and she sat back on her heels, shirt open, navy blue bra heaving. She looked at the startled look on his face as he was lying there on his side. She spoke firmly, gathering strength from his distance. "I said stop it. Do you hear?" And she added, "Pull yourself together, man." It was all she could think of, and it was the sort of thing she'd heard her father say.

He was on his hands and knees, their separation undermining his attack.

"Hold me; let me hold you, Beatrice," he pleaded.

She stood up but hadn't time to move away before he grabbed her legs and embraced them. It was a last and despairing attempt at togetherness. She pushed down at his arms as hard as she could, and in resisting, they went up to her thighs, under her skirt. For the first time, she felt the indignity of it all, and it gave her strength for a push that sent his arms to her ankles. She freed one leg and stepped out of his arms as if they were underclothes. With one leg held and swaying to avoid toppling on to him, she was determined now to be determined.

"I will not have this," she said. She meant her voice to thunder, but it was soprano and shrill, "I will not have this sort of thing in the office, Mr Jenkins."

He held her leg and shuffled with her as she attempted to move away. His upturned face was a mixture of misery and desire.

"Forgive me, Beatrice. It was your father's address, that's all I wanted."

She didn't answer, she just looked down at him, and it gave him courage to add, "Or maybe his friends in the country."

She was moving slowly and laboriously backwards, dragging the wretched caretaker with her.

"I shall speak to Mr Bonnyweather about this."

She was determined to be cruel if that was the only way to stop the nonsense. She kicked at his arms with her free foot, and then she stamped his arms down from the leg he held. It was precarious for two or three moments, and he had his head down, grimly hanging on. She fell forward and grabbed at the table for support. Bent across him, her skirt covered his head and shoulders.

Before she could kick unseeingly at his arms, he'd released her. His head under her skirt brought home to him the indignity of his position. She straightened herself and stood back from him, breathing heavily and realising that she'd won. She fastened her skirt and shrugged her clothing back into place. He knelt by the table with utter misery on his face.

"Won't you tell me?" he pleaded, but she didn't reply. His voice changed to bitterness, "I should have known. He was right; I should have realised."

In spite of the situation, his words caught her interest, "Who was right?"

Jenkins pulled himself slowly and painfully to his feet, "He doesn't deserve your love, but he obviously has it."

"Who?" Errol?"

"Who?" It was his turn to query.

"Oh never mind," she said after adjusting her skirt. She was pleased to feel that it was all over. She was back in charge again, and she couldn't help feeling some pity for him.

"It's just that I can't stand you, that's all," she said, offering it like an explanation.

"I thought you were generous with your affections," he said like an accusation. Then he drew himself up, realising that the only way out was dignity. "I'm not good enough. That's it, isn't it? I have no qualifications, is that it?"

She just looked at him. She didn't answer because she thought he must be going potty. She didn't know what he was talking about.

"It is," he insisted, "I can see it in your eyes."

That made her turn away.

"It would be different if I was a vet, wouldn't it?"

She turned to look at him again. She'd never heard anything so stupid in her life. What on Earth had vets to do with anything?

"Tell me, Beatrice, is your horse a mare?"

The conversation was becoming bizarre. She really had to put a stop to it.

"What my horse is," she snapped, "is none of your business."

She went back to the rack for her coat, showing him that the conversation was finished.

"I find you totally unexciting, Mr Jenkins—either as a vet or a caretaker."

But he wasn't going to give in; it might be months before they were alone in a room again.

"Let me touch you, or meet me tomorrow dinnertime."

He really was the limit.

"I have told you, it's out of the question."

"Just to feel your body in my arms . . . I could be a really successful vet if I knew all your friends, if I did some work for your father."

He was appealing to her as a realistic, practical lover. Surely she could see the sense in what he was saying?

He had moved to her to emphasise his feelings, and she backed away. Her coat was only half on, one arm sleeved.

"If it's because I'm working class and I haven't any A-levels, just remember Lady Antonia. She could see there were more than just middle class qualifications."

He had kept on moving toward her with no harm in his mind—merely emphasis for the points he was raising. Nevertheless, she backed away as he neared and found herself against the door to the other room. He was still advancing, still talking as if he was telling her something. She hadn't realised the extent of his derangement.

"I can give you anything. I could give you anything if I had the right clientele—it's who you know not what you know."

She moved quickly into the other room and locked the door. He heard her say, "Go away, you horrible man. Go away."

He didn't know what to do. She was obviously scared, hadn't realised that he was in control of himself. Oh if only she knew the size of the love that he had to offer.

"Let me in, Beatrice. Or come out, love."

But she didn't say anything, and he didn't want to break the door down. That would be silly. God, he'd really cocked it up—and to think: the rarity of being alone in a room with her . . . and he'd cocked it up. Still, she was prepared to be kind to others, he knew. He'd heard it through the wall, but nobody, nobody at all could offer her the love he could. Oh what a fool he'd been.

He dusted the shoulder of his uniform jacket and cursed himself. She was obviously not coming out as long as he was there. He went dejectedly to the desk for his basket, and then he heartened himself with the thought that she wouldn't disturb him. The misery on his face relaxed as he searched a drawer. It was an ill wind that brought nobody no good, he thought.

Beatrice, amid cats and budgies, heard him move away. She pressed her ear to the door, but she couldn't hear anything. The office door had not been closed—she was sure of that—so he could still be in there, perhaps waiting. One could never tell what erratic plans were in the head of a man so consumed with lust. What an idiot! He'd never get anywhere acting like that.

She sat down on a sack of sawdust and wondered what to do.

CHAPTER 10

It didn't take Roy Jenkins long to push the failure of the last half hour into the back of his mind when the excitement of being alone with the Perry Ironside Agency records flooded through him. As the proverb has it, danger and delight grow on the same stalk. And although Jenkins never heard of that particular proverb, he had heard the one that said that to be alive at all involves some risk. And it was with that marvellous feeling of illicit endeavour that his hands trembled as he spun through the files.

All he needed was a comprehensive list of pet owners to add to his present half dozen clients, and he would be able to establish himself. He wasn't sure how he would be able to let those people know that he was there to service them, though. He couldn't advertise, that was unethical, and anyway, it would stand out a mile if his was the only advert. But there was nothing to stop him writing or even telephoning Bonnyweather's clients. The important thing was that with a list of pet owners, he would be better off than he was without such a list.

He was on the chair, anxiously trying to focus the camera and moving his head and the camera up and down to avoid including all the desk top in the photograph when the door burst open. The door ricocheted back from the rubber stop and banged Errol on the shoulder, causing him to stagger as he entered into the room.

Already suspicious because the office door was ajar, he was determined to make an entrance that would avoid a hail of bullets and give him the chance to utilise some of the techniques he'd watched so avidly performed by Starsky and Hutch. The thump from the door as it bounced back from the doorstop prevented him from throwing himself as far as he would wish to the right (down on one knee) to spoil the interloper's aim. But he was into the room, down on his knee, and holding an imaginary pistol at the man standing on Mr Bonnyweather's chair. It only took a couple of seconds. Errol was excited that he had been able to do it and thrilled because he had had to do it. After another two seconds, he saw that his adversary was the caretaker.

"All right, drop it," he commanded.

"Eh?" Jenkins was astounded, "Drop what?"

He looked at the grim faced Errol and believed that something threatening was being pointed at him. Soon, surprise gave way to shock.

"Don't give me that," Errol snapped just as terse as Starsky (or Hutch) would have been, "Come on, out from behind there."

He moved his imaginary pistol peremptorily to indicate that he wanted the caretaker down off the chair and round the desk.

"Round to the front of the desk and turn round."

Jenkins had slowly and carefully descended from the chair, never taking his eyes off Errol—or rather, at what Errol was supposed to be pointing at him—and he now moved crablike round the desk as he was bidden. At the front of the desk, he stopped, staring transfixed at the young man.

"I said turn round," Errol snarled.

"Oh," Jenkins said as if he'd forgotten, and he turned obediently (but twisted his neck to keep Errol in view).

Errol moved slowly from his crouch.

"Just keep it nice and steady; nobody wants to get hurt, do they?"

This was an observation Jenkins fully agreed with, and he squinted at Errol as he moved carefully toward him.

"No," Jenkins said, in case it was thought he might not be too worried about being hurt. He was taken by surprise again, and it gave way to a sort of fear because, without warning, Errol frisked him. He wrapped his arms around him and patted his chest, then heavily and not without a certain frightening sensuality, he moved his hands down Jenkins's body. This was exciting for a moment as the hands caressed his groin and legs. In fact, he squealed a little because so many emotions bombarded him.

"Okay," Errol said and clapped a hand on Jenkins's shoulder, "Okay, you're clean."

In Jenkins's mind, being clapped on the shoulder was associated with a sort of intimacy. And because Jenkins could speak frankly in intimate situations, he turned to Errol and snarled in a higher voice than he intended, "What do you think you're on?"

"That's my question," Errol countered, still looking severe. "And mine as well," Jenkins persisted.

"all right, all right, Mr caretaker," Errol said and sounded as if he were giving him a chance, "what are you doing?"

"Nothing," Jenkins blustered and reached for his basket. Once he had in hand his rightful possessions, he added, "Just checking. Checking, that's all."

Because the young man merely gazed at him without saying anything, he felt bound to remind him that he wasn't outside his purview, as it were: "It's my job to check, you know. I have to check."

He made it sound as if he would receive a dire punishment if he didn't carry out his duties, but Errol looked at him unimpressed. And as Jenkins had feared, he looked in the basket. Errol then pulled an object out and placed it between them.

"That's a tape recorder, isn't it?"

He looked up slowly to Jenkins's face, then he asked accusingly as if he already knew the answer, "Were you listening to something?"

"Me?" He sounded amazed that anyone could think such a thing, "Listening? No. Listening to what?"

Errol did not look as if he were being taken in.

"What should I be listening to, then?"

"I dunno," Errol replied. He was telling the truth: he didn't know what Jenkins could have been listening to, but he recognised the equipment so pursued his enquiry with statements rather than questions.

"You've been listening," he accused, "You've been taping private conversations, and you've been reading private files."

"I haven't." It was a deliberate lie; it was an instinctive survival technique that made him deny the charge. He could think of nothing else to say.

Errol looked severe and spoke with severity.

"It was just, well, bits," Jenkins explained.

"Bits?"

"Bits," he repeated.

"That is criminal," Errol announced, and after looking at a disconcerted Jenkins for a pause, he said very seriously, "A civilian has the power of arrest you know."

This statement took Jenkins by surprise, and he was surprised again when he was grabbed by the lapels and felt the basket bite into his abdomen as he was pulled close to Errol.

"Come on, spill."

"Don't," Jenkins was shocked, "Don't. You'll tear my jacket. I have to look smart, I'm on the door."

Errol did not think this was a reasonable plea, and he held the lapels tighter and said, "I said spill." His voice had menace in it.

Jenkins appeared to surrender. "All right," he said, "Come to the desk. I'm on duty, you know," he said and turned to go, pulling Errol with him until the fears for his jacket halted him.

"No," Errol said, happy where he was, "You can tell me here, but don't try anything, mister." That was how Starsky would have said it.

Jenkins did the only thing that he could do: he straightened himself as best he could and tried to look dignified.

"I can be trusted," he said, "You know that."

There was a pause before the caretaker's dignity undermined the young man's aggression. His lapels were released.

"Can I sit down?" he asked. After receiving a nod that was meant to be curt, he sat at Bonnyweather's desk and waited until Errol had perched himself on the edge of the desk before he spoke.

"I need to know, you see."

"Need to know what?"

"Names, you know—people who own animals."

It all seemed so sweetly reasonable, and Errol was puzzled.

"What for?"

"You'd never understand," Jenkins said in a sort of despair at making anyone understand. He put his chin in his hands and leaned on his elbows. His expression was lugubrious as he stated, "Never in a thousand years."

"Why wouldn't I?" Errol asked. He didn't like the inference that something was beyond his understanding.

The caretaker looked at him for a few moments as if working out the best way to communicate with the young man.

"Have you ever wanted to be different?" He didn't wait long for an answer before he went on: "Have you ever really desperately wanted to be something you weren't?"

"You mean like reincarnation?"

A flicker of irritation went across Jenkins's face. "No."

"Oh," Errol said, not quite clear what they were talking about.

"Do you want to be somebody else?"

"Not somebody," Jenkins was patient like a teacher with a pupil, "*something* else."

"Such as what, then?" There was impatience in his voice.

"A vet," Jenkins said simply. Then because Errol just looked at him, he added, "A veterinary surgeon."

There was still no response from Errol.

"I've got all the books, I've read all the books; I've got all the instruments, and I know how to use them," he said and looked away from Errol, "I've been studying it for years."

"Well why don't you be a vet, then?" he asked, unable to really grasp the caretaker's problem, "I would if that's what I wanted."

He was surprised at Jenkins's passionate response: "Why don't I? Why *don't* I?" Then his voice dropped back to normal as he digressed momentarily, "Mind those papers, you're creasing them."

Without thinking, Errol slipped off the desk and straightened the papers as Jenkins continued with bitter passion, "They wouldn't let me go to college, would they?"

The question was rhetorical. "Oh yes, I could have done Open University. I could have got up half past five every day and missed going out at night for eight years, but I couldn't go to college, could I?

"No, they're not interested in people who *know* about animals, people who are mature because they're older. No, they're only interested in kids with bloody A-levels, not in people who have lived life."

He looked at an uncomprehending Errol for a few moments until he was convinced that, once more, there was a brick wall he was banging his head against. He dropped his head onto his arms, a picture of despair.

Errol felt uncomfortable, and his innate concern moved him to the caretaker's side. He didn't know quite what to say or do but began, "You mean they wouldn't let you go?" He meant for it to be comforting.

"They wouldn't allow the likes of me to be better than them," he mumbled into his arms. He looked so dejected, then he startled Errol with the suddenness of the way he sat up and continued his bitter passion: "Bloody bits of paper. They won't give you anything, they won't let you do anything unless you've kept their bloody teachers in work. But they won't pay anybody who really wants to *do* something. They won't pay them any allowance, will they?"

Although he was not looking at him, Errol felt that it was all right asking all these questions, but it was no good asking him. Jenkins should be asking them down at the education office or somewhere. He did, however, recognise the frustration and unhappiness, and he helped Jenkins to continue by asking, "Wouldn't you get a grant, then?"

Again he was startled at the response. Jenkins swung round and grabbed his pullover and said, "All right, all right, I haven't got any A-levels, but I bet they can't tell if there's a distended bladder or a prolapsed rectum. Oh no, they couldn't neuter a cat, could they?"

Errol didn't know if they could do any of those things, but he knew that if Jenkins didn't stop pulling at his pullover it might be necessary to give him a bit of a nudge. Jenkins followed Errol's eyes and released the pullover.

"Did you write to all the people whose names you taped?"

"I have six satisfied clients," he said proudly.

"Did you write to the people whose names you spied?" Errol persisted.

"Don't keep talking about spying. I asked Ambrose. I've asked him time without number, but he doesn't even remember my name's Roy—never mind telling me his clients." He looked up at Errol and looked pleadingly, "I have to have access to that sort of information."

Errol could see that he had a point, but he had difficulty accepting that a caretaker could expect to be thought of as a vet. He didn't quite know what to say, so he just looked at Jenkins and waited for a more negotiable point.

"He wouldn't be in this office if I hadn't needed my special books—they're bloody expensive, you know—and the assistant director's already asking questions. One of these days he'll be told to be interested," he finished ominously.

Errol couldn't really follow what Jenkins was so excited about, but he did realise that the man was upset. It seemed sensible to change the subject for a bit, point the conversation in another direction. He searched his mind for an alternative subject until he remembered the caretaker's interest in art, particularly the way he'd got uptight about the statue.

"Do people who do modern art have to have A-levels?" he asked. But Jenkins was in no mood to be sidetracked.

"Just because you wear a uniform, everybody thinks you're thick, they despise you."

That was another new point of view for Errol; he'd never heard of anyone despising people in uniforms.

"Well I didn't take any A-levels. I told them, I wasn't going to take any," Errol said encouragingly and with some truth.

Jenkins was only concerned with uniforms, though: "Nobody likes uniforms." His voice was sad, despairing at people's foolishness, "Not now. Even women, if you haven't had any advantages."

Errol was mystified, and there was a feeling of relief when he heard Bonnyweather's voice: "Ah, what's all this then?" He was standing in the open doorway.

Errol explained, "He's upset."

Bonnyweather came in, took off his hat, and hung it on the rack. He then placed his stick carefully into the container at the base of the rack before he turned to them. Jenkins was sitting at the desk with a miserable look on his face, and Errol was beside him with a daft smile. *Dombey and Son,* Bonnyweather thought.

"Feeling unwell, eh? Had to come in here to collapse, had he?"

"I'm not collapsed, Ambrose, I'm just overcome." It seemed right to solicit sympathy.

"Well we can't all be supermen. There's always a failure rate."

He walked to his desk, a little irritated that the caretaker should be overcome in his chair.

"Right, let's have the chair, Bernard. Things to do, people to satisfy, you know." He was brisk; he knew he had to jerk things back into perspective. Once you let someone give in, they were like a rotten apple: they affected others. As he neared his chair, Jenkins stood up as a reaction. He wanted to prolong the possibility of sympathy and reduce the possibility of being asked what he was doing in the office in the first place. He put a hand wearily but gratefully on Errol's shoulder and looked at Bonnyweather with a wan smile.

"He's been a great help and comfort to me, this lad," he said.

Bonnyweather eased himself into the chair and Jenkins had to move aside.

"Well it's all good training."

"Come on," Errol said, "I'll see you back to your table."

Jenkins couldn't help it: he felt that the atmosphere would never have more promise of sympathy, and there was an urgency in him to give voice to his pent up feelings.

"You have so much, Ambrose," he said like a tender accusation, "The love of a woman, a great list of clients, and a room here with your own lock. All I ask is: is it fair?"

Bonnyweather looked at him, trying to guess what lay behind the caretaker's words. "Many are called, but few are chosen, Bernard."

"I can't understand it," Jenkins said, and there was despair in his voice because he couldn't understand what a woman like Beatrice could see in a Scotsman. Errol realised that Jenkins was not advancing his cause by staying in the office, and he tried to lead him away by gently pulling his arm, leading him to the door.

"Come on, I think Mr Bonnyweather's busy."

Jenkins allowed himself to be led a few paces like a casualty until he realised what was happening. He shrugged off Errol's helping hand.

"You don't have to help me, I'm not an old man—I'm only his age."

"Okay, okay, you don't have to get snotty," he said and took the caretaker's arm again, this time more firmly, "Come on, then," he insisted.

"There was a queue for postcards out there," Bonnyweather said matter-of-factly.

"Oh bloody hell," Jenkins said. Nothing was going right for him today, but postcards were only a perk: he made five pence on each one he sold.

"I knew I was chancing my arm being away."

He allowed himself to be taken by Errol, and Bonnyweather watched the door as it closed after them.

What on Earth had made the boy bring him into the office and have him sit at the desk? Surely he could see the serious possibility of undermining the whole hierarchical structure if he allowed a caretaker even a whiff of status? Ambrose decided he'd better have a word, stress the importance of security. Caretaker's should be allowed to collapse in their own place and not be brought into an office and sat at an executive's desk. No, at a company director's desk. He would definitely have to have a word. There was too much of this easy-come, easy-go attitude today. People should be made to realise that things have to be earned, that there were no increments and easy promotions in private enterprise. His thoughts flew on through a whole range of society's aberrations as he assumed his favourite problem-solving position: laid back in his chair, legs thrust out, and hands clasped behind his head. His body was taut with relaxation, and his face wore a sort of smile that might suggest he was condescending to be amused by what he expected.

He lay back in his chair for nearly a minute before his mind returned to Jenkins's comment that he, Bonnyweather, had the love of a woman. He assumed Jenkins meant Beatrice. He wondered idly—and a little conceitedly—what she could have said to him. His thoughts of what she said and how she might have said it were interrupted by the creaking of the door to the other room. The door was opened slowly until it revealed the anxious looking object of his thinking. Beatrice in her coat was peering cautiously into the office. Bonnyweather remained in his recumbent position. He didn't speak until their eyes met.

"Did you come in through the window?"

"Oh it's you," she said in near relief.

"A wise observation," he replied, and his smile broadened at his wit.

She closed the door, but she seemed reluctant to come any further into the office.

"Has he gone?"

"They've all gone."

"All?" She hadn't been able to hear much in the other room, and what she had heard was the caretaker's raised voice bewailing his educational hang-ups. She had thought that he was declaiming to himself, as she supposed all madmen did.

"What do you mean *all?*"

Bonnyweather came up into a sitting position and smiled at her without answering.

Finally, he said, "Have you been playing hard to get?" He seemed amused.

She went to the coat rack and took off her coat. She recognised his confident mood and argued with herself about the usefulness of continuing the conversation until she had hung up her coat.

She decided she had to talk about it: "That ogre, Jenkins, had the nerve to touch me. He attacked me."

He watched her go to her table, surprised at her news but not alarmed.

"Courage is the product of desperation, as they say at the war office," he said, and then, because the thought had piquancy, added, "Did he manage it?"

"What?"

Her answer told him enough. He lay back in his thinking position again.

"Poor old sod," he said, and there was genuine concern in his voice.

"He wanted father's address."

"Nothing permissive about Bernard—a very conventional mind."

She ignored what he said because she didn't understand. "Why do you think he wanted it?"

"Frustration," Bonnyweather explained, "Spirit of conquest, urge to be dominated. Not sure whether your lot was like his lot. Could be anything."

"But Daddy's address? Why?"

Bonnyweather chuckled at what came into his head: "Perhaps he wants to marry you?"

"But he wanted to know Daddy's friends as well."

"Just checking, I expect," he said. He was making everything seem perfectly reasonable. "Probably going to ask for a dowry."

He couldn't help chuckling again.

"Oh don't be ridiculous," she said. She realised that he found the whole thing incredibly amusing, and anything further she might say would only add to the amusement.

"He's a good man. He's honest, likes security, interested in safeguarding the nation's culture. I think your dad will like him."

"Oh stop it! How can you?"

She wasn't enjoying the joke, and he didn't really want to sour anything, so he permitted himself another chuckle before going to the other room.

"I think I know where that red setter is," he said as he went into the room. There was a clattering as if he'd knocked something over, and his voice rose so that she could hear him.

"I saw that twit that lost his horse. You know, I wouldn't mind betting the horse just got fed up."

She was a moment becoming aware of what he was talking about; all her mind was full of Jenkins.

"Oh Nicky you mean?"

"Yes."

"He's sweet, isn't he?"

Bonnyweather appeared in the doorway holding an ironing board.

"Very probably," he said before he came in and started to set up the board for operation.

"He gave me tea in a cup with legs on it and a bloody teapot with feet."

"They're marvellous, aren't they?" At last something she could enthuse about, something she understood—not like the madness of the last hour.

"I've met the man who makes them. I've got a teapot that looks like a tap."

He gave her a look—quizzical if perfunctory—before he went back into the other room. "Decadent," he said simply, "Toys for decadent drones."

She raised her voice, "Have you seen the one with the naked silver lady stretched across its top?"

There was no response, only the sound of things being moved noisily.

"I bought Daddy one for Christmas. He thought it was an absolute hoot."

He came out with an iron and an armful of clothes and asked, "Did you move the clothes horse?" He didn't wait for an answer because he thought he knew it, "I expect they were in a colour supplement, that's a sure way to get all you wholemeal twits going."

She watched him prepare a garment for ironing, and the morning's feeling of superiority came flooding back. She was sorry for him.

"As a matter of fact," she said, opening out a newspaper, "I saw them in Vogue." She pretended to be absorbed in the paper. After a suitable pause, she asked if he'd applied to employ Errol under the scheme he'd talked about earlier. And she couldn't help adding mischievously, "He's awfully sweet, isn't he?"

He ignored her description of Errol and said, "It's on its way."

She watched him fold a shirt carefully before spreading another on the board.

"What happens if they don't allow it?"

She was determined to keep the upper hand as long as she could.

"Don't be silly," he said, dismissing such a possibility, "There's no question about it."

"But they may not approve it, you know."

"Rubbish," he replied and licked his finger. He sizzled it on the iron and asked, "Not approve it?" He gave a short laugh and ironed the sleeve of the shirt before pausing.

"I'll appeal, that's what I'll do. I'll appeal."

But her question stayed in his thinking.

"There must be somebody you can take into her Majesty's Courts of Law." He looked at her and said, "Justice is truth in action." His tone indicated that she ought to know better, but she didn't reply.

He folded the second shirt and saw that she was watching him. "I suppose I could have a word with the chief constable."

She shook out the newspaper, "I think he's boring."

He didn't like the way she was capping everything he said.

"Oh yes," he persisted with the air of a man who is just a little wiser than most, "I know where the strings are. Typical, typical of this government. Typical."

She wasn't clear what was typical—personalities were more important than governments.

"My brother says he's an absolute boor, and he says it's common knowledge about his drivers." Then she added the ultimate insult, "They don't even have to be pretty."

But he wasn't listening. Surely they could see the advantages he could offer? He stood for a pause looking at the vest on the ironing board. She sensed his unresolved doubt, and her concern was aroused.

"You care too much," she said gently, "You mustn't care so much."

And she looked up from her newspaper and smiled at him because she knew he would like her to.

CHAPTER 11

There was a queue for postcards, six or seven people round the caretaker's table examining what was available. There were colour postcards of many well-known paintings, most of which were not in Marylebone Council Galleries. The postcards were bought in bulk by the superintendent, Mr Murphy, and he naturally chose the ones that offered the best discount. But because people who visit galleries tend to buy postcards from habit, their relevance to the collection in the Bloomsbury Gallery was not important. Jenkins had slid (looking agitated) into his seat behind the table, not deliberately and sedately, but with a slow patient check of his cashbox before looking up condescendingly at the customer. It was his typical behaviour. He still had that strange, out-of-tune feeling, and he was reluctant to let his newfound confidant go.

"Hang on, I won't be long with these," he said in an urgent plea to Errol before he turned impatiently to the people at his table.

"Right, who's first, then?"

Errol was feeling good. He was really into being a private investigator. He felt relaxed and refused to be in a rush to do things, so he leaned on the wall by Jenkins's table and folded his arms.

He felt good, and he could afford to wait. The people milling round the table just didn't bother him. Jenkins, it seemed, needed his protection. The caretaker had dealt with three or four of his anxious customers, and the rattle of coins into his box and the mental gymnastics of giving change had settled his excited mind a little. Glancing now and then to see whether Errol was being patient left him reassured. And it was after one of those glances that he noticed Mr Pugh come into the foyer. His immediate reaction was fear and annoyance.

He thought, *what the hell does the man want this time?* What he didn't realise was that Barrymore Pugh had hoped that the postcard buyers would hide his entry; he didn't particularly want to talk to Jenkins.

"Hang on, can you carry on here for a minute?" he asked Errol, and the urgency in his voice made Errol take his seat in front of a hand holding four postcards at him.

"Hey, what do I do?" How much are they?"

"Oh mainly 90p. Put the money in the box," he said and moved the cashbox nearer Errol. He then rushed over to Mr Pugh.

The assistant director had deliberately turned his head away from the caretaker's table and walked as nonchalantly as he could toward Modern Works & Exhibitions. He stopped when the caretaker grabbed his arm.

"Hello, sir, Mr Pugh. It's nice to see you again so soon."

"Yes, hello, Mr . . . Errr . . ."

"Jenkins."

"Yes, of course. Hello, Mr Jenkins."

There was a pause, each wondering why the other was bothering with him until Jenkins said, "Is there some special reason? I mean something special you've come to see?"

"Errr, no. No, not really. It's, um—I thought I'd better have a look at what's available. I mean, on display. Familiarise myself with what there is, sort of thing," he said and laughed in a rather staccato way, which made the caretaker copy it without thinking. They sounded like the background noise in a wildlife documentary.

"I could also, I suppose, have a look at the staffroom, eh?" Pugh said, extending the humorous aspect.

"Staffroom?"

"You know, washroom, staffroom," he continued, and because Jenkins was looking at him with his mouth open, he felt a need to explain. "You remember the last time I came; you were quite concerned about, well, the staffroom."

"Oh," Jenkins said, baffled, "Oh yes."

"You busy, then?" Pugh asked. He tried to reinforce the cheerful unimportant nature of the conversation via his tone.

"Oh yes, oh yes. Its postcards—they're always popular."

"Are they?" Pugh asked as he turned to look at Errol, happily dropping coins into the cashbox. The sight and sound of cash brought his mind back to his job—he'd forgotten that there was a cash factor.

"Who's the young man at the table. He's not one of ours, is he?"

He knew one ought to be relaxed about appearance, but there was a certain formality that was normal to galleries, and Errol didn't look formal.

"Why hasn't he got a uniform?"

"Oh," Jenkins replied, he had not thought about having to explain Errol. "Oh well . . . you see, sir, he's not one of us. I mean on gallery staff. He's, he's from the treasurer's department," he finished, a surge of pride going through him at being able to think of that. "He's just doing a check, a spot check."

"A spot check?" Pugh knew that the treasurer's department had a penchant for spot checks, but he was surprised: he'd never seen a local government clerk who looked so young and, well, so informally dressed.

"Can you change a tenner?" Errol shouted at the caretaker, and Pugh was shocked at the raucousness of the young man's informality. Treasury clerks always seemed to be low-voiced and pussyfooting characters when he went to have his monthly expenses checked.

"In a minute. Won't be a minute," Jenkins called back, and then he lowered his voice, "I'd like to come and see you, if I may. At your office, sir."

"Oh."

"I know it may seem unusual, sir, but I was wondering if I could use you as a reference. You see, it's about going to college—I need references."

"A what?" Pugh was amazed, "Well maybe so, but I think we should have a little talk about . . ."

Mrs Hepworth had just come into the foyer and had looked straight at him with the briefest of smiles before closing the glass door in a deliberate way. Pugh's voice tailed off, and he looked at his watch. She was on time and he should be in Modern Works & Exhibitions, not chatting to some fool.

"About what, sir?" Jenkins asked. He didn't like people who left sentences unfinished. He was interrupted by Errol at his elbow.

"Look, I don't know whether you're interested in selling these flipping cards, but I haven't got any change," he said and flourished a ten-pound note.

"Well I haven't either," he said as he remembered the presence of Mr Pugh. "Oh this is the assistant director," he said as meaningfully as he could to Errol who gave Pugh a nod.

"Well what about the change?"

Pugh vaguely patted his pockets, "I don't think I . . . Look, I must press on. I want to see these pictures."

In turning to look at who might be the idiot who was offering a ten-pound note for a few postcards, Jenkins saw Mrs Hepworth. Then he saw the quick look that passed between her and Mr Pugh, and a great dawning came over him. He turned to Pugh and gave him a wordless smiling look before he leaned closer. The assistant Director bent his head to him as if mesmerised to hear his whisper.

"Don't you worry, sir, I understand. You can use the staffroom if she'd like a cup of tea," he said and winked. He then jerked his head in the direction of Modern Works & Exhibitions.

"Hey, what about this change? I think I'll just give her the postcards," Errol said. He was not Jenkins's assistant, and he couldn't give fourpence about postcards and stupid women with no change.

"Yes, yes, of course," Pugh said and pulled himself together. He was irritated by the caretaker's confidential manner, and he was flustered. "Now these pictures. I mean, treasury spot check," he began and looked at Errol, "How often is this? I mean, I suppose I'll hear if there are any discrepancies and so forth?"

Errol said "Eh?" then to Jenkins he asked, "What's he on about?"

Jenkins said hastily "Oh about every two or three months," and he turned to Errol and contorted his face into an exaggerated wink, "That's about it, isn't it?"

Errol looked at him for a pause before he said, "If you say so." Then he returned to his query, "But what about this? I can't stay here all day, you know."

"Quite so, quite so," Pugh said quickly. He thought, *so they have cocky buggers in treasury as well, did they?* "I think Mr—errr—Jenkins, you should see to your customers. I'm sure this, um, gentleman has other things to do."

"Well yes. I'm going, I'm going now, sir," said Jenkins and he jerked his head again, this time to Errol to indicate that he should leave the table. As a parting shot, he said to Pugh, "I think there's enough milk. You should be all right in there."

Pugh didn't answer, but he felt distinctly apprehensive about the caretaker having any inkling about what he was about. The only thing he could do was glance quickly at Mrs Hepworth who was examining a postcard before marching off into Modern Works & Exhibitions.

"What was all that about?" Errol asked, but Jenkins was travelling with great speed to the table.

"Ah good afternoon, madam. Can I help you?"

"What about this lady's change?" Errol persisted.

"Good afternoon, Mr Jenkins. You see? I remember your name." Jenkins smiled fondly at her before turning to Errol's customer.

"Have you anything less than that?" he asked sharply.

"Afraid not. I only have fifteen pence in change."

"All right, just this once," he said and took the note from Errol. He gave it to the woman, and she was delighted with her bargain.

"I thought you said they were 90p each?" Errol couldn't misunderstand such largesse.

"They are," Jenkins said as he turned to Mrs Hepworth and put on a strange smile. "It's nice to see a regular visitor, madam," he said unctuously.

"Tell me, how long has Mr Pugh been here?"

"It's about . . ." Jenkins began and seemed to think hard, "about three, maybe four weeks now."

"No, I meant today."

"Oh not long. A few minutes, I would say," he said and then lowered his voice and bent to her, "I think he was expecting you, wasn't he?"

She smiled at him, but her eyes were cool. She didn't like to think that Barrymore Pugh would share confidences with the caretaker. Jenkins, for his part, had a mind that was running amok with mischief. "Actually, he's just getting over a bit of bother, I believe. But I understand he's quite fit now."

"A bit of bother?"

He chuckled at her like a two-stroke motorcycle and said, "He's obviously been a very active man."

She looked at him uncomprehendingly. "Has he?"

Jenkins was prepared to elaborate further when he saw Mr Pugh looking back into the foyer, perhaps wondering if Mrs Hepworth had left.

"Ah there you are, sir," Jenkins announced loudly.

"Oh yes," Pugh began, flustered. His eyes lit on Errol, who was leaning against the wall not really interested, and Pugh felt he should say something to him.

"Ah the treasurer's. Is it just postcards, or what else do you do spot checks on?" He came to the table because he felt he must. He didn't want to be left out of anything. And in any case, he wanted to show his status.

"No nothing else this month, unless you know . . ."

He was getting used to playing parts.

"What?"

"How do you mean?"

"You said *unless*. Unless what?"

Mrs Hepworth gave the anxious Jenkins a smile, and with a deliberate and elegant walk she went into Modern Works & Exhibitions. She walked past Mr Pugh as if she didn't know him.

He turned and watched her go.

"Well I mean, unless there's a theft or . . ." Errol began but was interrupted by Jenkins saying cheerily, "Did you want the exhibits checked, sir?"

Pugh had a strong feeling that he was vulnerable, so he glared at Jenkins's grinning face and turned on his heel to follow Mrs Hepworth.

Jenkins called after him, "Try not to use all the milk, sir." He grinned at Errol, and Errol grinned back without really knowing why.

She was looking at a creation by Willy Nowowski "After Hockney," as the caption said, when she felt the presence of Barrymore Pugh.

"Interesting, isn't it?" he said, and she didn't answer. He looked at the painting with her for a pause.

"I didn't think you'd come."

"I'm not sure why I did," she said.

"Oh," he said as he tried desperately to think of something chatty.

"There's a place where we can have a very private cup of tea if you like."

"Is there?" She looked at him in mock surprise.

"You look incredibly beautiful," he said. He couldn't help it, it was what he thought.

"Thank you," she said and moved to the next picture. She sounded pleased. He moved to stand behind her, and greatly daring, put his hands on her hips.

"Would you like some tea?" he asked, his voice low.

She didn't answer, but she didn't move, so he allowed his hands to feel the firmness of her hips and put his nose into her hair. She smiled at the painting.

"Come on," he urged quietly, "Let's go somewhere private."

There was a pause before she turned suddenly, smiled, and said, "Okay, let's have an exciting cup of tea."

He didn't risk an answer. He led her to the door marked "Staff only," and he ushered her in.

It was a small room, narrow with a toilet bowl at one end beyond a sink. There was a scruffy, stained cupboard upon which was placed a kettle and a teapot.

He was more surprised than she was. He'd thought Jenkins staffroom was just that—not a loo.

"How intimate," she said.

"I didn't know. I thought . . ."

She stroked his face and said, "You are sweet," and he looked lost for what to do next. The smell of her perfume was intoxicating. She stayed close to him.

"Would you really like some tea?" he asked.

She looked at him and started to giggle.

There were still two shirts to iron when Errol walked into the office, and Bonnyweather nearly scorched a cuff as he paused to look with cold amazement at his assistant.

Beatrice lowered her newspaper and smiled at Errol after he'd closed the door.

"I didn't hear a knock, did you, Mrs Thompson?"

"Miss," Beatrice corrected, looking at Errol.

"There is little point in having security if every Tom, Dick, and Harry can walk in here, is there?" He realised that he should move the iron and did so. "Little point at all."

Errol smiled happily because he felt good. He went to the armchair and asked, "Have you been busy?"

"Don't be impertinent."

Bonnyweather and Beatrice watched him make himself comfortable in the chair, then he looked at Beatrice and said, "You know, with the right clothes, you'd be really fantastic. It's a great body."

"Thank you," she said modestly and folded the paper. This was interesting. Bonnyweather snorted and carried on with the shirt. "You're going to have to learn, young man," he said severely, "Security begins with a capital S in this game."

Beatrice cupped her chin in her hands and looked at Errol. She said, "You seem very pleased with yourself."

"I've found the cat," he said simply.

She was silent a moment before she said in wonder, "Oh how terribly exciting! So soon?"

Errol looked smug; he knew he'd been good.

"It was the satisfaction that gave me the MO."

"MO?"

"*Modus operandi,*" Bonnyweather said to the ironing. He refused to be impressed.

Beatrice gave Bonnyweather a puzzled look before giving her attention to Errol. "And is it satisfying?" she asked.

Errol was loving this. He crossed his legs and let his hands hang down each side of the chair, exuding relaxed confidence.

"I thought I'd suss out the streets round about—you know, look for the obvious *Stones* fanatics then check which of them were cat nuts." He moved his look to the ironing man and asked, "Do I get bus fares back?"

Bonnyweather didn't look up from his ironing, and Beatrice was gazing at him with admiration. He continued, "It was three streets away. There was this freak who was really into fish—you know, said it was organic protein and that. I knew I'd cracked it when I could smell all this room odour—you know, like fish is when it's all you eat."

He paused to put his hands behind his head and ruminate a bit more.

"You know, they're not all students, these health food nuts. This bloke was old, about thirty or something. He was a 'Friend of the Earth,' he said. And he was really into growing cabbages and things in the park instead of flowers and you know. He said there would be no pollution if people stopped using trees for paper and no whales were killed for armaments."

It was a long speech to be allowed to make, and he glanced suspiciously at Bonnyweather. He was apparently oblivious to what he'd said, or maybe he was thinking deeply about it while he was ironing. Beatrice looked as if she could listen to him for ages.

"They don't use whale meat for armaments, do they?" This was something that had puzzled him since he was told it.

"It's the sperm oil," Bonnyweather said, folding the shirt.

"Sperm oil?" A light dawned on Errol and he said, "I remember that from biology. You mean the male seed in conception?"

"That's human biology," he said as he spread the last of his shirts on the board. Things were becoming more interesting for Beatrice, and dramatic if rather erotic pictures had come into her head. "Whales don't copulate like humans, do they?" she asked and added in awe, "But they're enormous."

"You were talking about a cat," Bonnyweather reminded Errol.

"It must be a majestic sight," she said as she closed her eyes at the thought.

"Why whale sperm?" Errol asked, wanting to get to the bottom of it. "Do they inject it into bombs, then? Like artificial insemination?"

Bonnyweather didn't care for the way the conversation was going. "Where did you find the cat?" he asked curtly.

"This freak had this bedsit that was all fish like I told you—you know, real fish. I would have thought that was really pollution, that stinks. Anyway, he had three in there, but I only took Norma. I thought I'd wait until somebody put tabs out for the others," He concluded and looked at Bonnyweather for approval. "Okay, eh?"

The ironing man turned the shirt to do the sleeves and asked, "Where is it, then?" as uninterestedly as he could.

"How do you mean?"

"Where," Bonnyweather said as he looked up at him and spoke slowly, "is the cat?"

"I took it back."

"Took it back?" Bonnyweather was now all attention, "Five days' search fees, pfff?" And he snapped his fingers at the second attempt as he said, "Just like that? What sort of business studies did you do at that technical school? Eh? Eh?"

"Well," Errol began, not knowing what to say—he'd only expected admiration. "I didn't know, did I?"

"Of course you didn't," Beatrice dismissed Bonnyweather's ingratitude, "Do you think I should wear more red?"

"I'm not sure about bright colours," he said. It was easy for Errol to give her attention: "I mean, the outline's okay, isn't it? You don't have to be more obvious."

"How the hell do you think I can earn a living, pay taxes?"

"You don't," she interrupted tartly and changed her tone for Errol: "I often think of not bothering to wear a bra, but I don't think I have the confidence. I mean, I know it feels nice . . . ."

"Never mind about bras," Bonnyweather said. It was his turn to interrupt. "What about consumer satisfaction? What about that, eh? If people think they can get just what they want just like that, pfff." And this time his fingers snapped the first time.

"You're the last person I would have thought to be unconcerned about bras," she said dismissively. "I have a sort of cheesecloth shirt my brother bought me in Turkey. I think he really meant it for a bit of fun, but I'd love to have the confidence to wear it openly."

"It's nice, that. Nice material, isn't it?" Errol remarked. He was an expert on clothing. "I wonder why they call it cheesecloth?"

"Because they wrap bloody cheese in it, that's why! Are you listening to me?" It was outrageous, the lack of attention.

"Course," Errol said, recognising the need to be subordinate but needing reassurance, "it doesn't smell of cheese."

The telephone rang, and it reduced Bonnyweather's response to a look as he waited for Beatrice to get up and answer it.

"The simple basis," he explained with irritated patience, "on which our whole economy is based, is that once a demand has been created, both sides have to keep on demanding."

"Hello, Perry Ironside Agency. Beatrice Thompson speaking."

"There is no point in building Everest if you are going to teach everybody to climb bloody mountains. Every economy needs the frustration of waiting, of waiting for . . . ."

"Will you please be quiet?" she demanded, holding the phone to her bosom, "Either get on with the ironing or put the whole thing away." After looking at her with surprise writ large upon his face, he started to fold the ironing board.

"I'm sorry, could you tell me that again?" she asked, her tone gone from peremptory to chuckling charm. "Oh you mustn't—but how nice." She beamed at Errol as she listened. "One of our bright young men," she laughed girlishly, "Oh yes, I'm sure he will—we all will," she said and nodded approvingly. She then simpered at what the caller was saying and said, "Of course, byeee."

She put the phone down and looked at Errol. She ignored Bonnyweather, who was taking the ironing board into the other room.

She raised her voice, "Norma, she's having a party," then she went to stand looking at Errol fondly and added, "and you're the guest of honour."

"Hey, great. I wonder if she has any more *Stones* records."

"Party?" He came back in and had the feeling that somehow things were being taken out of his hands. "Party? he asked again. I run a business, not an amusement arcade. I've not sweated my guts out climbing from obscurity just to be a guest of honour at a party for a cat."

"I'm the guest of honour," Errol said smugly.

"It's Norma's party," Beatrice said as she went back to her table, disappointed at Bonnyweather's unwillingness to be joyful, "and she wants us all to go."

"There's no reason at all why you should go." It was the only way he could think of to reassert his status.

She stared at him dumbfounded by the unkindness, "Well of all the cruel things to say . . ."

Bonnyweather was determined to have his authority back and said, "However unpleasant it may appear, I have made a decision." And then, with gentle firmness, he placed the ironed garments carefully into a plastic carrier.

"That's the trouble today: nobody is used to decisions, decision-making is . . ."

"Oh stop talking balls!" she interrupted furiously, "You're jealous. And you're cruel, sadistic, and ever-so-stupidly pompous." She marched to where her coat hung. Errol felt uncomfortable. He wanted to help, but he didn't wish to jeopardise his job.

"Maybe it could blow your cover? Couldn't it?" He said as he looked hopefully at Bonnyweather.

"My cover, I can assure, could only be blown by a man. And I said a *man*. I think you're a pig, a rotten, chauvinistic, sexist, nasty pig"

"Don't be silly," Bonnyweather said. He'd never seen her so cross before.

"It's nice stuff, cheesecloth," Errol said, trying like mad to mediate, "Why don't you try your cheesecloth shirt?"

She was at the door, and they watched her struggling into her coat. She paused for just a moment after Errol had spoken, and she said with some vehemence, "Oh fuck cheesecloth." Then she pulled her coat round her, glared at Bonnyweather, and said, "I am going to have to consider my position here." She spoke with militant dignity. When she left the office, she slammed the door.

Both men turned their eyes from the door to the other, then Bonnyweather went into the other room.

Errol called out to him in a last effort to bring normality back: "Mr Bonnyweather, can you do A-levels in investigation?"

CHAPTER 12

The early evening sun was yellowing and flooding Bonnyweather's view from the office window. Bricks, slate roofs, chimneys, fall pipes, buttering—everything looked as if it had been crayoned: it was all soft and matte, not like paint. He was filling in time until Errol returned with his corn beef sandwich, and he was at his favourite place for thinking: right by the window.

As usual, he had been interrupted by his eyes, and they'd insisted that his thinking concern itself with his view and move away from colours and the mellowing day. That man with the ladder was in Percy Mews again. It was rare to see anyone for more than a brisk couple of seconds from the office window, so it was something of an occasion. It gave the man with the ladder a rarity value, made him interesting. His ladder was up against the wall, not fully extended, and he was laying back on the propped up ladder, smoking. Bonnyweather watched him. He couldn't see any tools or equipment. If he'd been a window cleaner, there would surely have been a bucket or a cloth or a leather—something like that hanging from a belt.

But he didn't seem to have any tools; he was just laying back on his ladder, and he didn't even look dirty or dusty. Maybe he was just waiting for someone? He had the look of a workman.

Bonnyweather squinted down at the man trying to see his face. It couldn't be Jenkins, could it? Maybe his brother? Cousin? But why should he be laying back on a ladder smoking in the one part of Percy Mews that was visible from his window? As an investigator, he was always interested in why people did things, why they should let him see things they were doing.

Bonnyweather rubbed at the window to clear his view, and he was surprised at the dirt. No wonder he couldn't see clearly. And all the muck was on the inside—God knows what the outside was like.

He must have a word with her. As he enlarged the cleared part of the pane, the desire to have a clearer view of the stranger overcame his reluctance to soil his hands. He saw the man looking up at him, and he looked older than he thought. He had a narrow face—a face with a cap that could have been the face of a gent or aristocrat . . . it was horsey.

The man smiled up at the window (a charming, happy smile), and he waved, perhaps thinking that Bonnyweather's window clearing had been a wave to him. It seemed as if it were a signal. The time had come to get on with the next thing. The man threw his cigarette away and moved away from the ladder. But he turned to look back up before he moved out of sight and waved again, cheerily and energetically, up at Bonnyweather. He wanted to move back a pace, seem unconcerned, but he didn't. He was fascinated by the man's cheery familiarity, and he didn't know why. The man had gone and left the ladder propped against the wall. It gave no access to any part of the building—it merely ended two thirds of the way up the wall.

The man had been leaning idly; the ladder was propped idly. Together and separately, they had been—were—part of some inactivity, and Bonnyweather wondered now why the man had waved so cheerily. He also wondered why he had waved back to the man. He felt a compulsion even though he wasn't the demonstrative sort, never had been. And it was perhaps the word demonstrative that brought his mind back to Beatrice—and there was an irritation. He'd said to her earlier, before all the childishness when she'd left: "I just might be able to get round tonight or tomorrow."

She'd said, "Oh not tonight. No, I don't think it would be advisable. I don't think I'll be there." It had been a surprise.

She was always the one who had had to ask before; it was the first time he'd actually asked. And there it was: a rebuff.

Surely it couldn't be to do with the other night? She'd said herself that he'd been too tense, should have been more relaxed, should have been more aware that it didn't need worrying about. It was there for the asking, and he had stopped worrying. She'd said that—well more or less. Of course, it was tenseness that had been his undoing. He could see that. But it had always been there for the asking, and he'd asked and been told, in effect, to piss off. He closed his eyes in exasperation at allowing these phrases from his past to keep summarising his situation. Nevertheless, he'd been told in no uncertain terms that she wasn't as easy as she had been. Why? Somebody else? It couldn't be Jenkins? Surely to God?

He gave a disdainful yack of a laugh and had to swerve back into the correct lane when faced with annoyed pip-pips and flashing headlights. Eventually, the thought of Beatrice and Jenkins left him.

Errol pressed his foot on the floor and raised himself to look over the back of his seat to see who the horn blower was. He'd been working out an idea he'd had about fitting some sort of electronic device on or even in cats and dogs that would beep when they were more than half a mile away from where they belonged. All they needed was some equipment to pick up the beeps, and there'd be masses of satisfied customers. But Bonnyweather's explosive laugh had interrupted his thinking.

They were in the rover moving out to Raines Park, and Errol felt excited again at being able to go out and be recognised—admired even—as an investigator. Bonnyweather was more concerned with seeing that Hanson man again and meeting a satisfied client. But the Beatrice business? Was there somebody else? Surely not. She'd always been impressed with him—he'd hardly had to try. But she'd been different, sort of distant—even argumentative. And she didn't give him all her attention like she used to over the last couple of days. In fact, since the boy Errol had been with them . . . Errol? Errol? *Oh God, no!* he thought, and he erupted into a short, sharp laugh again. But he didn't swerve.

It was a niggle all the same. He glanced at Errol and saw sufficient to stop him thinking such a bloody stupid thought. But they had been talking about clothes or something—cheesecloth, wasn't it? They must have gotten to know each other pretty well to talk like that; he would never think of talking about clothes. It was ridiculous. He was a bit of a kid. No, it would be somebody more like himself if it were anybody—she needed maturity. They drove on toward Norma's party.

"I'm hungry," Errol said, I hope there's going to be some nosh."

Bonnyweather glanced at him but didn't reply, so Errol said it again, "I'm hungry."

"Oh," his employer said, "interesting."

"You've had a sandwich," he said accusingly.

He'd been surprised and a bit hurt when Bonnyweather hadn't offered him some of his corned beef sandwich. He didn't even offer to lend him the money to buy one. It had hurt watching him eat that sandwich. Thinking about it made him feel hungrier.

"Do you think there'll be some nosh?"

"I am sure there will be (what you call) nosh," Bonnyweather finally replied with heavy disapproval.

"Good," Errol said in a satisfied tone.

At the Hanson's there was an air of festivity and excitement—at least there was for Mrs Hanson. She was so happy to be rushing about, worrying about the sandwiches and the cakes and the special treats the dining room table was being loaded with.

The furniture had been pushed back to give the table prominence, and she'd made Arthur wear his new suit. She also warned him about putting the television on. Tonight was Norma's, and it was more than a celebration—it was the only opportunity she could remember when she could invite people *she* wanted to invite and show her love so openly. She was excited and thrilled.

"Do I have to wear this damned silly thing, Josie?" he asked like a little boy.

"Of course. We're all going to wear them. Now put it on and don't be silly."

He put the party hat on reluctantly. It was a blue paper mobcap, and he had to wedge it further onto his head when it nearly blew off after a couple of paces.

"We'll all have hats. Do you like mine?" A high green crown was perched on her freshly washed and set hair. "Oh it's going to be such fun."

The doorbell chimed, and she rushed into the hall before he could answer or even look as if he were volunteering to see who it was. Arthur Hanson pushed his hat more firmly onto his head and looked longingly at the television. Although he meant to tell himself resignedly to enjoy himself during the evening, he wasn't enjoying himself. His mind was quite suddenly—and for the usual reasons, completely filled—with thoughts of Miss Anstead, his secretarial assistant. *Hazel,* she'd said he could call her.

"Here's Norma's doctor," Mrs Hanson cried as she ushered in the vet, "Mr Campari has come early just so he can see little Norma."

Hanson came over to shake his hand and bared his teeth in what he hoped was a welcoming smile.

"Oh please don't call me doctor. I'm not, you know."

"Hello Mr Campari," Hanson said, never intending to call him doctor. Campari was a stocky man with a short neck. He looked ponderous in tweeds.

"Here's your hat, doctor. We're all going to wear hats."

"All?" he asked, taking the hat from her and looking at it very unsure, "Who else is coming?"

"What about a drink, eh?" Hanson said. He felt like a drink. Josie would be pushing whisky around like lemonade, and he was determined to get his share. "Let's have a whisky, eh, doc?" He was going to try hard tonight to keep Josie in her good mood.

Mrs Hanson, Josie, hadn't heard Campari's query because she was busy rearranging the plates and things, and he felt just a tiny bit apprehensive. It hadn't occurred to him that there would be other guests. She'd rung up only an hour ago, and he'd been delighted to say, "Yes, of course I'll come." Mrs Hanson was his best client.

"Put your hat on," Mr Hanson urged, "There may as well be someone else looking a Charlie. Water or soda?"

"Either—it doesn't matter." Campari was gingerly placing a pink crown on his head when Hanson thrust the drink at him and said, "Now we must let Norma hear her record just once more" He stopped beaming after his wife went to the record player; she didn't see the pained look he gave the vet.

"Well Mr Campari, how's business?"

"Quite good," and because the music came on loudly, he raised his voice and said again, "Quite good, thank you."

"Do we have to have it so loud, Josie?" Hanson shouted at his wife who was already on her way to the kitchen to fetch the vol-au-vents. There was no answer, and so, greatly daring (with glances toward the kitchen and quick grins at Campari), he turned it down three or four gradual turns.

She appeared in the kitchen doorway. "Have you thought of joining rotary?" Hanson asked when he saw her. "No," Mr Campari said honestly, "no, I've never thought about it."

"Could be good for business, you know."

"Have you turned it down, Arthur?"

"Just a mite. Couldn't hear what Mr Campari was saying."

She looked at her husband without speaking. The plate of vol-au-vents in her hand could have been a missile, and he went to turn the music up again.

"The doors are open. She can hear it out there, you know," he said.

She ignored what he said, but she went to the French window to be sure that "Satisfaction" could be heard clearly in the garden.

He gave in, turned back to Campari, and said very loudly, "I could nominate you. It's quite straightforward."

Campari didn't seem sure of what to say, but he was saved by the door chimes, which played "Three Blind Mice." Mrs Hanson rushed back into the room, looking excited.

"It'll be him," she said, "Norma's Sir Lancelot." She ran into the hall.

"There's no vet in ours yet," Hanson was telling Campari, "I bet that fellow Herriot's in rotary."

"Who?"

"Hang on, I'll turn this row down a bit."

Campari wasn't sure about the wisdom of that. Mrs Hanson was beaming but cold-eyed in the doorway. "Don't tell me there's football?"

Hanson shouted back at her because of the proximity of the speakers, "I am not putting the television on, dear. It's the record player."

She didn't listen; she had turned back into the hall, and now she had her arm round Errol's shoulders. He was grinning with pleasure and trying to put a paper admiral's hat on with difficulty because of her embrace.

"No don't put it on, Arthur. Here's Norma's knight errant, the one who rescued her."

She brought Errol into the room, and Campari did a double take. He looked very surprised for a moment before he collected himself. Hanson was still trying to get the sound of "Satisfaction" down, and he bawled at her in irritation, "I was not putting the television on; I'm turning the noise down."

"Now I want you to meet Norma's other friend," she was saying to Errol as she ushered him to Campari. "This is Mr Campari, her doctor." The music was reduced in volume.

"How do you do?" Campari asked and smiled at Errol who held out his hand.

It was nearly two seconds before Errol realised who he was shaking hands with. "Hey," he said, "it's you." It was Jenkins in an expensive suit and false moustache. Errol, after all, was a private investigator and quick at recognition. The music surged up in volume again, and they all looked at Hanson who had leapt back to the player saying, "Oh shit!"

"Splendid job," Campari shouted, and then the music went off altogether quite suddenly. "Splendid job, young man. Splendid."

"Look, we don't need the television on, do we darling?" she said grimly but sweetly.

He came from the player and was terse: "I was not putting the bloody thing on. I was . . ."

"Haven't we met before?" Bonnyweather said from the doorway. He wasn't sure, but he was looking at Campari suspiciously.

But Josie would allow no chit-chat; she bustled about waving her arms. "Now are we all drinking?" she asked excitedly, "Sit down. Come on, everybody, sit down." To emphasise herself, she pushed Errol down onto the settee and went to pull Bonnyweather from the doorway as Jenkins hurried to an easy chair. Like the last time she was close to him, the thought came to her from nowhere that that man must be different—he would know what animal loving really meant. He was so different from Arthur. There was a sort of thrill of possession as she took Bonnyweather's arm tightly and pulled him into the room.

"Come along. Norma doesn't like to see her friends standing."

When she pulled him to the settee, she put her hands on his shoulders and paused just a moment before she pushed him down hard so he was sitting beside Errol. Throughout the operation, he had been staring at Jenkins, transfixed with dawning recognition. But before he could say anything, finish righting the bishop's mitre he was wearing, the door chimes went off again.

"Oh now I wonder who that can be?" Mrs Hanson said and scurried out of the room.

Hanson had plonked himself down heavily into an easy chair, and he gave Jenkins a quick, matey grin.

"Another thing: have you thought of taking a youngster under the youth training scheme, Mr Campari?" he asked and smiled benignly.

"We would look very favourably at the chance of a young person getting experience with a professional man."

Campari glanced nervously at Bonnyweather before he answered: "I'm not sure, Mr Hanson. It's just that . . ."

"I'm a professional man," Bonnyweather said challengingly, looking balefully at Jenkins.

"You mean him taking on a trainee vet?" Errol asked, and there was some amazement in his voice.

Hanson ignored Errol and Bonnyweather. He carried on looking at Jenkins with a fixed grin on his face as if they were the only two in the room.

"I don't think I could," Jenkins said sorrowfully (though he was grateful to have been asked). "I'm only a one-man business, you know."

Errol had been thinking, and now he sounded eager.

"Oh it doesn't cost anything. I could be a trainee for . . ."

"Just a minute!" Bonnyweather interrupted with a snap, "You're my trainee. Whose side are you on?"

He was annoyed, not least because there was some new competition—and it was from a surprising and unworthy source.

"It isn't allowed," Hanson said sternly, for the first time acknowledging Bonnyweather's part in the conversation, "Not if you're his father. I mean, that would be nepotistic, wouldn't it?"

Hanson, Errol, and Jenkins didn't really break off conversation at that point, they just looked up in wonder at the woman who had followed Mrs Hanson into the room. They didn't take much notice of Bonnyweather's loud denial either.

"I am not his bloody father!"

It was Beatrice, and she looked nothing at all like the Beatrice they knew. Sleek, silk ankle-tight trousers, and startlingly, a tight, cheesecloth shirt open almost to the waist and so obviously all that was trying to hide her bosom. She looked beautiful and extremely provocative. She was smiling as she adjusted her matador's hat.

"Oh," Mrs Hanson said to Bonnyweather in mild reproof at his loud denial, "well I'm sure Norma won't be interested in that." Then she beamed at Errol and said, "Here's someone to see you, Errol."

"Hello, Errol," Beatrice said and simpered.

Errol was the word that locked itself with the speed of light into the minds of both Bonnyweather and Jenkins.

Bonnyweather's mind lit up. He was amazed at first, and then the realisation sunk in that she must be toying with him. She must be trying to make him jealous, even excited. He didn't really approve of her giving all and sundry glimpses of her body. He resolved to be stern and mature with her.

Jenkins mind took the word *Errol* like a slap in the face. He knew Bonnyweather was a rival, but he never thought she would go for a boy. And that shirt: it was fantastic. God, how desirable! He stood up gentlemanly—and because his tweed trousers were tightening.

"Oh hello, Beatrice," Errol said, unaware of the furore in other men's minds. He was only concerned about how good she looked and whether she would get into bother since Bonnyweather said she couldn't come.

For all his knowledge of what was the right gear and what constituted an ideal female form, Errol was merely an acute observer—not a user. His experience of females entailed being as wise as any comprehensive schoolboy was in terms of the nomenclature of various parts. He was not expert in terms of experience. Errol had only handled—or perhaps *explored* is a better word—the female form on three occasions, and each time it had ended abruptly by what seemed to have been boredom on the part of the chick. It was difficult putting into practice what he'd heard in the bog: girls didn't seem to want to be silent show-offs who enticed plumbers and milkmen upstairs. They weren't, in his experience, eager. But he had his magazines, and he had seen movies and knew what they could be like—it was just a matter of finding that sort of girl. So far he hadn't, and he'd become blasé about females—he could take them or leave them. And leaving them was less complicated.

But here was Beatrice: all floppy like he used to advise the girls at school to be. She looked like a picture in the Sunday times colour supplement, and she'd actually taken his advice. He didn't really feel sexually stimulated, he just felt pleased.

Bonnyweather was stern. "What are you doing here?" he asked.

Hanson had not stood—he hadn't thought to do so. He hadn't thought of any sort of movement that might interfere with his view of her breasts. It was breathtaking, exciting—like standing on a plant pot and risking a fall to see Mrs McCardle in her garden.

He didn't need a plant pot now, and he heard himself say, "I'll get a chair. Is there a chair, Josie?"

Josie gave her husband's glassy-eyed face a contemptuous glance and took Beatrice's arm.

"There's no need for you to move, Arthur," she said and gently propelled Beatrice to the settee. "Now you can come and sit next to Errol."

Errol and Bonnyweather moved apart without thinking to allow her to sit between them.

"Oh," it was a cry from a maternal heart as Mrs Hanson looked down at Errol, "And he looks so young."

She clasped her hands in happiness. "Well I must say," she said, but she didn't expand. She instead went off into the kitchen saying, "Oh Norma will be happy."

Bonnyweather glanced at Beatrice, determined to look no lower than her face, and said in a fiery whisper, "I thought I said . . ." But she interrupted, still smiling, low voiced: "The Borzoi's been seen. I came as soon as I could." Then she linked her arm through a surprised Errol's and said, "I'm sorry if I've surprised you, darling." She smiled and looked round the room. "What a super house. Where's Norma?"

Hanson moved quickly, half stood, and poised himself in eagerness to serve. "In the garden," he said. "She likes the garden," he continued and decided to sit down instead of going out and grabbing the cat for her.

"Oh I'm sure it's a super garden," Beatrice said, aiming to please.

"I thought she liked music," Bonnyweather said sourly.

"Only if she's inside," Hanson said, prepared to chat to Bonnyweather if those breasts were next to him. "At least that's what Mrs Hanson says," he noted and laughed in a sort of strangled way. "I think there's something psychosomatic about it all myself," he said and carried on with his laugh.

"Excuse me for a moment," Errol said in a low voice to Beatrice, and he took her arm from him, "There's something I want to do." But before he stood up, he whispered, "I told you, didn't I? You look fantastic!" She smiled at him, pleased. She then watched him go to the French windows. She had felt a little nervous once her fury had calmed down—the fury that had made her remember Errol's advice and given her daring. And when she'd taken her coat off in the hall, she'd felt like an actor in his first part. Now, she felt good, daring, and strangely proud of herself. Errol was amazing; she was so glad she'd met him and been able to change her mind so radically about people from state schools. She knew that to him she was a woman. And he was right: she would be what she wanted to be, not what she was. Errol had said she was all right, and she believed him.

He'd said more loudly as he went out, "I'll just have a quick chat with Norma, see how she is."

"Oh how sweet," Beatrice said and smiled happily after him. He was a fascinating boy.

Only glancing suspiciously at the departing Errol, Bonnyweather decided to keep their host's attention: "How do you mean psychosomatic?" he asked, genuinely querying.

Hanson had seen Beatrice approved of what the young lout had said, and so he chortled happily as if approving. He too watched Errol go out, and he was taken by surprise when Bonnyweather persisted.

"How do you mean?"

"What?"

"You said *psychosomatic*."

"Well," Hanson began uncertainly. Beatrice had leaned across to pick something up from the coffee table, and she could have been nude—she was nude in Hanson's head. Bonnyweather's question seemed distant, and he didn't want to use the wrong word and make himself sound illiterate. "Maybe that's the wrong word, not what I intended. What I mean is . . ."

"Anthropomorphic?" Bonnyweather suggested.

"Eh?"

"Anthropomorphic. About the cat," he said and added, "Mrs Hanson" because the man was looking at him like an idiot.

"Oh," Hanson said, "Oh yes." He wanted rid of the conversation with Bonnyweather, wanted Beatrice to chat. "This is Norma's vet," he said, indicating the still-standing Jenkins. She smiled at Jenkins pleasantly.

"Hello," Jenkins said.

She looked back again—some note was sounding in her brain. But surely not? It couldn't be.

Jenkins knew that recognition was imminent and said, "You're looking very beautiful tonight, Beatrice."

"Good lord, it is. Good heavens," she said aghast, "it's you."

Hanson looked from her to Jenkins, not understanding.

Bonnyweather said curtly, "Yes, it's him all right."

"You know them, then?" Hanson asked.

Before Jenkins could elucidate, Mrs Hanson came in with a tray of drinks. "Here we are, everybody," she said gaily. "Oh it's such fun. Come on, it's party time!" she shouted and put the tray on the coffee table, beaming at them.

"Oh how sweet," Beatrice said again.

Hanson sounded relieved. "Ah the booze," he said and leaned to take a glass.

"The guests, Arthur," Josie reminded him.

Bonnyweather was seething, not just because Beatrice was displaying what he almost considered his personal possessions, but also because of all that chat about the scheme and Jenkins. The man was a fraud. But this buffoon, Hanson, was actually playing up to him, encouraging him. A professional man? Huh. It was bloody unfair and irritating. He must make a move, stand up, and be counted. He interrupted the allocation of drinks by saying, "Well I must confess I'm disappointed. Very disappointed, Mr Hanson."

They all looked at him, and Hanson said, "Eh?"

"I find your Norman, you approve my programme—that seemed fair," he said and looked at the uncomprehending faces. "However, it looks as if I was misconceived." He bowed to Mrs Hanson and stated, "You must excuse me. I had hoped," and he looked sternly at her husband, "at least a serious consideration of my application." Then he turned to Jenkins and meant his voice to be icy: "And as for you, all I can say is what the East Anglians say: a proud rooster today, a feather duster tomorrow."

He looked at their dumbfounded faces and turned on his heel.

Errol appeared at the French windows.

"Come along, Elvis," Bonnyweather said as he went to the door, "There's work to be done, clients to satisfy."

Errol didn't join in, he just said, "Eh? What's up?"

Mrs Hanson was first to do something. She felt rather than knew that Bonnyweather was hurt and said, "Oh no, don't go. Don't go yet." Then she turned grimly to her husband and remarked, "If this is all you're doing, Arthur . . ." She didn't finish, didn't have to.

"Just a minute," Hanson began, electrified into action (although *what* action he wasn't clear). "Just a minute. Nobody said anything about not being approved."

Errol had walked uncertainly into the room, reluctant to go and not knowing why his boss was so upset. Beatrice went quickly to him and held his shoulder. He faced her audience, saw their attention, and then looked at Bonnyweather.

"Errol and I will always remember what you did for us, Ambrose," she said simply, with feeling.

They were all—including Errol—looking at Beatrice, perhaps waiting for more.

"Pardon?" Bonnyweather said.

Her part seemed suddenly a major role. She left Errol, walked toward the French windows, and then suddenly spun round to face them: "Surely," she cried, "we should be rejoicing?"

No one said anything. It was theatrical and meaningful, if unclear.

"Of course we should rejoice," Bonnyweather said testily.

Mrs Hanson clasped her hands—she was moved. Beatrice was so right.

"Oh," she said with depth in her voice and went to Bonnyweather in the doorway. "Oh you're so right, Mr Ironside."

Reluctant to leave her stage, Beatrice grabbed Errol by the shoulders and said, "Oh Errol, I think everything is going to be super." She flung her arms round him, which startled him, but he liked the feel and the smell of her against him.

Mrs Hanson had Bonnyweather's arm and was pulling him back into the room saying, "Come along, Mr Ironside. Come along everybody, it's party time. Come on round the table." She gave her husband a look that indicated further comment when they had privacy.

"Arthur, do try not to be so dogmatic," she said.

Like a fool, he responded immediately. "I'm not being dogmatic; I'm not being anything," he said in hurt innocence.

But she'd said all she was going to say and left Bonnyweather near the table as she finally started to organise things.

"Come along. Not there, Arthur." He had been going to his usual chair. "Norma wants her Sir Lancelot there, doesn't she?"

She went to collect Errol, and Beatrice let him go. Happiness was beaming from both women's faces. "At the head—at the very top—that's where you are in Norma's eyes," she said as she held the chair out for him. "You sit there, Errol."

"Now I want you, doctor. Oh Arthur, I do wish you wouldn't be in such a rush." Arthur had seated himself, eager to please (and to eat) in what seemed to him the next most logical chair, one down from his usual head-of-the-table seat. Mrs Hanson and Jenkins stood by his chair until he stood up and rather churlishly said, "Well where do you want me?"

"You sit here, Mr Campari," she said and held the chair for Jenkins.

"Don't I get a seat?" Hanson asked.

"Don't be childish, dear," she answered calmly like a mother. "Now, Beatrice, isn't it?"

Beatrice smiled sweetly and came to her.

"Well now you must sit on Errol's left hand."

Errol was surprised. "How do you mean?" he asked.

Beatrice walked her now sultry walk to sit next to Errol and said, "I'm honoured." She stroked Errol's hair before sitting, smiling at him until she realised that Jenkins was opposite her and lost her smile. He couldn't believe his luck: actually eating with her at last, opposite her. Every breath she took moved those wondrous breasts, and he pulled at his trousers discreetly under the table to relax.

"Where do you want me, dear?" Hanson asked plaintively, hovering.

"Now shush a moment, Arthur," she said. She seemed to be considering something important, and then she smiled as a solution came to her. "No, nobody at the other end. Now then, Mr Ironside."

She turned to Bonnyweather who had been standing rather sulkily watching the proceedings. "Come on," she said as if she were indulging him, "you can sit between the ladies."

"Bonnyweather," he said, correcting her.

"Is that a Scottish saying?" she asked, holding his arm again and pulling him to the table. "You come and sit here, next to me."

Bonnyweather said rather sourly, "Thank you."

She sat next to him, brushed something off his sleeve, and gave him a smile before she noticed Arthur.

"Oh stop being sulky, Arthur."

"I am not being sulky." In fact, he sounded cross: "I'm waiting to see which chair will be left, Josie."

She pointed to the one opposite her and said, "Well it's there. Do sit down." She glowed a smile at Beatrice and stated, "I have a surprise for later." She then leaned toward her and couldn't help including Errol in her low voice: "She's got a birthday cake."

Errol thought she meant Beatrice and asked "Have you?"

"Don't forget Mr Campari, Arthur," she said. She hadn't looked, but she knew exactly what Arthur would be doing. He took the sandwich from his mouth and passed the plate to Jenkins.

"Oh the wine, Arthur," Mrs Hanson said as she turned to look at him and then back at Beatrice. She lowered her voice again. "He's had so much on his mind," she said, as if he'd had an illness, "I think it's all this televiewing."

The only things on Hanson's mind at the moment were irritation, being the last to sit down, and being able to sit with a front view of Beatrice. He took the plate away from Jenkins and forced his eyes to his wife.

"All what?" he asked.

Josie merely flicked him a glance. "In the kitchen, dear. Where you left it."

"Oh," he said, standing. Then he asked, "What is?"

"The wine," she said plainly. "The wine, Arthur," she said and smiled apologetically at the others.

Arthur went reluctantly to the kitchen.

"What a super meal, Mrs Hanson," Beatrice commented.

"Oh do call me Josie. I don't like being formal."

"It's lovely, Josie," Errol said and meant it. She smiled at him, happily indulgent.

"Jolly good," Jenkins said, "Jolly good." He was using his new accent.

Mrs Hanson had noticed that Bonnyweather was only picking at his food, obviously without appetite. "Aren't you hungry?" she asked, and he turned what he felt was a hurt look to her, "I'm too surprised, Mrs Hanson."

"Oh please call me Josie, Mr Ironside."

"Bonnyweather," he replied automatically, "I'm too surprised. I used to know a caretaker once," he began, putting more bite into his voice and looking at Jenkins.

"Friend of yours, was he?" Jenkins asked, feeling the confidence of a beloved vet in the home of his best client, "Did you a favour, did he?"

Hanson brought in the wine and went straight to Beatrice to fill her glass.

"Ah," cried Josie, "The *vino*." She was so glad everything was going well. "Oh don't let's have any protocol, Arthur. Serve our hero first. Fill Errol's glass first."

He was filling Beatrice's. Beatrice smiled at Mrs Hanson and put her filled glass in front of Errol who said, "Thank you." He had a sip before he said to Mrs Hanson (because she was watching him), "Nice. Why does Norma like 'Satisfaction?'"

She simpered and clutched Bonnyweather's arm. "Why do any of us, eh, Mr Ironside?"

"Bonnyweather," he said. He still looked morose.

"Oh, och, aye," she cried gaily, "I love Scotsmen." And she grabbed his knee in her glee. "Oh you must be very proud of him. I'm sure you'll both become very famous." She held on to his knee, and he felt unsure. He realised that there was the possibility of more than a business relationship if it suited him. And because he was a man who hated to throw anything away, he paused before he spoke.

"A job, Mrs Hanson . . ."

"Josie, please."

"A job, Josie. Just a job of work—no chance of us being famous." And he couldn't help it, he added sarcastically for Beatrice, "We weren't at school with her brother."

"Oh I'm sure Jeremy couldn't help," she said. She hadn't noticed the sarcasm; she was above noticing things like that now. "He's a 'Friend of the Earth' now," she said as if that explained everything.

"I agree, I agree entirely," Jenkins joined in, wanting to show Bonnyweather that he agreed—as a fellow professional should. Jenkins continued, "If you'd had a great mass of A-levels and a degree, you could have been like David Attenborough or Mrs Thatcher now." As the others paused to listen to him, he went on, allowing bitterness to colour his words: "Oh yes, you have to be able to take the mickey out of the working classes—not belong to them."

He had all their attention now. "It used to be like prostitution, but it isn't now. It's your bits of paper."

They realised that this was something he felt really passionate about, but none of them looked as if they were clear what his something was.

"What used to be like prostitution?" Mrs Hanson asked, taking her hand from Bonnyweather's knee. "Are you a socialist, Mr Campari? Oh do sit down, Arthur."

Arthur had been pouring wine by reaching across the table for the glasses, filling them while standing beside Beatrice. He had, as it were, a bird's-eye view of her nipple-pushed shirt. He moved quickly round the table to his chair, "Socialist?"

There was scorn in Jenkins's voice, "I'm an individual. I'm not going to be dominated by governments and television and education officers.

You have to have GCEs if you're going to get really big customers."

Errol had seen Jenkins's statement in business terms. "Like hunts who've lost their beagles," he added in explanation for Bonnyweather.

Bonnyweather had a taste of the wine and became aware that, if this was the level of chat he had to compete with, he had no worries. He relaxed. "Ah-ha, beagles. We could do with some beagle cases," he said, looking at his empty glass.

"More wine, Arthur," Mrs Hanson said as she indicated Bonnyweather's glass.

"Dear, old Auntie Cashew had a beagle—a darling dog, lovely," Beatrice said. She was on a ground she knew. "They get terribly fat though, don't they?"

"That's a funny name: *Cashew,*" Errol said.

"Yes, I was going to say that," Beatrice said.

"Oh we've always called her that since we were teeny tots,"

Beatrice had a girlish giggle, which endeared her to Hanson and Jenkins. "I think it's because her name was Nutt."

"There are plenty of nuts about," Bonnyweather observed.

"Are there?" Beatrice was truly interested, "Auntie Cashew lives in Wiltshire." Then she turned to Errol and asked, "Do you know Devises?"

"Who?"

"Have you thought of rotary?" Hanson asked Bonnyweather, "We haven't a private detective in ours."

"Or a vet," Jenkins reminded him.

Now that some conversational link had been forged between them, Bonnyweather wished to develop it. "When will I hear about my application?" he asked Hanson.

"Well," Hanson said uncertainly. He didn't want any dramatics again from Bonnyweather—or from Josie—so he said cautiously, "I'm not sure. There could be complications—father and son."

Bonnyweather echoed him, "Father and son?" This nonsense really had to stop. "Look. Once and for all: I am not his father."

"Poor boy," Mrs Hanson said, looking sorrowfully at Errol. The association of Errol with the reason for the meal reminded her of something, and she looked toward the French windows. "I wonder where Norma is?" she asked.

"The thing is," Bonnyweather said, ignoring her, "that as a qualified—" and he glanced at Jenkins, "—and established professional man, I think I can be a great advantage to your scheme . . ."

Everyone was startled when Jenkins's control snapped. He threw his glass at the wall, just above the television and the record player. They all looked from the wall back to Jenkins, who was standing looking wild-eyed, his chair on the floor.

"You're all the same, aren't you?" he said in a taunting manner, like a man picking a fight. "What do you know about anything? Eh? Eh?" He didn't wait for an answer.

"All you can do is talk, talk, talk, talk. You don't care what happens, you don't even notice." He was walking round the table now, pausing at each in turn. The audience followed him like an audience at a cabaret. "Oh yes, oh yes: if you're under nineteen you can get all the sympathy, all the money—anything. Even without A-levels and bloody degrees. If you're under nineteen." He looked balefully at Hanson who felt uncomfortable even though he was over nineteen.

"But what about people who want to do jobs they want to do? And know what they're good at? Eh?" He seemed to be concentrating on Hanson. "Oh yes, you can do a top course if you're unemployed, but what about employed caretakers, eh? What about them?" This time he glared at Bonnyweather.

"Oh yes, you're laughing, aren't you? Oh yes, you're laughing."

He moved to Bonnyweather, addressing them all with a comprehensive wave of his arm. "No, none of you—none of you—give a monkey's toss if it doesn't affect your income tax. And if you talk right you're in the right, eh? And everybody thinks you're real; they just don't know about the arsehole creeping." He went over to Errol who looked back at him as if he didn't understand but was emotionally involved. Jenkins said aggressively, "Anybody can be an agent—anybody. All you need are punters. Get you're A-levels, lad. Buy 'em. Get your bloody A-levels and go to Oxford and lick arses with the right people. Then you'll get offers. Remember that." He finished with Errol and addressed the table at large.

"You're even better off if you're an immigrant—an immigrant. Like a Maltese or an Australian (if you're a white one)."

He rushed round the table to Hanson who looked decidedly apprehensive and demanded, "And you talk about fathers and fairness? Who's your boss? Who's your boss, eh? Go on, tell me?"

"Er, Richard O'Brien," Hanson managed, looking round but not feeling much support from the others.

Jenkins said, "Ah-ha!" in a shrill, triumphant shout.

"You see? A mick. Anybody, if they've got A-levels before they're nineteen, can buy anything. I bet he got a grant because he was an immigrant. Irish are immigrants, you know. Arsehole creeping and who you were at school with and how many Auntie Cashews you've got—that's all that matters."

He paused. He realised that he'd said a lot, and he was breathing heavily. It all just seemed a waste of time. He couldn't think of any more criticisms.

"I'm going now. I shall say goodbye to Norma as I go."

He drew himself up in order to be dignified. He felt dignified, right. He walked to the French windows and then walked out. It was some moments before the spell round the table was broken.

"What's a punter?" Errol asked.

Hanson asked, "Was that a glass from the presentation set, Josie?"

"No, Green Shield Stamps. It was only half a book," she answered absently. She felt so sorry for Mr Campari.

CHAPTER 13

It was Bonnyweather who had suggested that what they all needed was a drink, and he was now on his third whisky.

"It's probably overwork," he said to Mrs Hanson, "Overwork and frustration makes men into funny things, you know." He topped up her whisky.

"Oh no," she said, but she made no effort to stop him replenishing her glass, "I shall be tiddly." She held on to his arm again and said, "Oh I think I understand, Mr Ironside."

"Call me Ambrose," he said.

"So understanding Ambrose." She loved the feel of his nearness; it was such a brand-new feeling. There was a sort of power she could feel in the warmth of his sleeve, and it was exciting to feel that she could be daring.

"I think Beatrice looks beautiful," she said wistfully.

"Oh," Bonnyweather said dismissively, "she's okay."

"I wish I dared," she said softly.

He looked at her and she rubbed her cheek against his shoulder as she spoke, just for a second. She'd made sure that no one noticed.

"Dared to what?" he asked

"Oh," she said, feeling her cheeks were warm, "wear a shirt like that."

There. She'd said it. He thought he knew what she meant, and he felt a need to reassure her that a woman didn't have to be like Beatrice just to be attractive to him.

"It's cheesecloth, I think. I don't think it's so marvellous."

She started to giggle, and after watching her, he puzzled for a pause. He couldn't help smiling, it was contagious. Though he didn't know what he was giggling at. She tried to suppress her mirth and blurted out.

"It would be one in the eye for him, wouldn't it?" She nodded at Arthur, and she nearly spilled her whisky with the thought.

"How do you mean?" he asked quietly, putting his head close to hers.

She tried to whisper between spasms of giggle, "I mean, me showing," she began, and her shoulders shook, "showing these off." She pushed at her breast and had another paroxysm.

She must be half cut, he thought—or just abandoning herself to him.

"Oh I don't know," he said, but he did. "I think you'd look good; you're very shapely."

She carried on with her giggle, and greatly daring after having a quick look at the others to see if they were still engrossed in their conversation, he put his hand on her breast, gave it a gentle squeeze, and said, "Very shapely."

Her giggling stopped. She looked straight ahead, and he thought he'd cocked it up, offended her. Her mind was whirling round. No one had touched her breasts except Arthur, and he only clumsily and unknowingly. But the electric shock she'd felt from Bonnyweather's hand had been like a revelation: here was the man who could excite her as never before, simply by touching her breast. She glanced at Arthur; his eyes were fixed on Beatrice. She was surprised that she didn't even feel guilty, didn't feel anything for Arthur. She smiled at Bonnyweather, and he breathed a sigh of relief.

"You're so gentle," she said.

"And I'm sure you are," he said. They looked at each other, both wondering whether and how to go further.

At the other end of the table, Arthur was being as generous with the drinks as Bonnyweather had been. Beatrice had a large gin in front of her, which stayed the same level no matter how many sips she took, and Errol was on his second glass of wine. Arthur did not have the same motivation for refilling Errol's glass as he had for Beatrice's.

"I don't know though," Errol was saying in a tone of voice that showed no doubts, "I think something should be done about all this pollution."

"Well yes, maybe," Hanson said to Beatrice with a knowing smile, "but a lot of longhaired louts aren't going to change anything, are they?"

"My brother isn't a longhaired lout, Mr Hanson."

"Oh call me Arthur."

She leaned on the table toward him, and the shirt hung loosely. "My brother isn't a longhaired lout, Arthur," she said again.

He realised what she'd said and replied hastily, "No, well I never said he was, did I? Beatrice?" And he loved the daring taste of her name.

"Trees," Errol said, "All this paper. Forms, newspapers, government forms, and things—they were all trees, you know. And when they've gone, it'll be—" and he waved his arms to show the extent, "just a great waste."

She looked at Arthur accusingly. "You can't have forests if it's all paper, you know."

"Beatrice is right," Errol said, "You're right, Beatrice. It's like devastation—no, domination—by man. Like women suffer," he added.

"True, very true, Errol."

"Yes, but they like it, don't they?" Arthur said it like the punch line in a joke, and he laughed at himself.

"Sometimes," she said seriously. And when she sat up straight, a lightning message to her brain told her that it was an interesting sensation when cheesecloth passed across her nipple, so she leaned forward again. "Sometimes they like it," she said, and she straightened quickly again. "But not as a way of life. Our role is not just being subservient—the playthings of males—you know."

"I should say not," he began, and he said it as if shocked at the thought. "It's just that men are, well . . ."

"Pigs," she said with a glance at Bonnyweather who was listening to Mrs Hanson. "They can be pigs."

"Well I don't . . ." Hanson said. He felt a need to defend his gender, but he was interrupted by Errol.

"Like sperm oil for weapons. That's from a male whale—it has to be."

"Eh?" Hanson said,

"Sperm oil," Errol said, "Male sperm is vital in conceiving." He wondered why Hanson was going red. "In the act of conception," he explained, "the male sperm fertilises the female's ova, and whales' sperm is used for weapons."

Because they both merely sat and looked at him, he went on, "It's not right, and it's not fair, is it? That whales have to have this taken away from them, compulsorily, by killing them?"

Neither Beatrice nor Hanson were really listening. Each had stopped listening when Errol had mentioned sperm and fertilization. Both were watching pictures in their heads.

"It must be an incredible sight," she said as if to herself, and she was aware of (rather than saw) the great mountainous areas of white, pallid, sun-starved flesh, writhing and undulating in a salt water ecstasy. She closed her eyes and felt a great warmth of feeling for male whales.

Arthur's thinking was more lurid and practical. And his body reacted, readied itself to emulate the male whale.

"I think you look very beautiful," he said simply.

"Thank you," she said, and she gave him a smile.

Errol was deep into his subject, "I can't understand it," he said, "Why can't they make weapons from other animals' sperm—even humans?" They didn't offer explanation. "Why should whales be the only ones to provide sperm for weapons for human beings?"

"Because they're bigger," she suggested, but Errol was drinking his wine so didn't respond. "And have more of it? Lots of it? I mean they're huge, aren't they?"

"That's not sufficient reason," Errol said as he put his glass down. "I think there should be 'Friends of the Sea' as well as 'Friends of the Earth.'"

"So do I," she said.

"What if they took it all away from us now?" Errol asked with some fervour. "Well from Mr Hanson and me. What if he wanted to copulate?" he demanded, looking at Hanson.

"Yes," Hanson said and cleared his throat, "Yes, what if he did want to?"

"Humans have vasectomies," she said.

"Not all," Errol said, although he wasn't sure what she meant. "The thing is, who has the right to stop copulation, eh?"

"I agree," Hanson said warmly.

"So do I," Beatrice said and stood up. "It's jolly warm in here, isn't it?"

She walked to the French windows, stood in the open doorway for a pause, and went out of sight into the garden.

Hanson looked at Errol, then he quickly glanced at his wife who seemed to be listening to Bonnyweather. Dare he follow her?

"I think something ought to be done about it," Errol said. "It's nice, this wine, isn't it?"

"Have some more," Hanson said eagerly, "have some more." He topped up Errol's glass.

"Aren't you having any?"

"No," he said as he spilt some on the table cloth and got a quick glance at Josie. "No, I think I'd better see what Beatrice is doing. She might fall over something in the dark." And he walked as slowly as the speed of his thinking would allow him to the open French windows.

*   *   *

About five miles away, in Tottenham Court Road, in the Bloomsbury art gallery, the preliminaries of a relationship had in fact been completed. In the small staffroom at the end of Modern Works & Exhibitions, Mrs Hepworth had buttoned up her blouse, put her skirt on carefully, and brushed the dirty marks from it with her hand. She then combed her hair in the grimy mirror above the washbasin. The atmosphere in the staffroom was distinctly post-coital.

"You're a very beautiful woman," Barrymore Pugh said, and he meant every word.

"Thank you," she said to her reflection.

"I'm sorry."

"There's no need to be."

"It was just," he began—he felt a need to explain once again, "well the position."

She didn't answer but didn't look as if he should feel sorry.

"Oh God, if only we'd had a bed, it would have been great."

"Of course it would," she said and looked at him. "Don't worry, these things happen."

"It was the position. There wasn't room."

She finished her hair, turned to him, and asked, "Does it look okay?"

"Beautiful."

"That's a bit lavish."

"Oh if only we could do it again—properly." He couldn't help watching her every move. She was wonderful—and what a figure, what excitement . . . he'd never have believed it of a woman her age.

"Look, Barry, we had our orgasms. What more could we ask?"

That was another thing, the wonderful, matter-of-fact way she said things—words like *orgasm.*

"I wished we could do it again."

"Well it doesn't look too hopeful, does it?" she asked and laughed in a throaty way as she went to him. "Pull your trousers up; maybe it needs to be warm" she said and gave his penis a little flick with her finger. He hadn't realised that he'd been standing with his trousers round his ankles. He hadn't realised; he'd been too fascinated at the wonder of the situation—and he only realised it when he took a pace to her, wanting to hold her again.

"No, let's call it a day for now," she said backing away, "Get dressed. There's a dear."

She leaned on the washbasin and watched him adjust his clothes.

"I wonder what time it is?" She looked at her watch and said, "Good God, it's nearly seven."

"Is it late for you?" he asked, shaking then putting on his jacket.

"I'm meeting some people for drinks at 8:30. I must change."

She went to the door. "Come on, I'm going to have to sprint," she said, and she opened the door.

"Don't forget to look, see if anybody's about," he said, low voiced and anxious. But there wasn't—the gallery was deserted, lit only by shafts of yellow, summer evening sunlight from the slit windows high in the wall. Their footsteps echoed, and he started to feel nervous. A sort of anticlimactic apprehension. In the foyer, she went to the front doors. They were locked tight.

"Come on," she said, "let's get cracking."

He stood there looking vulnerable and said, "I haven't got a key."

"Oh," was her response, and she said it again, "Oh."

They examined the door, but it was locked securely. Three keyholes, three locks. It wouldn't budge when they tugged at the handles.

"Is there a back entrance?" she asked.

"I don't think so."

"Well let's have a look, shall we?" And she marched off, back into Modern Works & Exhibitions. Every door except the staffroom was locked securely. Jenkins was a stickler for detail.

"The bloody fool," Pugh said. He was allowing panic to make him angry. "He should have remembered we were in."

"Oh yes," she said with sarcasm, "he should have popped in and said, 'Shall I leave the door open?' as he admired your balls."

"There's no need to be vulgar," he said, sounding hurt.

"Well I would have thought the assistant director would have had a key." She wasn't really angry, just irritated at the way things were going.

"Can't you ring somebody?"

"Who, for Christ's sake? Who the hell can I ring at this time of night?"

She looked at him clear-eyed and fully aware that once you took the capacity for erection from a man, there was very little left.

"Look, we have to get out of here," she said slowly and carefully, "You haven't a key, but you are the assistant director, and you should be able to contact someone who has one."

"That's all very well," he said, feeling absolutely miserable and frustrated, "but who do I ring? And what are they going to think?"

"My dear man," she said and came close to him, "you wanted me to come. I did. Now I want to go." Her face was close to his and she stated, "I personally don't give a fuck what anyone thinks."

Again, he was thrilled and shocked by the freedom of her speech. "But it *is* important," he blustered, "Your husband. My career."

"Fuck your career," she said and went to Jenkins's table to bang the bell.

"No!" he said startled.

"No, don't do that. Somebody might hear," she said coldly. "In fact, I think I'll scream at the door."

"No," he said and grabbed her as she made for the glass doors. "No. Don't do that—you can't. I'll think of something."

She stopped and looked at his hands on her shoulders. "Well start thinking," she said.

*   *   *

"I think we should have some coffee, don't you?" Josie asked.

"Mmm," Bonnyweather said, his arms crossed as he leaned in close to her. His hidden hand was caressing her tight-braced breast.

"I think you're naughty."

He smiled at her, enjoying the illicit nature of the game.

They'd both looked up as Beatrice went out—and again when Hanson followed her. Neither of them mentioned what they'd seen, neither seemed really to care. "Where do you make the coffee?" he asked.

"The kitchen, of course," she said and simpered. "Where did you think?"

"I wondered," be began—and he knew he was pushing his luck, "whether you had a gas ring in the bedroom."

She looked at him with a sort of pleasant smile that included a sigh blown gently down her nose, but he didn't speak. He became braver.

"Why don't you go up, and I'll bring some coffee?"

It was incredible, amazing. She was loving every minute of this exciting new experience. There was a sort of you-can't-fight-it, numb acceptance of everything as it happened feeling in her head, and she could see herself smiling and leaning to his ear and saying, "I don't think I have a cheesecloth shirt."

He turned his face to hers, and he knew that he was on to a good thing. Awareness made him tremble with anticipation.

"All you need is a thin blouse."

"Chiffon?"

"That'll do. Have you got one?"

"Yes."

"Well go and put it on."

She turned her head away and closed her eyes. "Now?" she asked as if she were surprisingly being given permission.

"Yes," he urged, and she stood up. She didn't look at him; she just went through the door into the hall.

Beatrice was leaning on the wall just down from the open French windows. There was a half moon, and the grey, shadowy light made the leaves glisten. The shadows were fuzzy and mingled, and she thought she'd never felt so completely at ease with herself. So beautifully at ease, so composed. She heard him come out, and then she heard his sharp ejaculation when he stumbled over the rockery. She watched his shadowy figure go down to the garden and heard him call softly, "Beatrice, Beatrice." In some ways, she wished it had been Errol who had come out, but she knew she would have been surprised if it had been. The amazingly attractive thing about Errol was that he made no effort at all—and that fascinated her. It was big, clumsy Hanson down there, and in her confidence she thought, *Well there might be five minutes of fun.*

She walked quietly down to the garden. He must have heard her because he suddenly appeared at her side, startling her.

"Oh," she almost squealed, "Who is it?"

"It's me, Arthur."

"Oh, hello," she said as she grabbed his shoulder. "Oh it's lovely out here. What a super garden. Is that a summerhouse?" She waved at the cycle shed.

"No," he replied. He wished they'd had a summerhouse. "There's a greenhouse round the back, though," he offered, as if it was something worth visiting.

"Oh how super. Come and show me it." She put her hand in his and waited to be led. He was almost breathless with excitement: the small, cool, supple hand in his and the person attached to it who wanted to go to the greenhouse. It was like a dream.

"Isn't it warm?" she said, fluffing out her shirt with her free hand. He walked into a rose bush as the moonlight glinted on the paleness beneath her shirt, but he didn't feel the thorns.

The greenhouse was small—a door on one end and a broad shelf down one side. When they were inside, he was close to her—hot, eager.

"Beatrice, Beatrice," he said, and she moved her head this way and that way to avoid his mouth, tantalising.

"Oh Mr Hanson, you mustn't."

"Call me Arthur," he said, and his hands were on her.

He pulled open her shirt and said, "My God."

She felt mischievous. She wanted to shock him, egg him on.

"What are you doing?" she asked.

He pulled her shirt wide open and was gazing at her with awe. She pulled his head down by holding his ears and brought it to her breasts. She said, "Kiss me, then," and he tried to put his head back to her face. "No, here," she said, and she cupped a breast in her hand.

He was a moment understanding, and then he bent his head to the warm, scented softness of her. But she didn't let him linger long. She wanted more mischief.

"Oh Arthur, you're terribly passionate," she said. Then she felt a roughness of wood and a tickling of foliage where she was leaning. "Oh," she quietly squealed, twisting to see behind her, "What am I leaning on?"

She pulled at the seat of her trousers to examine them?"

He peered at her bottom and said, "Oh shit!" He was exasperated that the passion should be interrupted.

"Is it?" she asked in horror.

"No, no, it's only some soil. Just soil here," he said and patted her bottom and thigh. He felt the warm silky cloth on top of the firmness underneath as he dusted her awkwardly. His adrenalin was upsetting his coordination.

She turned again to face him and said, "Oh don't bother. I'm sure it's okay." He stayed bent for a moment, his brain not quick enough for her movement. She looked down at him and remembered Jenkins, and she didn't feel sorry for him. He straightened himself. He was breathing heavily, and it occurred to her that she felt bored.

"Are you excited?" she asked.

"Yes," he croaked.

"Take your trousers off," she gently commanded him.

He again said, "Eh?"

"Take them off, Arthur. Be free."

Like an automaton staring at her bared bosom, he unzipped his trousers and wiggled his legs so that they fell to his ankles. She could see how keen he was.

She pulled at the waistband of his underpants and said, "Shall I take mine off?"

"Yes," it was another croak.

"Turn round, then," she said—and he did.

She reached up for what she thought was a vine or something on a high shelf. She intended to break some off and twine it round his neck before scampering back to the house. But as she pulled at the foliage, it came away with its pot. And the pot hit Arthur on the head. He grunted and fell in a crumpled heap. She squealed in surprise, but it seemed so funny rather than frightening, and as she looked down at the insensible Arthur—a white-legged heap—she started to giggle.

He'd be so upset when he came round. What a hoot. And she couldn't help it: she looked for some further mischief to perform. She took a plant pot from the shelf and crouched to him. She pulled his underpants out, and giggling like a child, she poured soil from the pot into his pants. She noted with surprise that his stiffness was still there even though he was prostrate. This interesting physiological discovery soothed her giggling, and she left him and hurried back to the house.

Errol was still at the table when she returned. He was sitting there looking thoughtful at his glass of wine. He was the only one in the room. He looked up at her, not really curious.

"Hello. Been out for some air?"

"Yes," she said and sat next to him. "Don't you feel warm?"

"A bit," he said. Then he looked at her, smiled, and said, "I told you that you should be proud of those tits—but there's no need for all that."

She hadn't realised that her shirt was still wide open.

Automatically she pulled at the shirt to cover herself. She tucked it back into her trousers. Then it occurred to her that Bonnyweather was missing.

"Where's Ambrose?" she asked.

He said, "Dunno," and he went to look at the records on the rack. He didn't seem interested.

Ambrose was at the foot of the stairs staring at his watch as if timing activity—and he was. He was giving Mrs Hanson, Josie, exactly five minutes to do whatever she wished to do. The promise he had made about bringing coffee was already forgotten. His watch showed that four minutes had gone, and his patience was exhausted. He climbed the stairs and only then realised that he didn't know which room she'd be in. Bathroom, separate loo, spare bedroom, a pile of curtains and two rolled up carpets on the bed. And then he found her room: it had a bigger bed, and she was at the other side. She stood by the dressing table wearing a negligee and clasping and unclasping her hands as she looked at him. There was a fixture of a smile on her face, like an uncertain bride.

"Hello," he said.

"Hello," she said.

He moved toward her and asked, "I thought you were going to try on a shirt?"

"A blouse," she corrected.

"Well okay, a blouse then," he said. His mind was so uncluttered with sophistication that he was unaware that his accent was slipping back to its pre-London habits.

"Are ye no' going to try y'in then?"

"Eh?" she said, and he realised.

"Sorry, just a wee bit of Scottish," he said and smiled at her.

"Oh I love to hear the lovely way you talk," she said. In spite of her nervous expectation, she couldn't help saying that.

He went to the foot of the bed. It was only three or four paces from her.

"Are you going to try a blouse on?" he asked and paused by the foot of the bed. It seemed wise not to rush. "I have done," she said, and with her eyes fixed on his, she opened her negligee and showed him the blouse she was wearing. It was chiffon with a scalloped collar and three-quarter sleeves—and it was unbuttoned. More surprising to him was that the pretty blouse and a tiny pair of knickers made up all that she was wearing. His eyes were at her rounded hips instead of the blouse it had taken her ages to find. She pulled at the blouse to bring it tighter round her.

"What do you think? She asked.

"Terrific," he said, and he meant it.

"Oh I'm sorry," Beatrice said from the doorway, "Shall I close the door? Or is it an orgy?"

Josie grabbed the negligee she had thrown on the bed.

"Oh it's you," he said unnecessarily after he'd swung round. And he added rather roughly, "What the hell do you want?"

Before anyone could say anything, there was an outburst from downstairs: "Satisfaction" was blasting. Errol had switched the record on.

The music lurched down to a normal level of noise, and they knew he had worked out which was the volume control.

"No, please," Beatrice said to Josie, "don't get dressed. I'll go downstairs; I don't mind, really."

Josie held her negligee, arms in the sleeves, arms outspread like a statue on a mountain top. She was totally taken aback by what Beatrice had said.

"In fact, perhaps Errol and I could use one of the other rooms?"

"You what?" Bonnyweather was amazed.

"Well," Josie began. She didn't really know what to say. The situation was so new, and caring and uncaring didn't seem to mean the same things to her anymore. Beatrice was enjoying herself, and she threw a leer of a smile at Bonnyweather.

"You're impertinent," he said. I was discussing something, the case, with Mrs Harrison."

"Hanson," Josie said quickly.

Beatrice ignored him and came into the room saying, "What a lovely blouse, Josie. It's lovely."

"Oh," Josie said, nonplussed by the compliment, "I've had it ages."

"It's marvellous. Gorgeous colour," she said as she came round the bed. He stepped to let her pass, dumbfounded.

"Is it chiffon?" she asked and fingered the material of Josie's blouse.

"I just thought," she said bashfully, "I'd try on a blouse like you have yours. It looks so nice."

"Of course it does. You look lovely," Beatrice said, giving the impression that she always wore shirts like that.

"She looks pretty, doesn't she?" she asked Bonnyweather.

"Errr, yes. Yes, of course, she does."

She sat on the bed and said, "Oh do take your coat off, Josie. Come on, sit down." Josie did as she was bidden; she sat next to Beatrice and had no idea why she did.

"No, don't fasten it," Beatrice said as she took Josie's hands away from the blouse that she was grasping with a very distant modesty.

"There," she said to Bonnyweather, "You must think this is simply marvellous. You must."

And he did, but it was too strange—it was unnatural, two women.

"I'm sorry if I've spoiled things. Were you going to have some fun?"

Josie said, "I don't know," and she looked pleadingly at Bonnyweather who looked as if words weren't coming into his head in the right order.

Beatrice pulled her shirt out from her trousers and said, "I think you have a super figure, Josie—really." She opened Josie's blouse and turned to Ambrose as she said, "Don't you think so, Ambrose?"

Josie was smiling in a sort of apologetic way at him, and for the first time since Beatrice's appearance, his body was responding to the lewdness of the situation.

"I think you're both beautiful," he said fairly. There was a pause, and they all heard Mick Jagger singing, "I can't get no satisfaction."

It was more than a few seconds before they heard the door chimes incorporated into the beat.

"That's the bell," Josie stood up, alarmed, "It's the front door." She grabbed a skirt and struggled into it, and Ambrose realised that whatever might have happened was no longer going to.

Bonnyweather and Beatrice followed Josie down the stairs, and they paused to watch her smooth herself on the way to the front door before they went into the living room (or *lounge,* as the Hansons called it). Errol was sitting on the settee, and he was looking curiously if not too concerned at Hanson who was standing by the French windows holding his head. Hanson's suit looked as if it had been trampled upon.

"Haven't you got any aspirin?" Errol was asking him, and he looked round at Bonnyweather and Beatrice. "He's banged his head, got a headache," he informed them.

"God, where have you been?" Bonnyweather asked.

"Oh you poor dear, I didn't know," Beatrice said as if she really didn't.

"It was some variegated ivy. It fell on me. It'll need repotting," he said. He realised Beatrice was there and peered at her. "Did you see it?"

"Well no," she said, keeping her face straight, "You sat down. I thought, perhaps, well . . ." She didn't finish saying what she thought. There was a pause, and they looked at Hanson as he looked at her.

"Does it ache?" Errol asked.

"Course it bloody aches," he snapped and walked to the table to pour himself a whisky. He had gone but a couple of paces before it occurred to him that there was a frictional unpleasantness in his underpants. He saw they were watching him, and he manfully continued to the table. Bonnyweather slumped, almost disconsolate and certainly with a sense of loss, into an easy chair. Errol was not impressed with Arthur Hanson. It might have been because he looked and talked all positive and pompous like his old headmaster. In fact, he even looked and talked stupid when he was talking to females, just like his headmaster did. Errol thought Hanson was a bit of a berk, and he thought Mrs Hanson was really nice.

He could see why Hanson had tried to chat up Beatrice, but what he couldn't understand was why Beatrice let him. I mean, going outside? And why wasn't Mr Bonnyweather sorting her out? He was certain she was Bonnyweather's doll, no matter what she said. But why, Errol wondered, was she being matey to him, Errol? Not that he minded. He could see it may be because he was younger and things, and she certainly did look different just like he said she would when she was in the right gear. Errol thought she was maybe using him, you know, to make Bonnyweather jealous, make him pay more attention to her. But the more he thought about that, he couldn't really see it. He couldn't see Mr Bonnyweather as a man who really made it with the chicks. I mean, he was sort of old—and like his headmaster as well.

Errol paused as something he'd forgotten dawned on him. Mr Bonnyweather had been close to Mrs Hanson, and they'd both gone off together. He should have remembered that. Maybe they put something in his wine? Hanson? He'd been very keen to fill his glass and leave him the bottle when he'd gone out. No, he couldn't see Mr Bonnyweather and Mrs Hanson having it off. They didn't do things like that at their age—or did they? He knew when his dad did (or was going to), and he was about the same age. Maybe Beatrice really was making a play for him? They could be interesting, older women. They were supposed to be exciting, a friend of his had told him, and she'd called him darling and seemed dead easy about listening to him.

"Did you want to come and sit over here, Beatrice?" he called, shuffling along the settee to make room for her, "Eh, darling?"

All of them looked at him, and Beatrice smiled and joined him. Hanson and Bonnyweather looked at him with surprise, but Beatrice smiled.

"I think I ought to give that noise a short rest—it destroys conversation," Bonnyweather said, and it was Errol's turn to look surprised.

"You mean, turn it off?" he asked, amazed.

"Yes," Bonnyweather said.

Reluctantly, he obeyed. And the ensuing silence made Hanson look toward the player and notice the broken glass on the floor where Jenkins had thrown his glass. A sense of order overcame his need to stand and feel the anaesthetic quality of whisky. He went over to pick up the pieces of glass—again mystified by the grating sensation round his loins—and Mrs Hanson came in with a policeman.

CHAPTER 14

Hanson had crouched to pick up the pieces of glass whose glint had caught his eye. There was a thick feeling behind his eyes, a thickness of ache that was a sort of platform for the oscillating throbbing at the side of his head where it had met the plant pot. He didn't feel well. His stomach was making strange noises inside him, and he couldn't understand the grittiness round his genitals—a grittiness that was painful when he moved.

He remembered lying on the earth floor of the greenhouse, the strong, pungent smell of tomato plants, and the gossamer light material over his head. He remembered the coolness under him, the softness that was freshly turned soil under his head, and the light tickling featheriness on his face. His mind still held the picture of breasts. His mind's picture was battling against the new surging sensations that were rushing in from the rest of his body. He moved his legs, straightened them, and felt the exciting coolness of their unclothed contact with earth. Without opening his eyes he knew it was dark, safe.

It must be Friday, the environment told him. Friday, the night he reserved for the half hour of supreme privacy in his greenhouse. He would tell her he was checking the heat, needed air, was studying the habits of an owl that he said shared their habitat. Fridays when, regardless of weather, he went to his greenhouse to fire his imagination, stand, turn up the volume of his fantasies, and undress slowly. Sometimes he would be completely naked, sit carefully, and hold his breath until he truly felt the chill earth. Then the plunge of feeling would come as he threw the whole of himself flat, writhed for more feeling of alien surface—the chill and primeval feel of his naked body on earth—and masturbated silently and seriously. And he did so with the luxury of knowing he was being wicked.

The fast-changing temperature, chill, and scratching irritation of earth were combined with the comforting revulsion of feeling soiled at the finish.

The tired feeling of being dirty was his end of the week culmination. Friday night was bath night.

But this time, he was lying there and he felt hurt. He had struggled to his feet while his head felt as if it were splitting open, and he fell down again—tripped by his trousers he'd discovered round his feet. This time had not been like usual times. This time the memory came flooding in through his pain that he had brought Beatrice into his sanctum, and he'd made a complete fool of himself. He wondered where she was.

The broken plant pot—the straggling young ivy—had been under his hand when he'd pushed himself back up on to his feet, pulled his trousers up, and clothed his legs. Where had she gone? What sort of things had he said, done? How long had he been there? His greenhouse seemed cold and unfriendly in the moonlight when he'd stumbled back to the lounge.

Now, crouched by the television, his mind searching for reasons for uncomfortable genitals, he told himself it couldn't be *that*—he'd had a bath earlier. When he came home, he had foregone the greenhouse. Maybe it was something he'd caught, maybe it was an allergy? He'd seen a programme on allergies, and they could happen anytime, there didn't need to be obvious reasons. But he felt sore—inside his head and inside his trousers.

"When will I know, Mr Hanson?" Bonnyweather asked.

As he bent under the television and reached out for the pieces of glass, he noticed the red scratches on his hand and couldn't remember being hurt by glass. It was a few moments before he realised that Bonnyweather had spoken to him.

"Know about what, for Christ's sake?" he snarled, anger welling up in him. He turned as he snarled and hit his head on the television above him. "Christ, oh shit," he added as pain seared through his head.

His wife said coldly and loudly "Oh no, not television, Arthur?"

Ambrose stayed calm and said, "I thought you would have got it this morning. I sent it first class."

Hanson was sitting back on his heels and holding his head. There was a sort of sob in his voice when he said, "I'm not putting the television on."

"Football, football," Mrs Hanson said. She couldn't take her eyes off him—and her eyes and face were filled with distaste. "I think he's a fanatic."

"I think Starsky and Hutch are on now, Mrs Hanson," Errol said. He felt an undefined need to say something helpful.

"Come away from it," she ordered.

He lurched painfully to his feet, holding onto the set, and he sounded weary and dejected: "I was not putting the bloody thing on."

She turned to the policeman at her side who had been an interested observer of the scene, as policemen are trained to be.

"I think it's dreadful the amount of football and all those hooligans on television," the policeman nodded in agreement. It was a law-abiding thing to say.

She turned her back on the others and smiled at Beatrice and Errol on the settee as she announced, "It's our policeman friend back again." She took his arm and escorted him into the room.

"Good evening," he said, nodding at them.

At the word *policeman,* Hanson's concern with his feelings and his automatic searching for the glint of glass fragments was interrupted. He turned to look with dull surprise, and because the policeman only gave him a cursory glance, he didn't say anything.

"Good evening," Bonnyweather said, tightening his mouth into a brief welcoming smile.

"Evening officer," Errol said, knowing the right way to great a policeman.

Mrs Hanson ushered him to an easy chair and moved it slightly to reduce any effort he might have required to sit.

"No, no, I'm not staying," he said as he sat, "Well," and he beamed at her before adding, "well this time you really are having a party."

"What on Earth have you been doing, Arthur?" she said. She had just noticed his soiled trousers.

"Eh?" he said. He had bent to another glint and now straightened himself quickly, the effort being felt again in his head.

"How do you mean?" he asked, looking down at his trousers and dusting his knees.

"I said where have you been to get into that state?" But she lost interest almost immediately. She dismissed the fool and smiled at the policeman.

"Well we are having a bit of a celebration. Would you like some wine?" She didn't turn her head as she raised her voice, "Arthur, what about a glass of wine for the, errr, constable?"

"PC one-one-oh Bauer," he said and smiled back at her.

She repeated in the raised voice for Arthur, "For PC one-one-oh Bauer, Arthur."

"Well it looks more like a party than it did last time I came," Bauer said and chuckled. Mrs Hanson, who'd gone to sit at the table, joined in his chuckling.

"No, this is specially for Norma," she explained.

"Are you a friend of Norma's?" Beatrice asked him. The constable looked at her clearly for the first time, and he was pleasantly surprised to see that she, too, was one of those permissive, modern females. He'd been surprised when he'd seen Mrs Hanson at the front door—he wouldn't have thought it in a woman her age, but he had to admit she looked all right. She didn't look all tarty like some of them did, and why shouldn't she be a sort of glamorous granny? But this one he wasn't sure—she looked more like, well, one of those trendies from up west. She had a snotty voice too.

"Pardon?" he said.

"I said, are you a friend of Norma's?" Beatrice was reinforced in her opinion of the police.

Hanson was coming to the table with pieces of glass cupped in his hands.

"Some wine, Arthur," she reminded him and shot him a cold smile.

"All right, all right," he said testily, "I'm just getting rid of this glass." He went into the kitchen, and Mrs Hanson looked at Bonnyweather for sympathy—maybe in apology—and he smiled back. She poured the remains of the wine left in the bottle on the table into the nearest glass.

"Now you mustn't," PC Bauer said, watching her fill the glass. His taste buds prepared themselves and he said, "Really, I'm here on business." Nonetheless, he took his hat off and placed it on his knees carefully. "I shouldn't be sitting here."

Mrs Hanson had brought the wine to him, and she pushed at his shoulder because she thought he meant what he said. "No, you must. We're celebrating." She gave him the glass and said, "Yes, we're all together again." And because she felt a need to explain the rudeness of Arthur, she looked toward the kitchen and raised her voice, "My husband would like you to have a glass of wine."

He was looking at the movements under her blouse as he took the glass, and he had to force himself to look up at her face.

"Oh he's back, is he?" Bauer said, and his sympathies were all with the woman in front of him. He turned to Bonnyweather, who was obviously a friend of the family, and asked, "Was there any trouble?"

Bonnyweather, taken by surprise, said, "No, no, not at all," and he went to the table to get a whisky. He felt a need to do something. Errol, who had been studying the constable until his attention was interrupted by Beatrice linking her arm through his and squeezing, decided to take full advantage of being an equal.

"Did you sort out that business the other day?" he asked

"Well no, not really," the constable said as he turned back to Mrs Hanson at the table. His gaze interrupted a fond smile she was beaming at Ambrose. "There have been two more telephone calls today, Mrs Hanson."

"Oh," she said and turned at the sound of her name, "Oh I'm sorry. It's my fault, I should have told them." She then transferred her smile to him.

Hanson came back in with a bottle of wine. He had resolved to make the best of everything. No point in souring things up for the future. He tried to look pleasant at the policeman.

"Right, now," he said. He was used to dealing with officials. "And what can we do for you?"

The constable looked at him coldly and didn't say anything. He was becoming less and less impartial about this man.

"Oh you've got a drink," Hanson said and put the bottle on the table.

"Mrs Hanson very kindly gave me a glass."

Hanson noticed the smile that passed between him and Josie, and he was momentarily at a loss. He stayed by the table, holding the back of a chair.

"You know my wife, then, do you?"

PC Bauer didn't care for the look of Hanson. He sensed a trouble maker—the man was acting very casually and arrogantly considering the worry he'd been causing. He'd met Hansons before, many times, and the thoughtless, selfish way they went through life (causing misery to their wives and unpleasantness for police officers) was something that a considerate person like himself found appalling. Particularly when they had nice ladies like Mrs Hanson for a wife. And this other female—permissive, toffee-nosed trendy—she'd be the one he'd fallen for. He could tell the sort of man he was, bringing another woman into his wife's home.

"Of course he knows me," Mrs Hanson said, "And Mr Ironside and Errol as well."

PC Bauer noticed that she didn't include the other woman, and Ambrose nearly corrected his name but decided not to.

"Oh," Hanson said. Bauer was looking at him.

"Your wife," he said coolly to Hanson, "wasn't too certain when you'd come back."

"Eh?" had he called whilst he was in the greenhouse? Did Josie know what he was up to in the greenhouse? What the hell did he mean?

"Wasn't too certain? What do you . . . ?"

"Now, sandwiches. These are salmon and cucumber, and there's a sort of pate." She was explaining the dishes, waiting to see what he would like. "Or there's some minced chicken there," she said. She noticed her husband holding onto the chair and told her husband, "Oh sit down, Arthur."

"You're celebrating?" the constable asked, and he took three salmon and cucumber sandwiches from the plate she offered.

"I am sitting, Josie," Hanson said, sliding into the chair that he'd been holding.

"Oh I've just realised," she was loud in her apology, "I haven't introduced Beatrice."

"Hello," Beatrice said.

"Pleased to meet you," he said civilly because Mrs Hanson looked so happy. He attempted to stand with a plate of sandwiches in one hand and a glass of wine in the other, and his hat rolled off his knees onto the floor. He sat down again after nodding. "Did you come with Mr Hanson?" he asked as innocently as he could, hoping to catch her out.

Beatrice looked at Hanson, the smile disappearing. "Mr Hanson?" He followed her look to Hanson and said deliberately and seriously as he held a sandwich halfway to his mouth, "I thought you might have both come back together."

"Oh," Hanson said, sure now that he'd known they were in the greenhouse. Perhaps they'd had a camera—infrared or something? "Why?" he asked, and he heard his voice high. He looked quickly and guiltily at his wife. She turned to meet his look, and he knew she knew from the coldness of her expression.

"Arthur, do be a lamb and pass Constable Bauer some watercress." She then turned to smile at Bonnyweather who was sipping whisky, pondering whether to top it up before he returned to his seat. He returned her smile and lost it when he met Hanson's look.

Bauer was a very pleasant young man, and he had to struggle—even after all his police training—to be suspicious of people like Mrs Hanson. He liked her and wished there were more people he had to deal with who were more like her. He wasn't going to let his antipathy toward this girlfriend of Hanson's spoil the good lady's evening if he could help it.

Her husband was obviously a slob, and he thought she knew it, so he didn't mind being a bit acid with him.

"Is this your first visit here then, Miss . . ."

Beatrice waited to make him ask what her name was, but he didn't.

"Thompson," she said, "Beatrice Thompson. Yes, lovely, isn't it?

"Oh yes," he said, finishing the sandwiches on his plate.

Mrs Hanson handed him more, and he smiled at her. To be polite, he took two. He looked around the room at the others watching him eat, and he stopped looking round when his look arrived at Hanson. He lost his smile and said, "Well as I said, there have been phone calls again."

Hanson didn't know what to say; he felt apprehensive.

The constable turned to Mrs Hanson and couldn't help smiling. He said, "I think some people think this is a real way out place."

Mrs Hanson wasn't sure what he meant, but she returned his smile.

"Oh," she said as if she understood, "way out."

"You mean us learning to dance?" Errol asked, "Phone calls about that?"

"Well yes," Bauer said as he looked at Bonnyweather who seemed to be letting his son do a lot of asking, "I suppose that's the gist of it."

Because he was being looked at, Bonnyweather lowered his whisky and said, "There's nothing wrong with dancing," and he added and knew not why, "It's a healthy, innocent pastime."

"I agree," the constable said nodding, and he and Bonnyweather looked at each other for a pause before Bonnyweather said, "Dancing is a very crude attempt to get into the rhythm of life." He smiled knowingly at the policeman.

The policeman didn't look knowing and nobody tittered. "Bernard Shaw said that," Bonnyweather told him. The response didn't indicate a Shavian admirer, so he said, "You've had phone calls about dancing? It's a pity people haven't anything better to do."

"I agree, I agree."

"I mean, what possible harm," Bonnyweather said, warming to his subject, "can dancing do? You like dancing, you said so."

"Oh I do, I do. Love it," Bauer said, quite definite.

"I think it's great," Errol said, "if I can do it properly."

"Anything's great," Bauer said with seriousness, looking at Hanson, "if you can do it properly. I agree."

There was a pause, and because the policeman was still looking at him, Hanson felt an urgent need to say something.

"Absolutely right. Oh yes, absolutely right."

The constable seemed satisfied with that and turned to Beatrice, "Are you a dancer, miss?"

Beatrice was startled out of her baffled apathy. "Me? A dancer?" And she laughed, maybe too loudly, before saying, "Oh I know a number of people who would think that hilariously funny." But there were none in the room, no one joined to support her laughter.

"Oh," Bauer said, looking serious because he thought she was trying to make him look a fool. "Oh do you?"

Her laughter ceased. They watched him finish his sandwich before he looked up and glanced around the room, puzzled.

"Which is Norma?" he asked. "Is she here?"

And because he was looking at him again, Hanson said, "She's in the garden."

"I should have rung and told you," Mrs Hanson said.

"Didn't you ring?" Hanson forgot momentarily his promise to himself about Josie and his sense of guilt. "Oh Lord, no wonder you think we're wasting your time, officer."

"You're not wasting my time," the officer said meaningfully, and he stared at Hanson, waited for him to go on.

"She was found yesterday," Hanson said lamely.

"Found?" He looked at Hanson as he handed his plate back to Mrs Hanson. "Yesterday?" he asked and sat back, looking at Arthur for a pause. "Were you here?"

"Me? No, I wasn't here."

Bauer moved to look at Beatrice and said, "No, I wouldn't have thought you'd be."

Hanson didn't like the inference, and he didn't like the way he was the one who was being questioned—and God knows what Beatrice might say. He decided to put his usual brave face on things. "Well what about that? It didn't make any difference me being here."

"No," the constable said and gave Mrs Hanson a sympathetic look before returning to her husband, "No, I don't suppose it would make any difference, eh, sir?" These last two words were addressed to Bonnyweather. Bauer knew he'd know what he meant.

"Eh?" Bonnyweather asked. He was thinking that he ought to write a book, a funny book, about the way police operated. "Oh no. No, you're right, officer."

"She was found, was she?"

"Yes, thank goodness. We're all together again," Mrs Hanson said cheerfully. Even she, with her respect for this young policeman, thought things were getting just a bit gloomy.

"Was she abducted?" he asked Hanson sharply.

"Eh?" Errol said, feeling the need to intervene again, "It was just, well, accidental. She was only three streets away."

Bauer moved his gaze from Errol to Beatrice and asked, "How old is she?"

"Three, I think," Hanson said, looking at his wife for corroboration, "Isn't that right, dear?"

"Three years and five months."

The policeman looked at her disbelievingly, and she folded her arms. She was aware of what she lacked.

"And she's in the garden?" he finally asked, "In the dark?"

He'd turned to look at Hanson again who replied, "Well yes."

The policeman couldn't believe it, and Hanson couldn't stand his stare. "She's in the garden every night—every night, isn't she, dear?"

But before Mrs Hanson could join in, they all turned to look at Jenkins at the open French windows. He came in and shut the doors noisily. He was carrying a suitcase.

When he'd left, Jenkins felt dignified. He felt dignified until it dawned on him when he was out in the dark garden that he didn't know the way round to the front of the house. The routes down each side seemed, in the dark, to be impenetrable and large. Plus, free growing shrubs appeared to bar his way. His dignity turned to anger as the need to climb the fence into the next garden made it obvious to him that it was yet another imposition he'd been singled out for. If he'd been middle class—or even if he'd been a fully qualified vet—this sort of thing wouldn't be allowed to happen to him. It would not be tolerated, no way.

His fury at the indignity of having to scramble and be scratched just to leave the house and its occupants was increased to the point of rage. When he got to his car, he found some imbecile had parked an ancient limousine only a foot away from his bumper, and a Mini behind was almost in his boot. It was nearly five minutes of gear changing and engine roar before he shunted his way out onto the freeway of the road. So much for making a dignified getaway.

It was not good. He had lost his best client, insulted Bonnyweather (and above all, Beatrice), and life as he knew it was finished. It was now or never: he must fight for what he wanted and be prepared to lose—*Shit or bust,* he thought. And a plan that had only been a germ—not even a real thought in his pre-breakfast dreaming—began to look more feasible. He was going to win, going to show them he could come up trumps.

He'd read about other people doing it all over the world—mostly airliners, of course. He drove home quite fast to assemble his equipment and put it in a suitcase. He hoped that the look of it would have the same effect on people as his tweeds and moustache: acceptability. Going back to the Hansons, he didn't drive quite so fast because he needed just a tiny bit more time to convince himself that what he was doing was right.

Determined not to have to climb in from the next door garden, he slammed his car door shut after having parked halfway into the short drive of the house and halfway across the pavement. This time, if he had to make a quick getaway, there would be more chance of success. To his surprise, the path from the front of the house to the rear was obvious: there was a gate in the trellis he hadn't been able to discern from the other side because of a shrub, a philadelphus. He had straightened himself, poised himself, as if readying for a parachute jump, and he walked briskly round the side of the house to the open French windows.

When he closed the windows, he turned to them and said, "All right, I've come back." And then he saw there was an extra man, a policeman. "Oh," he added.

To Hanson, in his vortex of confusion and irritation, Jenkins's entrance was a godsend. At last he could vent his pent up frustration.

"What do you want?" he demanded angrily, "I thought you'd gone."

The policeman was interested—in spite of his impartiality—in anybody who could make this Hanson idiot lose his rag. The man must have a defence.

He needn't have been concerned. Jenkins didn't see Hanson as a problem.

"Oh yes, that's what everybody thinks. That's what you'd all like, isn't it?"

It was a question but didn't sound rhetorical. And once again, his listeners were unsure what he meant. "Well I'm fed up of going away," he said before pausing and gazing at them.

"No, do stay, Mr Campari," Mrs Hanson invited.

He gave her a quick, grateful smile before saying, "I have decided to stay and sweat it out. And you're staying with me."

Again his listeners were puzzled; they hadn't intended to leave just yet. Only Bonnyweather thought he knew why Jenkins had come back. He had empathy for a situation that was based upon the principle: "There but for the grace of God go I."

Nevertheless, what he was going to say needed to be said. "Look, Bernard, you can't expect me to be pleased when I find you with one of my clients." He was trying to sound reasonable and added, "By all means, if I'm not there—I mean, what the eye doesn't see et cetera—but I think I had every right to be niggled."

"You've no right at all," Jenkins responded. It was too early for him to accept sweet reason. "You promised me names and addresses when I let you have rooms, and God knows what they'll say when they find out. The buffoon, Pugh, couldn't be kept away forever. But you never gave me one—not one—address. That's not fair play, Ambrose."

"Oh," Bonnyweather said. He did see his point of view, and he had no desire to wash too much linen in public, so he made the supreme gesture: "Well I'm sorry, then. I apologise." He rather enjoyed saying it, "I apologise, Bernard. You must have been hurt."

"Have you come back to join us, Mr Campari?" Mrs Hanson asked, glad in a way that he had. Jenkins was looking at Bonnyweather, distrust battling in his head with what could be sincerity.

"What!" Hanson almost shouted, "After this disgraceful exhibition?"

"Don't shout, Arthur," she said.

"Yes," Jenkins said. He hoped Arthur would do some more shouting—you know where you are with a shouter. "I've come back after that disgraceful exhibition, and this time you're all going to dance to my tune."

Having heard the word *dance,* PC Bauer didn't feel so uneasy. After all, it was the reason he was here.

"Well Mrs Hanson," he said as he stood up and took a pace toward her. Too late he felt the hat under his foot but continued talking to her: "I think I really ought to go." He picked up his hat and banged it on his sleeve as if punishing it. He made his voice pleasant and confidential to her, "Look if you're going to dance, keep it down a bit, keep the windows shut."

"Dance?" she said unsure.

Jenkins had taken a cycle lock from his pocket and was fastening the handles of the French windows together. "Yes, and it's to my tune," he said and turned to look at Hanson. Then he'd turned the key in the lock, smiled menacingly, and said, "You'll not be going out tonight." Hanson thought, *My God, he must have been in the garden all the time, seen everything. Him* and *the policemen. How the hell did I fail to notice?*

Jenkins had turned to the others and folded his arms. His back was to the locked doors, guarding them.

"We're going to sink or swim together this time," he announced. PC Bauer realised that the newcomer was a friend of the family, was unknown to the others, and was obviously a bit of a comedian. He decided to ignore him like he did children and other precious things. He took a pace toward the door into the hall.

"Well enjoy yourselves," he said in the fatherly way that young policemen have. "And not too loud," he reminded them, "otherwise I'd really have to do something."

"What not too loud?" Hanson asked, baffled.

Beatrice tittered and said, "That was really strained English."

"Eh?" he said to her, his lust forgotten.

"Music," the constable said to him as if he were a Ballymena idiot. Loudly and clearly he said again, "Music. You have a couple of neighbours who don't like pop music."

"Don't like pop music?" Hanson left his mouth open, agape.

Again Errol felt the need to be a peacemaker. "*The Stones* are a bit strong for some people," he admitted.

Hanson looked at Errol as if he'd introduced a brand new topic. "What stones?" He asked.

Josie felt annoyed that her silly husband was not only making a fool of himself but was probably complicating things.

"Oh stop being difficult, Arthur," she said and turned back to PC Bauer. "Who are they? Do you visit them as well?" She was trying to think which neighbours would feel strongly enough about pop music to bother telling a policeman.

"I don't think I should tell you that," the constable replied and smiled at her kindly. "It's just a matter of keeping it down a bit; do you do it in here?"

"What?" she asked.

"Yes, what?" It was no good—Arthur couldn't help himself. He felt an urgency to know what the hell they were talking about. "Do what?" he demanded.

Bauer looked at him coldly and said curtly, "Dance, of course."

"Dance?" Hanson asked. He didn't know whether the policeman was taking the mickey, and he was as bewildered as he sounded: "You mean dancing?"

Again Errol attempted a rescue mission. "Josie—I mean, Mrs Hanson—is learning to dance," he said and he smiled at her. "Aren't you?"

She looked at Errol so maternally, kindly. He could have been her son. Then she said to the constable, "Of course we do it in here," and without thinking too deeply, she took hold of Bonnyweather's arm. "Don't we, Mr Ironside?"

"Oh," Ambrose said to her, "yes, we certainly do."

"Well you must consider the neighbours," Bauer said fatherly again. He looked kindly to Mrs Hanson before he looked at her husband.

Hanson felt so many things from the policeman's look: aggression, impertinence, and—God forbid—the possibility of blackmail. How long had he known about the greenhouse? Had he watched every Friday? Even one or two Fridays recently could have been enough. *Oh my God*, he thought. The constable seemed to be more concerned about the two of them coming back together, though. He was obviously out to trap him. Hanson looked at Bauer like a man with a speech defect, and he wished the man would say straight out what he was thinking—not talk a lot of bullshit about neighbours and dancing and try to make everything confusing just talk to him. He met the constable's look and didn't say any of the things he'd been thinking. He just blurted out the truth, loudly and plaintively, "I don't know what you are talking about."

Jenkins, who had a similar sense of grievance and feeling left out, also spoke loudly from his position by the locked French windows. "And what about me?" he called, "Don't you realise I'm threatening you?"

The constable didn't look past Hanson, and he said again slowly and carefully: "Dancing, Mr Ironside, and your wife."

"Bonnyweather," Ambrose said, and Josie patted his arm affectionately.

"While you were away," Bauer added coldly and accusingly.

"Dancing while I was away?" Hanson repeated in disbelief. Then he looked at Bonnyweather and asked, "With him?" His tone indicated that the suggestion was outside the bounds of possibility.

"And why not?" Bonnyweather said. He didn't like the way he said that. Looking at Bonnyweather as if he'd just entered the room—seeing him, as it were, in a brand new light—Hanson noticed the affectionate proximity of his wife to this dancing Scotsman. The thought processes that were occurring were amazing, surprising, and worrying.

Errol tried once more to explain, mediate. He came to Hanson and spoke confidentially, "The "Satisfaction," that's why the officer called. The music was too loud. They thought it was a party." He looked at Hanson as if he should now understand.

"Hey, what about me?" Jenkins called, "Are you listening, you middle-class parasites?"

But no one was listening. They were concentrating on Hanson with a mixture of pity and irritation. Only Josie turned to give Jenkins a loyal smile before she hugged Bonnyweather's arm and laughed at Arthur.

"They thought we'd been having a party for two days—two days!—can you believe it?" she asked Hanson happily, and he didn't know whether he could or he couldn't. His eyes were riveted to the Scotsman's arm she was hugging. "And they thought we were away and didn't know," she said as she turned back to the constable to include him. "In fact, you thought it might have been Errol and his friends, didn't you?"

Errol and Bonnyweather joined in the laughter, feeling that they should. Beatrice merely smiled and felt a little left out, as if she'd missed something. But to Hanson they were laughing, and his wife was on Christian name terms with this Scotsman, and things had been happening while he was away.

"Away? Away where, for Christ's sake?"

"When you," Bauer began and repeated himself sternly, "when you were away, Mr Hanson." Then he included Beatrice. He turned to her and said, "I expect you were enjoying yourself with somebody?"

"Me?" She was taken by surprise. "Well yes, very probably." He was still looking at her and she added, "I suppose I could have been."

"Who was enjoying themselves?" Hanson was frightened into aggression now that they were including Beatrice with him. Why couldn't they come straight out with things?

"Who was enjoying themselves?" he demanded again.

"We were, dear," Josie said and gave him a pitying smile before her face straightened, and she explained with a grim fervour, "so that Norma could hear her tune." Then she repeated herself: "Norma her tune."

Again PC Bauer's faith in Mrs Hanson was shaken at the thought of a three-year-old out in the dark, but they didn't seem too concerned. They thought it wasn't out of the ordinary.

Jenkins was not only feeling hurt, he was getting very annoyed. He thought, *Right, I'll make these buggers pay attention.* He took a square tin from his suitcase and threatened, "I'll make you listen." He put the box on the floor near his feet.

"You've been dancing with my wife for two days?" Hanson asked, determined to pursue the improbability. "In here?" he demanded and glared at Bonnyweather.

"Well," Ambrose said as he looked guiltily at the policeman, "almost."

PC Bauer had had enough. He didn't mind helping, but however nice she was, if she had a thick husband, it was her affair. Her friends were with her, so there shouldn't be too much bother. The man was obviously stupid.

"Well I'll have to leave you to it," he said, and he moved toward the door, "Although, I wouldn't mind staying for a bit, I can tell you." He meant it; he loved dancing.

"I think you're going to have to," Jenkins said.

"But why with him?" Hanson asked his wife. His pride, his security—everything seemed to be cracking. "For two days?"

"Goodnight, then," the policeman said, putting on his hat, "Enjoy yourselves."

"I think I said that you're going to stay!" Jenkins shouted, and they all looked at him.

"Sorry, can't be done," Bauer smiled, "I'd like to, but it just can't be done."

Jenkins took a pistol from his pocket to emphasise his wishes and said, "Just hold it." He tried to mimic the drama in Errol's voice from when he pointed his fake gun before: "Just hold it right there." He pointed the gun at PC Bauer.

"Oh that's a gun," Mrs Hanson said unnecessarily.

The policeman still only half believed the situation. He'd read about things like this, of course, but he'd never expected it in Raynes Park. He decided to be pleasant. "Now, then, sir," he said to Jenkins, and his faith started to slip when he examined the look on Jenkins's face, "I don't think there's any call for that sort of thing."

Jenkins disagreed, and his gun was wavering. "Well I do."

They looked from him to PC Bauer, and the PC met their look. He realised that they were expecting some action from him, so he took a couple of slow paces towards Jenkins and said, "I wouldn't play with things like that, sir," he said respectfully, "Give it to me."

"I will," Jenkins said. He was quite calm. "Straight through the pectoral and into the breathing gear if you walk another step."

PC Bauer remained still. He tried frantically to remember the techniques for this sort of situation but couldn't.

"Now I'm sure there's no call for all this unpleasantness, sir."

The only thing he could remember was that you were supposed to humour people like Jenkins, keep them calm and act reasonably.

"No call?" The sheer unthinking banality of what the constable had said outraged him. He shouted, "No call?! After what I'm going through?" But they didn't understand his outrage.

CHAPTER 15

PC Bauer felt that he should drop the sweet reasonableness because he couldn't think of anything reasonable to say. He spoke as he normally did as a policeman when faced with someone defying the law. He was stern when he said, "You realise that it is a criminal offence to carry a firearm?"

Jenkins smiled at him. In fact, he felt a bit sorry for him. "Yes," he said, "and I know it's a criminal offence to hold people as hostages."

Hanson was first to understand. "Hostages?" he asked.

"Yes," Jenkins replied and looked at him. If his lip could have curled, it would have done so. "I'm going to hold you all as hostages until the authorities give in to my terms."

"You never did have much of a sense of humour, Bernard," Bonnyweather said.

"Roy, if you don't mind," Jenkins reminded him.

"And if they don't?" Hanson asked. He had no wish for the conversation to digress.

"Then, Mr Hanson," he said, giving him his full attention, "I'll shoot you, or—and this I have to decide yet," he continued and tapped the tin box with his foot, "I can let this off, and we'll all go together." He enjoyed seeing the expression on Hanson's face.

They were all suitably impressed with his threat and seemed reluctant to speak. Except Errol. Errol was interested in details.

"Is it a bomb?" he asked.

Jenkins looked at him, but for once he was in a position of power and didn't have to answer individual questions—he could generalise. "If they're slow giving in to me," he said, "I'll just shoot them one at a time to hurry them up."

"Oh dear," Mrs Hanson said, "When will we know? When they're being slow, I mean."

Beatrice, in spite of herself, was becoming just a little impressed with Roy Jenkins. He obviously had more to him than she thought. He was mad, though.

"You couldn't," she said, sure in her heart, "You couldn't do that; you're not an Arab."

He smiled at her and said, "You really are lovely, Beatrice. Lovely." His smile was appreciative—a man's smile at a less-than-equal woman—then his face became sterner. "All right, Mrs Hanson, don't worry before you have to. Will you please sit down?" And he indicated the settee to her with the pistol. "And you, constable," he commanded. They joined Bonnyweather on the settee.

"I think we'll have that big armchair next to it—have you all in line, better targets," he said and laughed.

"Come on, then, get it moved."

Errol had pushed the armchair to the settee, pushed it up close to the side where Bonnyweather sat.

"No, not close up. I think we'll have one of these chairs," he said and indicated a dining chair from the table. "You," he said, and he meant Hanson, "put that between the settee and the armchair."

Hanson looked at him sourly and took the chair, waiting until Errol had moved the armchair to make room. He stood in front of the others and made a face at them that they didn't understand. It was like a party game where they weren't allowed to speak, had all come to a party on their own, and were too nervous to break rules. Jenkins had come closer to supervise the arrangements. Hanson didn't turn round, but he knew Jenkins was there, closer. As he picked up the chair to place it in the space, he suddenly raised it upside down above his head and turned quickly to Jenkins. Jenkins fired a shot into the ceiling, and Mrs Hanson shrieked. The others jumped, and Beatrice was even more impressed with this new Jenkins. The seat from the dining chair had fallen out when Hanson upended it, hitting his head. It reminded him painfully that he still hurt there from before.

"Don't play about Hanson," Jenkins said, backing away a pace, "This is serious."

The pain in Hanson's head was nothing compared to the rage he felt when he looked up at the ceiling and saw the bits of plaster drifting down from the hole.

"But you shot the ceiling," he gasped, almost speechless. His householder's burdens outweighed, for the moment, his pain and fear. "That's damage. Malicious damage. Who's going to pay for that?" he demanded.

Jenkins ignored him. He looked at Beatrice. She had seated herself in the armchair.

"You really do look beautiful tonight, Beatrice," he said, and it was the calm considered way he said it—not part of any ramblings about sandwiches and things—and the way he presented himself—tweeds and a moustache and prepared to shoot pistols—that made her accept it as a real compliment. She felt flattered, in fact. She smiled at him and crossed her legs.

"You won't get away with this, you know," the policeman said, disappointed that Hanson had not been successful in felling the gunman, and more than a little nervous about flying bullets. "Now why don't you be sensible and give me the gun?"

It wasn't just that he was being reasonable, Mrs Hanson's warmth next to him made him feel just a little bit safer somehow.

Jenkins looked at him and lowered his gun, smiling sort of pityingly. They looked at each other for a few moments before PC Bauer felt constrained to say, "I think you ought to consider your position carefully."

"I will," Jenkins said, still smiling, "when you're all sitting down."

Errol took the dining chair from Hanson's unresisting grasp, and after replacing the seat, put it between the settee and the armchair, all in a line facing the table. Errol sat on the chair he had placed. Hanson saw that there was no seat in the row for him, so he sat on the arm of Beatrice's chair.

"I'd rather you didn't sit there, Mr Hanson," Beatrice said and looked up at him coldly, "You seem to be something of a prime target."

He slid off the chair at the mention of targets and stood looking at her. His eyes registered nipples, but his brain made him turn to Jenkins.

"How do you mean? What do you mean?"

She gave him a look to dismiss him and sat back comfortably, smiling. "Well I must say, I do find this terribly exciting," she said, "You know, Mr J—Mr Campari," she began. Even the name made him more acceptable. "It's amazing how different you look out of uniform."

"Some women love uniforms," he said.

"No one I know does. I mean those silly people in Knightsbridge only wear them to work in and when they're galloping about with the Queen and things." She leaned forward in an attempt to see Ambrose face to face and asked, "Don't you think he looks different, Ambrose?"

"Hummph," he uttered and sipped at his whisky. He was thinking.

She turned to Jenkins and said, "I love that moustache."

All this idle chatter seemed quite irrelevant to PC Bauer—toffee-nosed tarts flaunting their tits and chatting away when the situation should be kept serious. It was ridiculous not to discuss and admonish the serious and obvious consequences of deliberate law breaking. More of this and it could make the man wild with lust or something. And then he might start flailing about with the gun. *And oh God,* he remembered. He didn't have his radio with him. He'd unclipped it and left it in the car. He thought he'd only be a few minutes. Christ, he'd get a real bollocking if they ever found out. He was determined to be cool and severe.

"Have you thought of the consequences of all this?" he asked sternly.

Jenkins smiled at him and backed to the sideboard.

"You're very kind, Beatrice. My feelings for you haven't changed, I'd like you to know that."

She wasn't quite sure whether to be pleased, but it was flattering. Jenkins took the telephone from the sideboard, pulled at the lead to see how much of it there was, and brought it over to them. He thrust it at PC Bauer who took it as a reflex action.

"Here, I think this might be quicker if they know I'm holding a policeman."

"What's all this?" Bauer asked.

"It's a telephone, constable," Beatrice said, "A telephone." Bauer glared at her. And then it startled all of them—and particularly PC Bauer—by ringing shrilly.

In the Bloomsbury art Gallery the intimate and passionate relationship that had existed in the staffroom had almost disintegrated. Mrs Hepworth, if she had ever seen Barrymore Pugh as anything more than a brief sexual adventure, no longer viewed such an existence as possible. For his part, of course, he was still fascinated by this incredibly good-looking, middle-class woman. She had miraculously allowed him to take her into a loo where she had exhibited all the sexual athleticism any fancy of his could have wished.

He still fancied her, but she was being a pain in the arse right now. Each, in fact, saw little of interest in the other when their minds were occupied with more mundane reality. She was furious, and he was frightened. She'd made him telephone Mr Murphy, the superintendent. But of course, he wasn't there. A cleaning lady answered, and he couldn't bring himself to say what the predicament was. And of course, the cleaning lady demurred about looking for a key and bringing it down to the gallery. She had, she said, to cook a meal for her husband and son when they returned from the dogs at Catford. That duty seemed to be all important to her. But as Mrs Hepworth said with fervour afterwards, if he'd told her exactly why they were locked in the gallery, being a woman she would have understood and been more helpful. She was also angry because he wouldn't let her pull the telephone out of his hand whilst he was talking to the woman—and indeed; he had given her an ungentlemanly shove. It wasn't the sort of treatment she was used to.

The drawers of Jenkins's table had been more than rifled—she had emptied them onto the table in her search for phone numbers, particularly the number of Jenkins's home. Tissues neatly folded, two hankies with the monogram *B,* a camera, a loose French tickler contraceptive, and a bicycle pump were the more interesting items among the bric-a-brac of his drawers. They searched through everything. But it was only when Pugh was putting the drawers back into the table that he noticed the desk diary hidden under the reserve packets of assorted postcards of Michelangelo's cartoons.

Mrs Hepworth had her arms up on the glass doors, staring abjectly out at any passer-by who may have looked. None did.

"Hey," he said, "I've found a diary."

"It's eight o'clock," she said in despair, "I don't suppose there are any blankets?"

"No, this might have something in it," he said before hesitating. "Although I don't like breaking into anybody's personal possessions."

The word *breaking* moved into her head and within seconds had clicked, fired a spark.

"Of course," she said, coming away from the doors and looking round the foyer agitatedly, "Of course. We can smash the doors."

She searched for something to smash with.

"You what?" he said and looked up from the careful writing—every item had the letter *B* somewhere, usually with asterisks after it. "We can what?"

She'd found a fire extinguisher and was struggling to release the clip that held it to the wall.

"The doors," she said, breathless with effort, "We can smash the doors with this extinguisher."

"Don't be so bloody silly," he said and rushed to her. Together they wrestled with the extinguisher, her trying to get it off, him trying to ensure it stayed where it was.

Because she'd started before him, she was winning. It came away, and the unexpected weight made her drop it. And when he grabbed at it, it somersaulted before hitting the floor, landing on the knob, and depressing the activating head. Thick, powerful, creamy liquid whooshed its way up the wall. They'd both bent to grab it—his head hitting hers and causing her to sit quickly, legs splayed—and he'd grabbed and only half held it. He spun it round and it was now spraying thick, creamy foam over his trousers and most of the floor up to the doors.

"Fucking hell," he said and immediately regretted it—it wasn't the sort of thing he usually said, but he was angry. How the hell could he explain this mess?

"Pick it up, pick it up!" she screamed, "Pick it up, aim it at the door. People will see."

He was all too aware that people might see, and also that his trousers were ruined and he hadn't the faintest idea how to turn it off. She was scrambling to her feet in an uncaring rush. "Hold the fucking thing, can't you, you fool."

He managed to grab it and started to pick it up when it magically stopped gushing. The foam now came jerkily in blobs—custard-thick foam dribbling down the extinguisher and on to his sleeves.

"Give me it, give me it, you prick!" she screamed and tried to pull it out of his hands.

He twisted away and dropped it. She jumped on his back, and he fell to his knees. They were both wrestling in the foam on the floor. It was a couple of minutes before he was sitting across her, sitting on her, holding her arms out above her head. His hair was awry, and he was sweating. "You stupid cow," he said.

"Prick," she almost spat at him, and they glared at each other, neither struggling. He looked down at her taught blouse; she looked up at his wet face and heavy breathing chest.

He felt her under him—hip bones, soft belly, and breasts that moved with her quick breathing. The feel of his weight and the strength of his hands as he held her wrists struck her—along with the feeling of being in a taking position, both wet, untidy, disarranged.

"What time is it?" she asked.

He twisted her wrist to look at the watch on his own and said, "Twenty past eight."

They looked at each other's face for a pause.

"It's too late now," she said.

"For your date, you mean?"

"Yes," she said and gave him a fleeting smile. "Will your wife be worried?"

He lifted his shoulders in a shrug and said, "Too bad."

"Did you find his number?"

"No, but I saw an entry for today. He was going to see somebody called Norma. There was a phone number."

"Oh," she said and seemed to be thinking. Then she said, "You're hurting my arms."

"Are you going to do anything stupid?"

She smiled at him and said, "Not unless you want to."

The feel of her under him was already sending messages to his head, now her smile among the tousled hair, perfume, and closeness increased the messages into warm epistles. It dawned on him that what she'd said had been an invitation. "You mean?" he said unsure.

She just smiled at him, and he took his hands from her wrists, still leaning over her, hands on the floor.

She reached forward to him—this fantastic, brazen woman—and felt his crotch. Her smile was pure invitation. "Let's do it fully clothed," she said, unzipping his flies.

And they did. Squelching with the foam and moving with the energy of animals in a muddy field. But it was a beautiful happening, both of them thought.

He wasn't wearing his trousers. He'd put them on a radiator to dry, and she had done the same with her skirt. He was jacketed but lacked trousers; she had a blotched, damp slip under her open blouse. They were friendly because they were intimate. They felt a sense of being together, and experienced no desperation to change the situation. He was dialling the number Jenkins had written after the word *Norma*.

PC Bauer looked at the telephone shrilling in his hands for quite a pause before he lifted the receiver, looking at Jenkins.

"Hello?" he said cautiously.

"Oh hello," Pugh said, "I'm not sure whether I'm going to make sense, but is there someone there called Norma?"

"Norma?" Bauer repeated, and he looked at Mrs Hanson.

Mrs Hanson said, "Norma?"

"Someone wants to speak to Norma."

"Speak to Norma?"

"Is she still in the garden," Bauer asked.

"Well yes, I suppose so," she said very unsurely. And once again, Bauer was surprised that a nice lady like Mrs Hanson could be so unconcerned about a three-year-old out in the dark.

"Hello, hello?" Pugh called, "You still there?"

"Yes," Bauer said, "Errr, I don't think it's going to be possible."

"What?" Pugh asked.

"To speak to Norma," Bauer said. He looked and shrugged at Jenkins.

"Get that line cleared," Jenkins snapped, "There's more important things to do with that phone."

"Hello?" Pugh intoned. "Look, I believe a Mr Jenkins is there—or seeing her tonight. Is he still there by any chance?"

"Errr, no," Bauer replied, totally at a loss. "No, I don't think so." He looked for help to Mrs Hanson, and she said, "What about Norma?"

"Is she expecting anybody? Is anybody visiting her?" The constable asked.

"Anybody visiting her? Who is it?" Hanson asked crossly.

"Somebody wants to speak to somebody who's visiting Norma," Bauer explained.

"Somebody visiting Norma?" Mrs Hanson asked, looking mystified at the French windows.

"It's Mr Jenkins," Pugh said.

"Jenkins?"

"What?" Jenkins asked automatically

"Is Mr Jenkins visiting Norma?" Pugh asked, his ire rising. He turned to Mrs Hepworth and said, "There's an absolute bloody imbecile at the other end." She said, "Here, let me have a go," and she took the phone from him.

"A Mr Jenkins who is supposed to be visiting Norma," Bauer explained.

Mrs Hanson shook her head. "No, I don't know a Mr Jenkins."

"Here, give it to me," Jenkins said, taking the phone from Bauer.

"Hello," he said. And then he remembered to step back a couple of paces to keep distance, and PC Bauer had to grab the part of the phone that was on his knee to prevent it falling.

"Hello," Mrs Hepworth said.

"Who's that?" Jenkins asked.

"Never mind who I am," Mrs Hepworth said briskly in a businesslike manner, and Barrymore Pugh looked at her admiringly. "Have you got a Mr Jenkins there?" I understand he is visiting Norma."

"Is he a vet?" Jenkins asked cautiously.

"No, he's a caretaker."

"What do you want?" Jenkins asked, unsure whether to admit anything.

"Look," Mrs Hepworth said, getting annoyed, "can I speak to Mr Jenkins?"

"Speaking," Jenkins admitted.

"Oh," she said and turned to Pugh, "it's him." Then she spoke into the phone, "I'm speaking on behalf of Mr Pugh, the assistant director. Have you got the key for the gallery with you?"

"With me? No."

"Well can you get one?"

"Why?"

"Because we're locked in your bloody gallery, that's why," she replied. She could only take so much of this sort of thing.

"You and Mr Pugh?" he asked in disbelief.

"Yes."

"Oh," Jenkins said, torn between curiosity, loyalty, and his new role of gunman. "I'm afraid I can't come," he finally said.

"But you've got to. You're the only one with a key."

"No, I'm not."

"Let me deal with him," Pugh said, and she gave him the phone. "Jenkins?"

"Yes, Mr Pugh?"

"Yes, now look here . . ."

"It's no good. I can't get down," Jenkins insisted.

"Well how the hell are we going to get out?"

PC Bauer was not normally heroic, and in fact, usually approved of members of the public having a go rather than himself, but it seemed that their captor was engrossed so he threw the part of the telephone he was holding. Because of the limited length of lead, however, it hit Jenkins's knee. And because he was still holding the pistol, it was fired as a reflex of sudden pain. The shot went over their heads and shattered a picture on the wall. It was a copy of an eighteenth century print of *St Martin in the Fields.*

"Hello, hello?" Pugh called, "You there? What's all that noise?" He thought he heard an explosion and a scream before the line went dead.

"I've been cut off," he said to Mrs Hepworth.

Jenkins was as shocked as the others. He dropped the receiver he was holding onto the floor and backed away, rubbing his knee angrily. Some inner safety mechanism had prevented Bauer from following his action with a rugby tackle or something similar. He had not moved from the settee.

"Look, I've told you," Jenkins snarled, "Pick it up. Go on, pick it up."

Bauer knelt to retrieve it, looking apprehensively at him. "Two calls," Jenkins said, "One to the chief of police. Another in an hour to the papers."

Bauer clutched the phone and was unsure. "I'll have to ring the station," he said, "go through the switchboard."

"Well get cracking," Jenkins said and sat at the table, glowering at them as he rubbed his knee. PC Bauer balanced the phone on his knees and dialled.

Hanson couldn't hold his feelings any longer, he was breathless with anger. "That's more malicious damage! That was a valuable picture."

"Shut up," Jenkins said.

"I will not shut up," Hanson said, finding his bravery in his fright, "It is extremely valuable and means a great deal to us . . ."

"It didn't to me," Mrs Hanson interrupted.

"I wasn't terribly impressed either," Beatrice said, twisting round to view the shattered print.

"It's been in the family for years . . ."

Again his wife interrupted, "Ten years. Your mother bought it ten years ago in Brighton. You should have let your Elsie have it." She looked at him accusingly and said, "She wanted it."

Ambrose decided to test out his thinking: "Are you going to let the ladies go to the toilet, Bernard?"

Beatrice's face had a pained look as she said, "I thought you weren't going to use that silly word again?" She was lying back in her chair, not looking at him.

"How do you mean?" Jenkins asked Bonnyweather.

"Well," he said, slightly put out of his stride by Beatrice, "I mean it's important, isn't it?"

"Are you planning something, Ambrose?" Jenkins asked suspiciously.

"Me, Bernard?" Bonnyweather said innocently, "No. Painstaking attention to detail—that's my job, you know."

"Hello, hello?" PC Bauer had had an answer to his ringing, "Oh yes, can you put me through to the night office please?"

"When did you last go to the . . ." Bonnyweather began, and he glanced towards Beatrice before saying, " . . . lavatory, Bernard?"

"That has nothing to do with you," he responded, but it worried him. He was wise to Bonnyweather's game; he knew what he was trying to do.

"But what about Mrs Hanson?" Bonnyweather persisted.

"Hello," Bauer said. He had a loud telephone voice. "PC 110 Bauer, is the sarge there?"

Hanson, already upset and convinced that he was surrounded by madmen, snarled at Bonnyweather, "What about Mrs Hanson?" He looked from him to his wife, and for the first time, he noticed how flimsy and transparent the blouse she was wearing was. He was amazed.

"When did you get undressed?" he asked.

"Bauer 110. Yes, Panda, G Section."

"You look very attractive, Mrs Hanson," Jenkins said, having himself just noticed her attraction and wishing to be on her side.

"Never mind all that—" Hanson began, but he was interrupted again.

"What about the ladies, eh? Bernard?" Ambrose was using psychology. "What about Beatrice, eh?" he asked snidely, knowing Jenkins's feelings. "They're not like us, Bernard."

"Just stop talking about it," he said, but he looked at Beatrice who was lying back in her chair, apparently deep in thought.

"When did you get changed?" Hanson insisted, and his wife turned away and moved closer to Bonnyweather's side.

"Of course I'm on duty," PC Bauer sounded as cross as he dared. "Well I left it in the car," he added more lamely.

"They'll need to use the loo," Bonnyweather said, unwilling to give in, "Won't you, Mrs Hanson?"

"Just what the hell are you talking about?" Hanson demanded.

It was all becoming impossible—his wife in a half-dressed state . . . and when had she done that anyway? Hadn't she been close to that Scotsman when she went out? *When he went out,* he thought, *Oh my God: the policeman, everybody knows.*

"And why can't I sit next to my wife?" he asked, talking to her without having to include everybody else.

"Because there's no room," she said.

"Look," PC Bauer's said, his anxiety was giving him courage, "is Sergeant Jackson there?" Oh I didn't know that was tonight."

"I don't think I want to go to the loo, Ambrose," she said, smiling fondly at him.

He returned her smile, and she took his arm again, holding it tight.

"Well who's on, then?" The constable looked at Jenkins hoping he would understand the bureaucratic delay.

"What's all this about?" Jenkins asked Bonnyweather, knowing the answer.

"Well get him," Bauer said tersely.

"Oh nothing," Ambrose said lying back with Josie. He waved a hand nonchalantly and said, "I was just wondering what you would do if someone wanted to leave the room."

"Shoot them," Jenkins replied simply.

"What? Even if they were going to the toilet?" Hanson was aghast, and Beatrice winced at that terrible, working-class word again.

"Look, let's just have less of this sort of talk," Jenkins said. It was making Jenkins feel uncomfortable and a little embarrassed.

"Hello? Sergeant Bissell?" Bauer said and looked encouragingly at Jenkins. "I know," he said and raised his eyebrows in a sort of *my God* way at Jenkins, "I left it in the car. It was just a quick enquiry. I thought . . ." He had to listen for a few moments. "It's all very well you talking like that, but I'm being held hostage," he finally said. He could take a bollocking, but not at a time like this.

"How long do you think you can keep up this nonsense?" Hanson demanded. He was fed up with standing. Why couldn't he have a chair? Twice he'd tried to sidle back on to the arm of Beatrice's chair, and each time she'd given him a look that put him off. And bullet holes all over the place. And who would pay for the damage? They're not just a Pollyfilla job. Who the hell did Campari think he was?

"I'm sorry, yes," Bauer said and either sighed or took a deep breath, "I'm being held hostage. In fact, there's . . ." he began but had to pause to count them before continuing: "five of us." He listened. "Five," he said again, "No, I'm the only policeman." Again, he had to shut up. "Yes," he said tersely, "members of the public."

"Tell him you'll be shot if the chief education officer doesn't meet my demands," Jenkins reminded him chattily.

"In a house. Errr 27 Kipling Close." He had to wait until there was a pause in the speaking at the other end before saying, "He says we'll be shot . . ." He had to pause again, and it made him irritable. "Well I know that, but it's in my car . . . What?" He looked down at the phone and said, "Errr, double-five, oh, four, eight." He heard it repeated then said, "Right," and he put the receiver down.

"Well?" Jenkins asked.

"He was annoyed because I didn't use the radio," he said sulkily.

Hanson's frustrated irritation showed again: "Well why didn't you use the radio?"

"Because, like he said," Errol explained, "he left it in his car; you're not deaf are you?"

"Now one thing I am not going to stand for is impertinence . . ."

"Sit down, Mr Hanson," Jenkins ordered.

"I'm fed up, really fed up," Hanson said, feeling that he'd had enough, "You come in here breaking glasses . . ."

"Only one, it was only one," his wife corrected.

"Shooting at us, and then this," he said as he waved at PC Bauer, "this policeman comes in and says you've been dancing." Again he waved—this time at Bonnyweather—and said, "Dancing with that Scotsman . . ."

"Sit down," Jenkins voice was louder and Bonnyweather glared at Hanson for making his nationality sound like an insult.

"And now this," Hanson said. He could not be stopped: "Policemen who leave their radios in cars and you shooting the ceiling and a valuable picture." They followed his look as it went up to the ceiling and to the wall. "I only decorated in March."

Jenkins shouted, "I said sit down, Mr Hanson."

The phone rang again and PC Bauer sat up startled. He rid himself of it quickly, handing it to Mrs Hanson. She held the ringing telephone for a pause; she seemed to be unsure what to do. "Oh do sit down, Mr Hanson," Beatrice said. The word *Arthur* never entered her head, and because he was now balancing himself again on the arm of her chair, she appealed to Jenkins.

"Can't he sit on the floor or something, Roy?" She'd been thinking about Jenkins, revising one or two things, and she had quite unconsciously used his Christian name.

Jenkins felt as if he'd won a prize, hearing her say his name.

"Hello?" Mrs Hanson said warily into the phone, "Who? Oh." And she passed the thing back to PC Bauer.

"It's the tea office or something," Mrs Hanson was explaining to Bauer, "I think it might be for you."

"I see no reason why I should sit on the floor," Mr Hanson said, but he did see a reason however defiant his tone.

"Hello? Oh hello, Alan." PC Bauer sounded relieved.

Jenkins aimed the pistol at Hanson and he sat on the floor. "Oh all right, then, but I protest strongly."

"Where's Sergeant Bissell, then?" Bauer asked chattily, "Oh good." Then he listened. "Yes, five of us. And he's got a gun . . ." Jenkins interrupted, his patience being tried as well.

"Get the chief education officer. He's the one I want to talk to."

Bauer looked at Jenkins—particularly at his pistol—as he spoke on the phone. "He says he wants the chief education officer," he said, and he listened to the response to what he'd said before he lowered the phone and stated, "He won't be at his office now; do you want his home number?"

"I want him at the end of the line, quick," Jenkins barked.

"But I'm talking to the divisional office; he's not there." Bauer sounded as if he thought that Jenkins was being unfair.

"Tell the divisional office," Jenkins said, his voice cold and menacing, "that one of you parasites will be shot every half hour until he listens to my terms."

"Oh dear," Mrs Hanson said.

Jenkins quickly changed his tone to reassure her, "Don't you worry, Mrs Hanson, I'll do the others first." Then he looked grimly at Hanson, whose anger had cooled into nervousness and snatched the phone from the constable. "You've got half an hour," he shouted into it, "Just half an hour before I start shooting people. Get him."

He slammed the phone down onto its holder in Bauer's lap, and it made him wince. Jenkins went back to sit at the table, looking at the plates of sandwiches as if deciding something.

There was quite a long silence and no one spoke. Ambrose and Josie lay back. She was holding his arm tight to her. Errol was watching Beatrice's breasts as she breathed. He had never noticed before that women could be seen breathing so clearly. And Mrs Hanson and Bauer watched Jenkins as he pulled a plate towards him. "They're minced chicken," she said, and the phone rang again.

In the Bloomsbury art gallery, the viewing couch in the post-renaissance room was really not a couch at all, it was made up of four leather cushion-topped pouffes. Sometimes they were all separate, sometimes three were pushed together (or they were in any other permutation the caretaker could think of). At the moment, they were all together: a long couch with lateral crevices caused by the bevelled edges of the individual pouffes not meeting to form an unbroken plain of surface. And a couple of these crevices were almost six inches wide because Barrymore Pugh and Audrey Hepworth had made love on them, and his knees and the general movement had pushed them away from their fellows.

It was just, well, absolutely fantastic, Pugh thought. Not just the amazing fact that this woman was so exciting and eager, but three times! Three times in one night. He'd never, ever thought that would have been possible. To hell with locked doors and missing keys, they were the outside world, work, and boring reality. Inside, locked inside the Bloomsbury art gallery, it was like being locked in a bubble—a fantasy that he'd never fantasised about. And it was fantastic.

The phone number that, ages ago, they'd rung to track down Jenkins had been engaged on the two further attempts they'd made, and they didn't even feel annoyed. They'd looked at each other, commented on their luck that the place had central heating, and gone upstairs wantonly—taking off their clothes as they went. It was just like a dream in his head or a Ken Russell movie. There had seemed to be acres of space, acres of time, and he'd sung and danced naked round the post-renaissance room. Audrey Hepworth had done the same—at first stiffly and slightly embarrassed, then gathering confidence from his wanton cavorting, they'd flung themselves about. They paused only to laugh at each other, look at each other's eyes, and put their hands between the others legs. Sometimes, during a pause in the dancing, he would grab her and bend her backwards with a Valentino tango kiss, or he would try to bite her, suck her, with a mouth like a vacuum cleaner.

It was all so erotic. It was beautiful, like a myth. And then they had pushed the pouffes together, collapsed out of breath in each other's arms—hot bodies together—and stayed there. They were breathing heavily, looking at the cracks in the ceiling. She was the fittest, the first to forget the need for air, and she rolled over onto him. She kissed wherever her mouth could reach, and his breathing slowed. She was sitting on his belly giggling, and she felt his keenness behind her. They made love, moved some of the pouffes apart, and then let themselves cool down on the leather. It crackled as they moved their flesh to position themselves to look at each other.

"You're fantastic," he said.

"So are you," she said, and neither of them could think of anything else to say for a long pause.

"It's nice and warm; we're lucky," she said.

"No, love, not lucky—we're fantastically, amazingly, super fortunate," he said.

"I meant with the central heating."

"I meant having you *and* the central heating," he said. They both laughed, carefree, like people do when the world has shrunk to there being just them, just their togetherness. There was nothing else, just her nipples against his chest, her warm leg over his, and the funny way their skin stuck to the leather. They felt as though they were peeling themselves when they moved.

It wasn't love—not the love that had ideals and a sense of exciting companionship—but love that was Dionysian. It was making time into a luxurious moment, adrenalin, hormones, smoothness of flesh, and wanton pleasure. *Sub specie temporis,* Ambrose Bonnyweather might have said. Although he would have been talking about economics, the actions in the market place.

"Shall we ring again?" she asked

"Perhaps we should," he said and kissed her nose, "but we should get dressed."

"Yes, I suppose we should."

"Glass doors. Don't want to be an exhibit, do we?"

"They're easy to take off again."

"Glass doors?" he queried, pretending to be serious, and they laughed.

*   *   *

"Hello," Bauer said, "Sergeant Bissell?"

"Hello, Sergeant Bissell," Audrey said, "Is Mr Jenkins still there?"

"Who?"

PC Bauer lowered the phone and said, "It's someone for Mr Jenkins again."

"Who?" Jenkins asked, a minced chicken sandwich halfway to his mouth

"Mr Jenkins."

"Who is it wants him?" Jenkins said testily.

"Hello? Who wants Mr Jenkins?" Bauer asked.

"Who indeed," she said, meaning it jokingly, "I want him."

"But who are you?"

"Tell him there's trouble at gallery," she said, and then she did an impersonation of a Yorkshire mill foreman: "Tell him 'e 'as to come. There's trouble at t'gallery." She held the phone to her bosom, and she and Barrymore Pugh giggled as if they were drunk.

"It's a woman," Bauer explained, "who said there's" he started and then automatically impersonated her, "trouble at t'gallery."

"You what? Here, give me it," he said, and he took the phone from the nervous constable. Again, Bauer had to grab the other part as Jenkins took a couple of paces back to distance himself from his hostages. "Hello?" he said.

"Mr Jenkins?" Audrey asked.

"Yes."

She passed the phone to Pugh who said, "Hello, Jenkins?"

"Yes."

"Pugh here. Look, when can you get down with the key?"

"I can't," Jenkins said. He was short and to the point.

"Oh come on," Pugh said. He didn't even notice the intransigence. "We're locked in, Mr Jenkins. Surely you can help us?"

"I'm sorry, sir, it's just not possible."

"Well why not, for God's sake? What is more important to you than leaving us imprisoned?" And because there wasn't an immediate reply, he lowered the phone and grinned at Audrey. "Was that dramatic enough?"

After thinking, Jenkins said, "Well I'll be honest, Mr Pugh, I can't come because I'm holding some people hostage."

"Holding people hostage?" Barrymore asked, surprised out of his giggling.

"So you can see," Jenkins said apologetically, "I'm rather busy. I am, in fact, waiting for a rather important telephone call."

"Now look here," Pugh said, moving back to his old self, "Just cut out the jokes and let's have some help."

"I'm sorry, no can do," Jenkins said. He did sound sorry. "You could, of course, ring the police. They're supposed to have keys."

"The police?"

"With a bit of luck, they should have you out in a week," he said and put the phone down

"He said ring the police. He can't come because he's holding some people hostage." He looked at her in baffled amazement.

"Do you know any policemen?" she asked.

"No."

"I know a superintendent or something, but he's in the fraud squad—at least he said he was."

"What are we going to do?" he asked, feeling totally without answers. She put her arms round his neck, put her face close to his, and said quietly, "We could go to post-renaissance."

He looked at her until her eyes and smile pushed at his worries. "What? Again?" he asked and smiled.

"Come, lad," she said in her passable northern. She took his arm and pulled him out of the foyer. "Come, lad. Let's fuck."

Only fleetingly did he think that he must have a word with Jenkins tomorrow; he didn't at all think about the improbability of doing something for the fourth time in one night.

CHAPTER 16

Again, Jenkins plonked the phone down onto Bauer's knees, and again, he winced. Then Jenkins went back to the table and the minced chicken sandwich. He smiled at Beatrice—she looked comfortable in her armchair, and she smiled in a friendly way back at him.

"Well," she said to nobody in particular, "I think it's all terribly exciting."

"Absolutely ripping," Errol said.

"What?" she asked, looking quickly at him.

"Absolutely ripping. What that Monty Python bloke used to say."

"Oh," she said and put her head back against the chair and led a pause. Hanson broke it. He had pins and needles in his left leg, and it didn't matter which way he distributed his weight: it was either pins and needles or a burning grittiness round his private parts. He did not like sitting on the floor.

"I think the whole thing is outrageous," he said.

"Why haven't they rung?" Jenkins asked the constable.

"I don't know." He sounded aggressively defensive, and then he changed his tone and volunteered: "I mean, he might not be at home."

"I'm just being fobbed off," Jenkins said as he stood up, "If I'd done it on a plane or a ship or something, it would have been different." A thought came to him. "Ring the papers," he ordered.

Bauer automatically lifted the phone and awaited further instructions. "Which papers?" he asked.

Mrs Hanson said, "I think the *Daily Mail* would be best," and she added as a sort of reference, "We get the *Daily Mail*."

"Well ring them, then," Jenkins said, making a quick decision.

"What's the number?"

"I don't know," Jenkins said as if he'd been asked a daft question, "Where's the telephone book?" He looked at Mrs Hanson.

"It's in the kitchen," she said brightly, remembering, "I had it to ring Woolworth's."

"Woolworth's?" Hanson said as if she'd said the White House or Buckingham Palace. "What the hell did you ring them for?"

Ambrose stood up and said, "I'll get it."

"Sit down," Jenkins said. He wasn't born last week. "Sit down, Ambrose. I'm not falling for that."

"Because I wanted to ask them something," Mrs Hanson leaned forward to tell her husband, and her voice was hard, "That's why."

"Ah well," Bonnyweather said, sitting down again, "that knocks publicity on the head."

"We'll wait," Jenkins said, realising that the phone directory simply couldn't be got. "But we'll only wait for so long," he added meaningfully to Bauer.

"Oh I'm sure the sergeant will ring back soon," Bauer said, trying to sound cheerful. "He's seeing the chief inspector."

Jenkins gave him a pitying look and took another minced chicken sandwich. They all watched him eat it.

"I think you're awfully brave," Beatrice felt compelled to say, "kidnapping all of us." And the mention of kidnapping roused Errol's attention. He'd been wondering where Jenkins had got his pistol from and hoping that an opportunity might arise when he could ask him. Still, there was always the swordstick. If Bonnyweather had allowed him to bring it tonight, he would have disarmed Jenkins by now and been sitting on him, the sword point at his throat. And when they'd taken him away, he would have asked Beatrice, nonchalantly, to maybe go upstairs and, well, see what happened. But his attention was caught.

"Where will you go?" he asked with honest curiosity. "Where do you want to fly to?"

Jenkins looked at Errol. He vaguely liked the lad and was really starting to see him as a young adult, particularly after he'd been so decent to him earlier. But when he said things like that, he realised that Errol was maybe only a boy. He said without any irritation, however, "It's the chief education officer I want."

"For a grant?" Errol persisted.

"Yes," said Jenkins and he smiled. "He's not going to look too good if he has five shot people just because he refused, is he?"

Errol ignored this because he was more concerned with the logic of the situation. "Well you'll have to be sure it's a country where you can use an English grant," he warned.

"Oh and which are they?" Bonnyweather asked sarcastically, "Which are they, clever clogs?"

"Oh there's sure to be one," Errol said confidently, "Maybe in Africa."

Jenkins was surprised, "Africa?"

Bonnyweather seemed serious. "A good place for a vet, all that wildlife."

"I'd love to come to Africa," Beatrice said dreamily.

"You mean go?" Bonnyweather couldn't help correcting her.

"No, I mean as a hostage."

More irrelevance, always taking the conversation to themselves and talking as if it was all a big joke or something. "I'm not going to Africa," Jenkins said adamantly. I want to go to London University or Edinburgh."

"Has Edinburgh got an airport?" Errol asked. He had a passion for details.

Ambrose felt that the conversation had outlived its usefulness. "It's a lovely house," he said and smiled at Josie sitting next to him. She smiled happily back. "You have a lovely home, Josie."

Hanson glared across at this extravagant use of his wife's name, but Josie didn't see his glare. Her eyes were all for her new, thrilling adventure, and she held his arm again.

"Thank you," she said, nearly coyly, "I do my best." Maybe because she felt her husband's look, or perhaps because she wanted people to know that she wasn't responsible for everything in the house, she added, "There are a few vulgarities I could well do without though." She looked across at Arthur, and Beatrice thought she was looking at her so she put her smile on.

"Oh I agree," she gushed, "but I don't mind anything being, you know, terribly vulgar. It's all sort of super. I mean, I thought the musical loo paper an absolute hoot." She laughed appreciatively. "Mummy put one in Adamson's flat, and Fiona and I used to be absolutely poleaxed with giggles." Josie joined her giggling and said, "We used to hide in the laurels and guess who'd done what." Her laughter freed itself from the need to talk.

"Who's Adamson? Errol asked.

"Was," Beatrice said, still giggling, "He's left now. He was our chauffeur."

"Decadence," Bonnyweather announced sourly, "That's the word that marks the downfall of the upper classes: decadence."

"What exactly is decadence?" Errol asked.

"Ambrose is a ruminant," Beatrice explained.

Not fully knowing that word either, Errol said, "Is that because he's Scotch?"

"Scots," Ambrose said sharply, "Scots, laddie. Scotch is a drink."

"Oh och, aye," Josie said gleefully.

Errol merely looked at him and said, "Oh."

"I'll support that idea," Beatrice said as she lay back in her chair again, "I feel quite flamboyant tonight, terribly elegant." She looked expectantly at Jenkins.

"I told you," Errol reminded her, "you've got a nice pair."

No one said anything for a pause even though Jenkins looked as if he might. Beatrice seemed to think before she said, "Do you like ratatouille, Errol?"

"I don't know," he said, and he honestly didn't, "What are they like?"

The atmosphere in the room was quite relaxed now. Although each of them felt there was a sort of compulsion keeping them there, it was similar to waiting at an airport or a railway station. When they could move from the room it would be obvious, maybe even announced. Any tenseness that had been present had passed into a sort of relaxed companionship, each comfortable with the others, sharing.

Except Arthur Hanson. He was still tense, but that was because he was thinking about his wife and the Scotsman.

When had she changed? It was a different skirt as well—he was sure of it. And his murky greenhouse secret was eating at him. He glanced at Beatrice, and she seemed to be totally without memory of it. But if Campari and his policeman—and God forbid Josie—knew, they could have him over a barrel.

It was worrying, and he felt like a bath. But the others had accepted the situation, didn't feel too apprehensive now.

Jenkins was brooding. He was rapidly becoming disillusioned with his whole scheme. As always, he should have known that nothing ever worked out right for him.

"What about my application, Mr Hanson?" Bonnyweather asked, looking at Jenkins.

"Just apply, just apply," Hanson replied irritably, "The secretary will contact you; we only meet once a month."

"Once a month?" Bonnyweather said as if it were shattering news, "Well I think that's typical, emergency measures." He repeated the word for emphasis: "Emergency." "The country is in turmoil; thousands of Errols jobless, and the EEC is giving away money for young people, and the government is giving all this propaganda out . . ."

Hanson interrupted him wearily, "I thought you meant rotary."

"No Mr Harrison," Ambrose said sternly, "I don't mean rotary. I'm not talking about social clubs; I'm talking about urgent government measures to enable unfortunate, unemployed youths to earn twenty pounds a week to be taught skills by professional men."

"Thirty-five pounds," Errol said.

"It may not be thirty-five," Ambrose said curtly, "There are negotiations yet."

"It is," Hanson said, again with little fire.

"Mr Green says employers are only looking for what's in it for them; they're not rising to the challenge," Errol said. He had a good memory.

"This Mr Green, he's run businesses, has he?" Ambrose asked, annoyed on behalf of his fellow employers. "He's tried to make a living working with human beings? Has he ever been undermined by amateurs, eh? Eh?

"I don't know," Errol said."

"Shut up," Jenkins said loudly, standing. "Don't you care?" he asked, and he glared at them. "You don't give fourpence about me, do you? Talking about toilet paper and Mr Greens. And him," he said and indicated Hanson, "with this thing for unemployed kids, giving money away. And all of you thinking about yourselves. What about me? What about me, eh?"

Beatrice nearly applauded. "You know, you do look different. I think it must have been the uniform," she beamed at him.

"Oh you've realised?" Jenkins asked with enough bitter rancour to impress her. "You've realised because I'm wearing a posh suit—ninety-five quid just to pretend I was one of you lot when I ought to be one as of right. No, it's not enough just to know what I'm doing, is it? Not enough to have a good suit and make an animal happy—oh no! That's not enough for this society. You have to have special accents and bits of paper. Keep professors in jobs for six years while they teach you what you can learn in two—like I've done. Oh no, it's not enough to be able to do the job, you have to conform to middle-class rules."

He paused. It was a long speech, and he was a little out of breath. They all looked at him.

Ambrose tried to be sympathetic. "They're not rules, Bernard, they're values. Our whole education system is . . ."

"What rules?" Errol interrupted because he was puzzled.

"I think you should give me the gun," PC Bauer said, feeling intuitively that Jenkins was having second thoughts.

But Jenkins was scathing to him. "I'd rather give it to Mrs Hanson. At least she knows. She's a woman."

"Why don't you give it to her, then?" Errol asked.

"I'm a woman, too," Beatrice said.

"We can see that," Bonnyweather's retorted in an acid manner.

Jenkins was excited by what he'd said, and the sense of disintegration—his whole plan just fizzling out—was too much.

"Just get on that phone," he shouted at PC Bauer, "Just tell them that I can't take any more of this."

"Tell who?" Bauer asked quickly, nervously.

"Have a word with your chief inspector," Ambrose advised.

"Well I'll see." In spite of the situation, Bauer knew you couldn't rush senior officers. He just hoped they would understand. "I usually have to go through the sergeant," he explained apologetically.

"Ring, ring. Otherwise there won't be enough of you to go through a sergeant."

Bauer was dialling rapidly. "All right, all right, I'm doing it."

"Can't I feed Norma?" Josie asked because she was upset that she'd forgotten all about Norma.

"I wouldn't bother, Mrs Hanson," Errol advised.

"Hello?" Bauer was through. "Chief Inspector Spinelli, please," he said and watched Jenkins. "I'm just being put through," he said, and they all waited for a police conversation to begin.

"Hello? Oh hello, sir. PC one-one-oh Bauer," he said, and he had to say it again, "Bauer. I think Sergeant Bissell contacted you with regard to me being held hostage, sir."

Regardless of situations, the police have certain formalities. "Yes. Yes, sir, 27 Kipling Road," he said, and had to pause because he was being spoken to.

"No, I said road, sir. 27 Kipling Road." He had to listen again. He tried to show Jenkins with his eyes that it wasn't his fault. "Oh well, I'm sorry about that, sir, but anyway . . ." And again he had to pause.

"I know, sir, I left it in the car . . ." A cloud went across his face. "Tomorrow?" he said, sounding hurt. "With respect, sir, it's all very well for you to talk like that, sir, but I might not be here tomorrow."

"Tomorrow?" Jenkins was puzzled, "What's tomorrow?" "Excuse me, sir," Bauer said respectfully into the phone. He looked at Jenkins and stated, "They got the wrong address, and the marksmen are there."

Jenkins's look became a stare, a stare of amazement that synthesised into wide-eyed rage. It was too much, the last straw. Jenkins leapt at the policeman and snatched the phone. This time he dragged the cradle from Bauers knees, and it hit the floor with a bang.

"Hello. Now listen: fifteen minutes, that's all. Fifteen minutes and this gun is going to start shooting." He interrupted when the chief inspector tried to say something: "Don't give me any of your bullshit. I mean it, let's have some action." He threw the receiver at Bauer who caught it involuntarily.

"I just can't believe it," he said, and he looked as if he couldn't.

Jenkins wasn't merely furious—it wasn't all anger, it was frustration at the ineptitude and selfishness of others. His plan had been okay—of course it had been okay. It was just the stupid imbeciles he had to deal with. Jesus, no wonder there were traffic jams. He walked round the table, paced. They watched him; it was like watching a solo performance.

"Total stupidity. Totally stupid, thick-headed, stupidity. No wonder people think that people who wear uniforms are thick."

Bauer was hurt again. "Hey now, just a minute. There's no . . ."

"Shut up," Jenkins snapped, and he did. "I just can't believe it." He certainly looked as if he was shocked, his voice took on a weariness laced with despair: "You can't fight things like that," he said, "you can't fight idiots, fools like that."

He stood still for a moment, his despair seemed complete. "You can't fight if they don't hit you." He looked at Josie Hanson as if making up his mind. And he did; he went to her.

"That's it; you can't do anymore," he said as if desperately weary, and he offered the pistol to her, "Here, Mrs Hanson, Josie."

She took it uncertainly. She didn't look at it, she kept her eyes on his face.

"Go on," he said, "use it if you want to." He turned his back on them and walked slowly to the hall door.

"Go on, shoot me as I go out, Mrs Hanson. There's only the Norma's of this world who'll miss me."

They watched him leave the room, leave the door open.

It was like the climax of a play, a movie. Prickly feelings ran down all their necks—except Arthur Hanson. He stood up quickly and changed the mood.

"Well go on!" he shouted at Bauer, "After him! Shoot him!" He shot his wife a look.

Bauer came to life. The gun had changed sides, and he went toward the door, still not a hundred percent eager, though. Hanson followed him, and then there was another shock.

The sound of the shot startled them into statues.

Josie Hanson had fired the pistol, and Arthur fell slowly to his knees, holding his arm. PC Bauer turned to her, amazement on his face. She lowered the pistol and gave the policeman a nervous smile.

"That's what Mr Campari would have wanted," she said quite simply.

Hanson was sitting on the floor, leaning against the wall, and he was moaning. A redness was already appearing on the sleeve of his jacket. His wife went over to him, not rushing.

"Does it hurt?" she asked, and she bent down to him.

The policeman collected his wits and did the thing that made most sense to him: he rushed out to get his radio from the car.

"I'll see if there's anything in the bathroom," Josie said as she left the room, but she didn't sound very confident that there would be. When she had gone, Hanson struggled to his feet. He'd stopped moaning when his wife had left the room, and they heard him start again when he laboriously climbed the stairs.

*   *   *

The rover was purring its way back to the heart of the metropolis, and with the comforting thud—the thud of its engine—and the smell of its deep leather, it was a comfortable capsule hurtling through reality at 35 mph.

Beatrice was reclining in the back. She could see the top of Bonnyweather's head above the high seat back and nothing of Errol who was at his side. But she knew he was there.

"He shouldn't have been so terribly rude and unpleasant." She had long forgotten the man in the greenhouse. "I think I would have done the same." And she meant it—she would have happily used a 12 bore if it had been her. "Why are men such fools, I wonder?"

There was a pause of no answer from the front seats.

"You still there, Errol?" she asked, raising her voice.

"Yes, darling," he called back.

Bonnyweather jerked to look at him, his interest quickened by the *darling*. Beatrice smiled at the reassurance; she was amused. She thought of Josie and having a husband like Arthur—and now, possibly, a lover like Ambrose. Poor Josie—even though she was not a cat lover herself, she could understand. Oh yes, she could understand.

"I never did see Norma. I wonder where she was."

"I put her in the boot ages ago," Errol's voice came over the high seat to her in a matter of fact sort of way. Ambrose took his eyes from the windscreen and actually smiled at Errol.

"That is what I call aptitude," he said approvingly, "Two or three days and we'll make everybody happy again."

Beatrice didn't say anything for a pause, then she said, "I think you're appalling."

"Laws of the marketplace, Beatrice," he said. And in spite of herself, there was a pleasure in hearing him use her right name. "Lame ducks can't swim, you know. Pay attention, my lad, and you'll find a lot of satisfaction in this game."

She felt a vague sense of being out of tune with the thinking around her, and it occurred to her that she must do something about being a minority viewpoint.

"I think you're a brute, an overbearing brute," she said without much rancour to Bonnyweather.

Errol was the one she could influence. Yes, it was worth hanging on and bearing everything to influence Errol.

"I'm a caring businessman," Ambrose said, and he really did sound hurt.

They drove on in silence for a longer pause, and Errol (who felt that some sort of reward was due to him) broke it. He said, "Can I use the stick tomorrow?"

Ambrose merely glanced at him, and Beatrice didn't really hear. The rover thud-thudded on into today's night.

In the Bloomsbury art gallery, Barrymore Pugh was snoring on a couch of pouffes, and Audrey Hepworth was lying on the floor in his jacket, near the radiator. They were both in post-renaissance.

Like the saying goes: days of wine and roses. Every life is like a song. There is an intro, a tune of words, and memories warming into humming—a comfort of remembering. Ambrose's world just couldn't be bettered in his estimation: a dalliance with two ladies (though Beatrice was working hard at the task of building Errol into a heady substitute for Ambrose). Josie's world was changed overnight. She had revived feelings from her past and enjoyed sharing a secret with Ambrose—on a regular basis. Hanson still tried to live a life as a fool, and P.C. Bauer was a regular visitor to the Hanson home. Barrymore Pugh was deservedly fired, and Mrs Hepworth, well, one didn't know what happened to her. Jenkins, of course, went to prison and spent his time on the prison farm studying for GCEs. And after six years of incarceration and study, he found his way to university and professionalism. So ends the story of a detective of sorts and the various people he helped and hindered. And who knows? He may be working for Errol soon.

About the Author

O'Brien has been a sailor.

Leapt from aeroplanes (with a parachute).

Led an expedition to search for the Loch Ness monster.

Took a ten foot python onto BBC Radio.

Increased attendance at a zoo fivefold in three years.

Did the Lyke Wake Walk—44 miles over rough moorland—twice (there and back) for a total of 88 miles in 22 hours.

Been an employer of 100 illiterate, criminal, and violent young people in Leeds.

Been a market trader, a parish councillor, and a village school manager.

Was the youth unemployment specialist in Stockport. (Obtained £100.000 offer from the Thatcher government to set up a cooperative.)

Befriended by Frith Banbury, who compared his writing to Pinter. And who asked him to rewrite an Iris Murdoch script (which he refused to do).

Was a successful odd-job man to the "carriage trade" in north Oxford for nearly 12 years, including being an odd-job man in a convent.

Counted (and still counts) patrons as friends.

Completed three novels (and another requires only the last two chapters) and wrote a number of play scripts and numerous short stories.

I live in Mid-Wales in the UK with my wife, Mary, who does all my administration for me.

I am the proud father of three outstanding children, several grandchildren, and even great-grandchildren.

About the Book

The story is about a specialist detective agency illegally located in an art gallery through the good will of the caretaker, Roy Jenkins (who has ambitions to be a vet). The characters comprising the agency are Ambrose Bonnyweather—a self-centred Scotsman—his secretary, Beatrice Thompson, and a seventeen-year-old trainee, Errol Billington.

The caretaker is madly in love with Beatrice—and she dislikes him. The visits to a client, Josie Hanson, regarding the loss of her cat, Norma, create many misconceptions, confusions, and cross purposes. This disorientation is highlighted in conversations and results in a total comedy of errors. It's filled with a froth of sexuality that culminates in total confusion and new discoveries within themselves by all the characters.

Lightning Source UK Ltd.
Milton Keynes UK
UKOW050343200612

194707UK00001B/49/P